NO ENTRY

Young George Micklejohn managed to have a British Cabinet Minister for a father, to cross the East-West German frontier, to get his hands on some top-secret Russian plans—and to disappear. Which was when Tommy Hambledon of the Foreign Office's Intelligence Service made his entry—into the search for the missing college student and into the East Zone.

The result of Hambledon's border crossing—and his capacity to put a Russian general under the table—is one of the best Manning Coles stories ever!

Setting: Germany

This novel has not appeared in any form prior to book publication.

Manning Coles

NO
ENTRY

DOUBLEDAY & COMPANY, INC., GARDEN CITY, NEW YORK

CONTENTS

Thomas Elphinstone Hambledon
George Micklejohn
General Vedovitch, of the Russian Army
Karl and Hans, German woodcutters
Andrey Lentov, a Russian civilian
Otto Neumann, a German field-worker
Hugo Britz, a taxi-driver in Goslar-am-Harz
Petersen, a Swedish tourist
Ludwig Kirsch
Dittmar
Tosen } his assistants
Lorenz Grober
General Ambromovitch, of the Russian Army
The late Gustav Ehrlich
West German Police, East German People's Police, hotel porters,
Russian soldiers etc.

TIME: Summer 1957
PLACE: On both sides of the Frontier between Western and Soviet-
         occupied Germany

NO ENTRY

excuse me again

GOSLAR-AM-HARZ is an interesting mediaeval town in the province of Brunswick in the Western Zone of Germany. It is a magnet to draw students of mediaeval domestic architecture since, though its larger buildings can easily be paralleled or excelled elsewhere, it is very seldom indeed that one finds a town with street after entire street of houses dating from the sixteenth and early seventeenth centuries. South of Goslar lie the Harz Mountains, not much of mountains for size but quite remarkable for beauty.

Thomas Elphinstone Hambledon came to Goslar on a summer afternoon, not because the town is interesting and the Harz country beautiful, but because the Zonal Frontier lies ten miles to the eastward.

Hambledon came, like a tourist, by air to Hanover and thence by train; he had a room booked at the Drei Bullochsen Hotel, room number 32. It was the room which young George Micklejohn had occupied before his disappearance three days earlier and it had been booked for Hambledon for that reason. Someone might associate it with young Micklejohn and visit it, or Micklejohn himself might return there, or there might be something to find in it—all rather unlikely, but the room was still vacant. Hambledon might as well have that room as another.

He walked into the hotel, produced his passport, and booked in; the porter carried his suitcase upstairs and showed him a pleasant but quite ordinary room at the end of a long passage.

"The Herr will be quiet here tonight; it so happens that the room next to his is unoccupied. The Herr will be tired after so long a journey."

Hambledon thanked the man for his kind thought, though in point of fact travelling did not tire him, and spent ten minutes rapidly and neatly unpacking his things and putting them away, after which he went out for a walk in the town. He loved foreign towns and this one was undeniably beautiful; also it was a lovely evening. He strolled along narrow streets with the westering sun slanting into attic windows and passed some time trying to decipher pious inscriptions, in Gothic lettering and mediaeval German, carved along the face of the great beam above the ground-floor windows. "Unless the Lord keep the house they labour in vain that build it A.D. 1621" with the 2 like a crooked capital Z. After which he sat down at a table under the arcade of the Kaiserwerth Hotel to drink beer and admire the gilded bronze bird—presumably an eagle, all heraldic birds are eagles here—which presides over the drinking fountain in the middle of the Markt-Platz.

He went back to his hotel for dinner and sat at table after it was over, drinking a cup of coffee and a glass of cognac and looking idly out of the window. Now that the children had gone to bed the street seemed oddly quiet; there were plenty of people about but they were not happily loitering in the evening light and still less strolling in groups singing choruses. No, they went steadily about their own business or talked together in quiet voices, two or three together and not more. Well, perhaps Goslar cheered up later in the evening.

He left the table to go up to his own room and crossed the hall to the porter's desk to ask for his key, room number 32. The man looked behind him at the rows of numbered hooks and said: "Not here, mein Herr. Is the Herr quite sure that he handed it in?"

Hambledon was morally certain that he had, but this is the sort of question which never fails to arouse doubt in any normal mind. He said: "Well—I thought so," and felt in his pockets. "No, I haven't got it."

"Perhaps the Herr left it in his room."

Again Hambledon did not believe it, but there was no point in arguing.

"The obvious solution," he said, smiling, "is to go upstairs and look."

"If there is any difficulty, the Herr has only to summon me."

Hambledon thanked him and walked away up the stairs. His first errand in Goslar was to introduce himself to the police, to whom he had been officially accredited; they would have had a letter from Foreign Office Intelligence about him by now, but all that would, he felt, do quite well in the morning. A quiet stroll, a harmless glass of wine in some café, a little conversation with some friendly stranger, and then to bed. Hambledon yawned and tried the door handle of his own room; to his mild surprise the door was not locked. He went in, switching on the light as he did so.

There was a man lounging in the one easy chair by the window, apparently asleep, but there was an unpleasant-looking hole between his eyes. He was not asleep, he was quite dead.

Hambledon shut the bedroom door quickly; the key was in the lock inside, so he turned it. Three swift strides took him to the windows, wide open upon a sultry evening, and he drew the curtains over them. Then he took a small chair from the dressing table, planted it down opposite to his visitor, sat down upon it, and took stock.

"You do surprise me," he said in a low voice. "I came out here to look for you and I seem to have found you. Or have I? English clothes, and they are not common in these parts. Age about twenty-two. I should have thought you a little older, but perhaps being killed has aged you, has it? It doesn't usually," said Hambledon, out of ripe experience. He took a photograph from his wallet and looked from it to the dead man. "No, if you're George Micklejohn I'm the Prophet Jonah. Just a moment—excuse me——"

The dead man's eyes were almost closed. Hambledon got up suddenly, lifted one of the eyelids for a moment, and sat down again.

"That settles it," said Tommy Hambledon. "Not even sudden death changes grey eyes to dark brown. You are not George Micklejohn. Who the devil are you? Some other Englishman? I wonder if whoever killed you left you with any identification papers. Excuse me again."

Hambledon went through his visitor's pockets. There was an inner breast pocket, closed with a button and buttonhole, and in this there was something flat and stiff. Hambledon drew it out; it was a British passport and the name on the outside was G. Micklejohn. Tommy's eyebrows went up. The passport had a rubber band round it; he slipped it off and opened the book, which had a folder inside containing five travellers cheques. There had been more—the perforations showed where others had been torn out—but those remaining bore the signature "G. Micklejohn" in neat, rather mannered writing. The passport itself was perfectly normal in every respect and the photograph in it was the same as that in Hambledon's wallet. No attempt had been made to replace Micklejohn's likeness with anyone else's; the visitor's, for example.

15

"You know," said Hambledon, addressing his visitor, "you are really very irritating. You have had some sort of connection with Micklejohn or you wouldn't have his passport. Did you bring it here yourself or did somebody plant it on you? How did you know that this was his room? Don't tell me that that was coincidence."

Hambledon looked round the room and rose suddenly to his feet, for one of the dressing-table drawers was ajar and the corner of a handkerchief peeped out of the gap. Hambledon, like most men who travel a great deal and who wait upon themselves, was almost finically neat in such matters. He pulled out the drawers to find that all the contents had been flung about and stuffed back at random; the suits he had hung in the wardrobe were tangled in a heap at the bottom; his suitcase also had been opened, for only one of the two catches was fastened.

Hambledon made a hasty search through the dead man's pockets to see if he had any identification papers of his own, but there was nothing to show who he was.

Hambledon went out, shutting and locking the door behind him, to call upon the Goslar police.

On the previous day, in London, Hambledon had been summoned from his office to an interview with his chief.

"Rather a nasty mess, Hambledon. There's a young man gone missing near the zonal boundary between East and West Germany and it is feared that he may have crossed over and be in the hands of the Russians."

"Serve him right," said Hambledon cheerfully. "Teach him to look where he's going. Why worry? It's not as though he'd infringed the sacred soil of Holy Russia. Or isn't it Holy Russia these days?"

"Some say one thing and some another, I understand. However, in this case there are complications. Young George Micklejohn——"

"George who?"

"Yes, that's the whole point. His father is the wallah who is now touring the capitals of Western Europe——"

"See Cook's Travel Brochures."

"—trying to co-ordinate plans for the atomic weapon defence of NATO. The Russians, naturally, don't approve of him at all and George is his only son."

"I see," said Hambledon thoughtfully.

"If pressure were to be applied it might be awkward."

"Ye-es. However much of a Roman father Micklejohn senior might be, one feels that—that his attention might be distracted, shall we say, from his work."

"Precisely. I would never admit that a man in Micklejohn's position would allow himself to be deflected from his course by threats of any kind——"

"How well you put things," murmured Hambledon.

His chief laughed suddenly. "Sorry. The manner is horribly infectious and I've had rather a lot of it lately."

"The solution is simple," said Hambledon briskly. "No one has to be a Cabinet Minister if he doesn't want to. Let Micklejohn senior resign from his high office and let another assume his mantle. Young George will then cease to be of any significance outside his loving family circle and all will be well."

"And the pressure will have succeeded to a certain extent. Micklejohn is a very capable man."

"Well, yes. There is that. You know, I have never been able, for various reasons, to take politicians very seriously. Box gives up and Cox takes on and in a week's time the eddies have died away and there's no change. I may be jaundiced," admitted Hambledon kindly.

"I think we're wandering from the point, which is——"

"That you want me to go and look for the wanderer, I suppose. Tell me about him."

"He is twenty-two years old and an undergraduate of Brasenose——"

Hambledon bounded in his chair.

"Oh, furies and all hell! Not another undergraduate. Of course it's the Long Vacation, I'd forgotten. Why don't they send them home with an iron collar welded round their necks and a strong chain to be attached to a post driven into the middle of the ancestral bowling green like cows in Normandy? Please, daddy, may I leave the room because this is where I came in?"

"Simmer down, Hambledon. This one is a quiet decent lad who went on a walking tour with a friend, but the friend broke an ankle and returned home. Young Micklejohn wasn't doing anything idiotic; he was staying at Goslar in the Harz Mountains, going for walks in the day and reading at night. He was there for nearly a week until one day he went out and didn't come back."

"When was this?"

"The day before yesterday, on Tuesday."

"Had any news of him from anyone?"

"Only that on that Tuesday he went by bus towards the frontier

17

and was last seen striding away into the woods. There's a camping site somewhere out in the wilds there and it was thought that he might have met or made friends there and be staying with them. But no one there has seen him."

"Then there's no evidence that he did cross into the Eastern Zone? No, then he's just as likely to have fallen down a drain somewhere."

"You know better than that, Hambledon. Remote country districts in Germany don't have drains."

"I still don't understand why there is so much anxiety," said Hambledon. "I was talking the other day to a man who had been up on that frontier with the British Occupation Forces and he told me that it was quite easy to stray into the Russian Zone—it wasn't very well marked—so when they saw a Russian uniform they used to run back. Of course they were in uniform, which might make it awkward, but a young man, a student in civilian clothes, couldn't come to much harm, surely? Of course if he turned nasty they might put him inside for a few days."

"I don't think your informant was there very recently."

"Well, no. About four years ago or so."

"Things are very different now, Hambledon. There is something like a cold war going on along that frontier; it is closed now, really closed. A barbed-wire fence, like that round a concentration camp, patrolled by armed men. People get killed on that frontier now."

"Oh, indeed," said Hambledon slowly. "No, I didn't know that. I've had no reason to take any interest in that frontier, you know, and one has a general idea that communications are getting easier all the time, not worse."

"That is not true of the East-West German Zonal Frontier."

"Evidently not, but it's surprising all the same. I shall be interested to see it."

Hambledon was supplied with a photograph of George Micklejohn and a full description of him.

On the following day Hambledon flew to Hanover and went on by train to Goslar.

He left the dead man in his room and went to the police station, where he sent in his card and asked to see the Chief of Police if he happened to be still on the premises. He was, as it happened, and Hambledon was received with some ceremony. But, of course, the Herr Hambledon's credentials had already been received; there was a letter, yes, yes. The Herr was most welcome; it was a privilege to meet one so high in the famous Intelligence Service of England. Let the Herr be seated, please. A little glass of wine, a cigar, or perhaps a cigarette was preferred? What a wonderful summer, really, the weather was excelling itself.

Hambledon responded suitably, took a sip of an excellent wine, and settled his broad shoulders comfortably against the high back of his chair. He then said that, repulsive as it must be to persons with any idea of manners to start talking business at that hour in the evening, he must ask whether the Chief of Police was aware that he, Hambledon, had come to Goslar to look for one George Micklejohn, unaccountably missing.

A slight cloud passed across the German's face.

"Yes, yes indeed. Enquiries have been received from the highest levels. This young man is the son of a member of your Government, is he not?"

"He is," said Tommy, "and a blasted nuisance you must think him."

The Chief of Police grinned suddenly.

"We like having foreign visitors in Goslar," he said, "but I must admit we prefer them not to lose themselves."

"Has he, do you think, simply wandered off into your wooded hills and met with some accident?"

"I wish I could think so—I beg your pardon. I should be very sorry if such a thing had happened to any visitor, but such evidence as we have does not suggest that." Hambledon looked expectant and the Chief of Police went on: "The last news we have is that he, or a young man answering to his description, went from Bad Harzburg by autobus to Eckertal on the frontier and was not seen to return. Our police there saw him alight and walk towards the frontier; that is quite a common occurrence. The Herr will understand that many people— mainly our own countrymen—find a painful interest in going up to the Zonal Frontier and looking across the barricades into Eastern Germany, particularly if they have friends over there. We have many refugees in this area from the Soviet Zone, as the Herr may have heard."

"Can I assume, then, that it is possible for this young man to have crossed the frontier?"

"It is possible," said the Chief noncommittally. "But highly inadvisable."

"I see. I have here," said Hambledon, putting his hand in his pocket, "Micklejohn's passport." He laid it upon the desk and the Chief of Police picked it up.

"I do not quite understand," he said. "Was it, then, at the hotel after all? We were told that it was not there."

"A man brought it to my room," said Hambledon. "At least, I assume he brought it."

"What man? Did you see him?"

Hambledon nodded. "He is still there. The reason for my disturbing you at this unseasonable hour was to ask you to be so good as to have him removed."

"But he—is he being held—what did he say—who is he?"

"I don't know who he is except that he is not George Micklejohn, and he said nothing. He is quite dead, mein Herr, of a bullet through the head."

"Dead," said the Chief of Police, rising to his feet and pressing a bell on his desk, "dead, in your room——"

"Without being unduly squeamish," said Tommy Hambledon, "I dislike corpses in my bedroom. Disconcerting. Unhygienic."

eckertal

THE POLICE took such thorough possession of Hambledon's room that he found it advisable, if he wanted any sleep that night, to move into the empty room next door.

"Just for one night," he said to the hotel manager. "Tomorrow, when the police have done with the room, I should like to move back. I like that room."

"The Herr," said the hotel manager, "has, then, no objection to sleeping in a room in which a violent death has so recently occurred?"

"Not in the least. Bullets through the head are not infectious—I hope. It is not as though the poor man had died of the plague, you understand."

"Heaven forbid," said the manager, edging away.

"I will not detain you," said Hambledon graciously.

The man pattered off down the long passage and Hambledon went back to the end room to talk to the Chief of Police, who had come himself to give the enquiry a handsome start. The corpse had been unobtrusively removed via the service stair; no well-conducted hotel conveys the evidences of its more serious crises through the front hall.

"I ask myself," said the Chief of Police, "for what object a search was made of your room."

"So do I," agreed Hambledon, "and I add to that the further question, who searched it? The late occupant of that chair or his murderer?"

"Fingerprints upon the furniture should tell us something. We have the dead man's; may we, merely for purposes of elimination, have yours also?"

"Certainly. And, of course, the chambermaid's. But do you mean to tell me that there are no traces of gloved fingers here? The criminal actually left fingerprints?"

"Indeed he did," said the Chief of Police, exhibiting a wonderful collection of superimposed prints which had been brought up with grey powder on the edge of a drawer.

"A beginner," said Hambledon disgustedly, "a novice, a rank amateur. Lives there a man in these days who does not read *romans policiers?*"

The Chief shrugged his shoulders. "You will be needing your things out of here, will you not? One of my fellows will bring them to your new room; the manager has found you one, no doubt?"

"Only my pyjamas and toilet things. I am sleeping next door for tonight. When you have done with this room I will come back to it, if you have no objection."

"Not the least, if you have none. On the contrary, I should be glad if you would. I am assuming for the present that the corpse was here because this room was young Micklejohn's—what a name—not because it is now yours?"

Hambledon agreed. "You think that possibly something else may happen here?"

"But not, I trust, another corpse."

"So long as it isn't mine," said Hambledon cheerfully, "I shall bear up. Or George Micklejohn's, of course."

The Chief of Police blinked.

"The armchair," he said, "shall be replaced. It is not what it was. By the way, here are the contents of his pockets. Not very informative, *hein?*"

There was a little collection of things laid out upon the dressing table: a rather grubby but good-quality handkerchief, a packet of Astor cigarettes with some missing, and an assortment of money. East German marks, quite a large number of West German marks, and a few Russian coins. Hambledon looked them over and raised his eyebrows.

"No English money," said the Chief. "Not even an odd coin or so, although he was wearing English clothes."

"So I notice. These West marks now, there is quite a wad of them, a hundred or more. Do you think that our departed friend cashed a travellers cheque in Goslar? And, if so, on whose passport?"

"I shall enquire as soon as we can get made a photograph of him which does not look too dead. But there is no reason I can think of why he should not have obtained them in any other town in Germany

22

or even have brought them into the country with him when he came."

"Quite so," said Hambledon.

"But it is worth trying and I will try it."

Hambledon gathered up his pyjamas and toilet articles and went to bed; he stayed awake only long enough to decide to go to Eckertal in the morning.

He went out directly after breakfast to see the Chief of Police again and get from him a written authority to show the Frontier Police—the West German force—whose duty it is to patrol the frontier on this side as the Russian-trained Volks-polizei patrol it on the other. The West German patrols wear a green uniform and are familiarly called the Green Police on that account; the Volks-polizei wear brown uniforms like the Russian Army dress but with narrower shoulder straps.

The Chief very willingly wrote out and stuck in Hambledon's passport an order to all Zonal Frontier police to assist, protect, and direct the Herr Hambledon as occasion might require—or words to that effect—and to answer his questions to any extent consistent with their duty.

"We cannot, of course," said the Chief, laughing gently, "let you into all our little secrets. But as regards Herr Micklejohn, ask what you will."

Communications with Eckertal are neither convenient nor frequent. Why should they be either since, except as the centre of a small farming community, the place is now dead? It is close against The Wire, as the frontier fence is called. Eckertal used to be a sort of suburb of Stapelburg, only a kilometre away as the free bird flies but now removed by the intervening Wire into another world. A railway ran through and is now stopped, a road went through and is now stopped.

Hambledon came to Bad Harzburg at noon to find he had forty minutes to wait for the autobus to Eckertal. Bad Harzburg is a spa and a tourist centre: there is a beautiful white *Kurhaus* sitting on formal terraces where a band plays; there are formal gardens with tidy gravel paths and gay flower beds; there are seats for the public to sit on; there are souvenir shops selling miniature witches of the Brocken and other mementoes; there are cafés with small tables under bright umbrellas.

Hambledon decided that he was not in the right mood for this sort of thing. He therefore retired into a restaurant to drink beer and eat sausage. Lunch at Eckertal seemed improbable.

The bus came at last and Hambledon got in. Other people got in also, not many, a dozen or so. They were evidently local inhabitants, for they nodded to each other, said "good day" to the bus conductor, and looked Hambledon over warily, for he was a stranger. In most parts of Germany fellow passengers in buses chatter freely to each other, strangers or no, but not anywhere near The Wire.

The conductor asked where Hambledon wished to alight and showed evident interest when he said: "To the end of the run." Some of the passengers glanced at the stranger and away again but no one made any comment. The bus rolled on, stopping occasionally to set down passengers, until at last there were left only Hambledon and two others besides the driver and conductor when the bus stopped finally in the weedy station yard at Eckertal Bahnhof. The other two passengers got out and walked away. Hambledon also got out. The conductor took a parcel to the stationmaster's house and a policeman in a green uniform stood at a little distance and watched proceedings.

Eckertal Bahnhof is a surprisingly large station for a very small place. Hambledon walked on to the platform and looked about him. There is a large booking hall, now closed, a restaurant surprisingly open until one realises that Eckertal has lost its inn beyond The Wire, and a waiting room fitted up as a chapel with notices on the door announcing the times of *Gottes-dienst*. There is also a stationmaster. He was sitting on his doorstep in his shirt sleeves, peeling potatoes. The whole place was uncannily quiet.

Hambledon walked across to look at the rails. They were corroded and eaten into by rust but they were not much of an eyesore because tall grass had grown up all over the permanent way, knee-high, and veiled the rotting lines. Sizable bushes and even young trees were flourishing between the rails. They went on towards the East and were lost in weeds and undergrowth.

Hambledon turned on his heel and left the place; as he crossed the station yard he saw the Green Police officer again, in another place, but still watching him; the man wore a large revolver holster on his hip and carried a pair of binoculars slung round his neck. The bus had gone.

Hambledon had studied a walker's map bought in Goslar and knew that the frontier ran east of Eckertal Station. He had, therefore, only to walk in that direction till he came to a barbed-wire fence, and that would be it. The woods came down to the side of the road and a path led off in the right direction. Hambledon took it and walked pleasantly among pine trees till he came to the bank of a stream. This, according to his map, was the Ecker, and the frontier should be just beyond it.

The Ecker is the sort of mountain stream which is a brawling torrent among boulders after rain and in dry weather merely a slender rivulet among stones. Hambledon chose a suitable spot and hopped across dry-shod.

The further bank is a tangle of bushes and small trees. Hambledon threaded his way for some time through the undergrowth which was thick enough to deny him a clear view in any direction. He did not find any wire fence but he was insistently and increasingly conscious of being stared at, though he could see no one. There was no wind to stir the leaves—it was a blazingly hot day—and here again it was uncannily quiet; no sound of traffic or of voices or of men working; no dog barked and it even seemed to him that no bird sang. "They wouldn't, anyway, in the middle of a hot afternoon," he said to himself, but the back of his neck prickled and he turned to go.

When he reached the stream again he saw, sitting on the bank and waiting for him, the same man of the Frontier Police who had watched him in the station yard. Hambledon instantly crossed the stream and walked up to him.

"*Guten Tag*," said Hambledon, with a smile.

"*Guten Tag*," said the policeman politely, and stood up.

"Were you waiting for me? I have been wandering about looking for the frontier."

"The Herr has found it," said the man calmly. "The frontier is the middle of this stream."

"What? Oh, is it? But it isn't marked, I was looking for a wire fence."

"The wire fence is further over. In winter when there is much rain, or when the snow melts, this river rises, as the Herr will understand. Then the land on the other side becomes flooded, so the Russians set the fence back to where it remains dry. A long way, in places, fifty or a hundred metres sometimes, but all that"—he waved his hand across the stream—"is East Zone territory all the same. I was very glad to see the Herr return in safety." He put up his binoculars and slowly surveyed the scene.

"Thank you very much——"

"It is very tiresome if there is an incident, it makes a great deal of work for us. I have to make out long, detailed reports, in triplicate." He sighed. "I do not like making out long reports and sometimes we do not get the body back for weeks. In this hot weather it can be an unpleasant business, the Herr will understand."

"Dear me," said Hambledon bleakly. "You do not cross the line at all, then, not even to recover a body on this side of their fence?"

"Not on any account. Such an action might start a Frontier Incident. Application has to be made to the Authority this side and by them to the Authority on the East side. Hence the delay," said the policeman, and put his binoculars up to his eyes again.

"And suppose the victim is only wounded?"

"Go back among the trees," said the policeman suddenly, "the Herr is too conspicuous standing up on this bank."

"But I am well on our side," protested Hambledon, removing himself quickly within the edge of the woods.

"Guns go off by accident," said the policeman, joining him. "There are two Vopos there now, they have just come. The Herr was extremely lucky that they did not come while he was still across the stream."

Vopos. Of course, a pet name for the Volks-polizei.

"There is a man in the watchtower now," went on the policeman. "Do you see him?"

Hambledon looked at a high platform above the tops of the trees. It had a sort of shelter upon it and was very like the watchtowers from which, in more civilised countries, a lookout is kept for forest fires.

"He is looking at the Herr through his glasses. He has a machine pistol beside him. If the Herr has now seen enough, there are many much pleasanter places in the Harz than this stretch beside The Wire."

Hambledon pulled out his passport.

"I ought to have shown you this at once," he said, "but events rather overtook me. There is a note inside from the Chief of Police in Goslar."

The man took the passport and read the order, nodding slowly. "I did not know that the Herr was anything but an ordinary tourist."

"How should you?"

The policeman looked through the pages of the passport at the numerous closely packed stamps of a dozen frontiers of Europe and America.

"The Herr has travelled extensively," he said with a note of envy in his voice. "It must be pleasant to be able to travel so widely."

"I have been fortunate in having opportunities," said Hambledon, "that is all."

"For me," said the policeman, closing the book and handing it back, "I have visited only Russia and for that I did not require a passport. Stalingrad," he added, and raised the binoculars to his eyes again with the now familiar movement which was plainly habitual. "The

Herr is still arousing interest. Take my glasses and look at the man on the tower."

Hambledon did so. They were excellent binoculars; when he had adjusted them to suit his own eyes the watchtower leapt forward to hang before his face and the man upon it was staring through similar binoculars at him—an odd sensation.

"Ugly-looking little blighter, isn't he?"

The policeman laughed and then turned to business.

"There was some matter about which the Herr desires information?"

Hambledon offered a cigarette and they sat down together, smoking companionably.

"I was asked to come out here to try to find some trace of an English student who seems to have disappeared in these parts."

"I have heard that a young Englishman is missing but I do not, myself, know anything about it. I only heard that enquiries were being made. When did this happen?"

"Four days ago. Last Tuesday."

The policeman thought for a moment and then said: "I was not on duty then, that was one of my free days. My colleague Ernst Schultz was on this patrol that day, if it please the Herr I will introduce him to Schultz and the Herr can ask him any question he pleases."

"Thank you, I shall be very glad if you will. There is an idea that the young man—his name is Micklejohn—may have strayed across the frontier and been taken prisoner, is that possible?"

"It is possible," said the policeman slowly. "Scarcely possible to stray across without being aware of it; there is always The Wire. The Herr has not yet seen The Wire? A young man could get through it easily enough, but not without noticing it, and there is also the ploughed strip to show footprints if anyone should walk across it. There is only one place I know of where there is no Wire and that is a short stretch beside the road at Neuhof, a long way off, south of Walkenried, thirty kilometres away and more. Nobody knows why there is no Wire at Neuhof, but there is nothing to take a visitor there, only a road leading nowhere; it is stopped."

"Assume that for some reason a man climbed through The Wire," said Hambledon.

"If he were seen by the Vopos in the act of doing so, he would be shot on sight, but even the Vopos cannot be everywhere at once. If somehow he avoided the Vopos and went on a kilometre or so beyond the frontier and were then picked up, I do not suppose they would shoot. He would be arrested, of course, taken in and questioned. If he seemed harmless and told a plausible tale he might be returned to this zone after a month or two. If they thought he was up to mischief he would be sent to Siberia or to the salt mines and no news of him would be forthcoming. They would say that they had never seen him."

"Finished," said Hambledon.

"Finished," repeated the policeman.

the wire

"I MUST RESUME my patrol," said the policeman. "Would it interest the Herr to accompany me? He would then see for himself what the conditions are on this stretch."

"It is very good of you," said Hambledon. "I should be very glad to see anything you care to show me."

"Good," said the man, getting to his feet. "My name is Ritter."

He led the way through the wood till they came to an iron bridge which used to carry the railway across the Ecker River towards Stapelburg. Ritter walked on to the bridge as far as the middle and there stopped. Hambledon made to pass him.

"Better not," said Ritter quietly. "The middle of this bridge is the boundary and they are watching you." His glasses went up to his eyes. "Do you see that tallest tree by the line with two bushes in front of it? There are two Vopos behind the bushes, can you see them? There, one of them moved. Take my glasses."

Hambledon did so and saw two men in brown standing together behind the bushes and looking towards him. He was seized with a mixture of incredulity and exasperation; how ridiculous it was in peace-time to have armed men skulking behind bushes glaring at one. They were like tiresome small boys playing at cowboys and Indians, trying to frighten people, they wanted their heads banged together. A stupid game. One of the Vopos moved across a gap and Hambledon saw that his hand was on his gun. No, not a game.

"There is The Wire," said Ritter, nodding ahead along the railway line. The Wire did not look particularly imposing at first sight, merely a fence five feet high or a little more, composed of strands of rusty barbed wire, red in the sunshine. The strands were close together, eight or ten inches apart, the posts supporting them were closer together than is usual with a wire fence and the strands were taut between them. All the same, the barrier was not impassable; if a coat were thrown over the top of it an active man would get over easily enough. Provided, of course, that the Vopos did not see him——

"You are right," said Hambledon. "A man would notice that fence if he came up against it."

"Shall we go on?" said Ritter, and took Hambledon for a brisk walk by the ways he himself used on patrol, from one vantage point to another, down narrow tracks like a double-row hedge, across strips of open meadow. For part of the time they were close to a country lane which ran parallel with the frontier; every time a cart or a car or a bicycle came along the road, up went Ritter's glasses as soon as it was in sight and every time he identified the vehicle. "That is the butcher on his rounds. That is the manager of the paper factory at Eckertal. That is the postman."

At one point they came to a road bridge with a red and white pole across it. Beyond the pole on the Eastern side, there were posts driven into the road and behind them again a pit dug across the road and the gravel from the pit piled up into a bank to stop escaping cars from crashing the barricade.

"This was an official crossing place at one time," said Ritter. "Before this frontier was tightened up, there were several such places, now there is only one, at Helmstedt." He jerked his head towards the north. "It is where the main road and the rail go through from Brunswick to Berlin."

"How long since they closed——"

"About four years." Ritter looked round sharply as a motorcycle with two young men on it came tearing down the road from Eckertal. They turned on to the bridge, saw the red and white pole, and skidded to an abrupt stop with a scatter of gravel.

"Are you in a hurry to get to Moscow?" asked Ritter pleasantly, but they did not smile.

"We—we took the wrong turning somewhere," they said. They turned their machine round in the road and went back the way they had come as though the devil were after them.

"Some people never see notices," said Ritter, and put up his binoculars again.

"That town across there," began Hambledon.

"Stapelburg. You see The Wire in front of us here with the branches stuck in it? This bridge is a favourite place for people to come and stare across and the Vopos got tired of being stared at, so they made a sort of screen there. There are always Vopos about here."

"I don't see any now."

"Where are the Herr's eyes? There is a man leaning against that tree not twenty metres away."

"It is their brown uniforms," said Hambledon, annoyed with himself. "The protective colouration is almost perfect."

Ritter nodded. "It is also a matter of practice." Up went the glasses again, again the slow sweep round. The country towards Stapelburg was open farm land and people were working in the fields. There was a cluster of small houses within a stone's throw and children were playing round them.

"It all looks so entirely peaceful."

"It does, but they will not speak."

"Who won't? The Vopos?"

"Neither the Vopos nor the people living across there. Sometimes, when we pass each other at points where there is only The Wire between us, I call across 'Good morning' or 'Nice weather,' but they never answer. And it is not as though they were Russians—they are all Germans like us—but they never answer."

"Do you ever see Russians along here?"

"No. Very seldom. Sometimes a couple of Russian officers. The troops are kept further back, but they are there if wanted."

"If wanted?"

"I have my wife and family in Eckertal—a man wants some home life—but sometimes I wonder whether it is right to keep them here so near the Russians." The binoculars went up again and Hambledon did not know what to say.

A little later on, Ritter said that he thought Schultz would probably be at home by now if the Herr still wished to see him. Hambledon said that he would. It was just to ask about that day upon which Micklejohn disappeared. Ritter nodded and they walked up the road towards Eckertal. At this point Hambledon did his best to induce Ritter to accept five marks for all the extra trouble he had taken, but the man refused, politely but quite firmly.

"At least," said Hambledon, "come and have a drink with me."

"The Herr is most kind, indeed, but I do not drink on duty," said Ritter. "Thank you, indeed."

"But when you come off duty, a round with your friends," urged Hambledon.

But it was all of no use and he had to give it up.

Presently three motorcycles together came down the road and stopped to speak to Ritter, who introduced Hambledon. These men wore black uniforms and their appearance and bearing were very smart indeed.

"These are of the Mobile Police," explained Ritter. "They do not have to wear out their legs walking all day like the poor wretched Green Police. No, they ride about like gentlemen all day on expensive motorcycles."

The Mobiles laughed and said that Ritter had only a pair of binoculars to service and maintain. He was not expected to be a motor mechanic as well as a policeman.

Hambledon realised at once that these men might be very useful and that he would almost certainly meet them, or some of them, again. He showed them his passport and permit and explained briefly why he was there.

Ritter said that the Herr had wanted to know about conditions there, so he himself had been showing the Herr round his area.

The sergeant in charge of the Mobile patrol said that perhaps Hambledon would like a little ride with them; it might be bumpy but at least one covered the ground.

Hambledon, assuming correctly that this suggestion was not meant to be taken seriously, said that, much as he would enjoy it, he had to go and see a man named Schultz at the moment and then he must catch the autobus back to Goslar. They parted with mutual courtesies and the Mobile Police swirled away.

At the entrance to Eckertal a small boy, aged about four, ran out of one of the scattered cottages and rushed at Ritter.

"My son," explained the policeman. "What hast thou been doing today?"

But the child looked at the stranger and turned shy. There was a wooden shanty at the side of the road where a one-armed man sold cigarettes, chocolate, beer, and lemonade; Hambledon went in and bought the biggest slab of chocolate in the place as a present for the boy, who proceeded at once to tear off the wrapping.

"Oh, no," said Ritter, "not all at once. Thou wilt only make thyself sick. Thank the Herr for his kindness. Thou shalt have a piece every night and so thou wilt remember the Herr for at least ten days. Here is Schultz's house, next beyond mine. Ernst! Are you there?"

Ernst came to the door, a giant of a man with a limp and three fingers missing from his left hand. Ritter introduced Hambledon, took his leave, and went away.

Hambledon once more explained his mission and showed the Chief of Police's authorisation. "I understand that you were on patrol the day the young man disappeared," he said. "Four days ago, last Tuesday."

"That is so," said Schultz in a slow deep voice. "I have been asked about this young man; English, was he not? Yes. I saw him get off the midday autobus at the station here and he walked along the road towards the frontier. Then he turned off by a path through the woods. I went on by the road and presently I saw him again on the road which runs south along the frontier. He was walking along it away from me. Then a car came along—they were strangers here, they stopped to ask me one or two things—and when I looked round again the young man had disappeared. That is all I know, mein Herr."

"Yes, I see. You have no idea which way he went?"

"I assumed he had turned off to the right, back into our woods here. If he had turned left he would have come to the frontier and there is no passage that way, as the Herr knows. I did not see the young man again though I walked on down the road the way he had gone. If he had gone to the frontier he would have had to come back again and I should have seen him. The Herr understands? He must have turned back into our woods."

"I understand perfectly. Tell me, did anything at all unusual happen that day?"

Schultz considered.

"Nothing, no."

"You did not hear anything?"

The policeman looked straight at Hambledon.

"The Herr means shots fired? No, I heard nothing and I should have heard if there had been. One is always looking and listening, the Herr knows."

"Yes," said Hambledon, "yes. It is so quiet here, one would say that even the trees were watching and listening."

"May it remain quiet," said Schultz, and at that moment there came from the cottage behind him the sound of a baby crying.

"Then there was nothing at all out of the ordinary?"

"No, mein Herr, I am sorry I cannot help you. If anything had happened, particularly on that day, we should have known it."

A woman's voice inside the cottage said something in a soothing tone and the baby left off crying.

"Why 'particularly on that day'?" asked Hambledon.

"Because they had a stretch of the wire down that day, replacing the posts. The Herr has seen the posts? They are only rough lumber, they do not last so long. There was a gang of men working on it, taking the wire down, replacing the posts and putting the wire back. They had Vopo guards standing over them all the time, they always do."

"To keep them at it?"

Schultz smiled slowly. "I do not suppose they would kill themselves with overwork, those labourers; they are not well paid nor well fed. Yes, the Vopos watch them for that and also to see that they do not slip across to us. Wages and conditions are better this side—everyone knows that—and if there is a gap in The Wire it is too easy, if the Vopos are not watching all the time."

"I see," said Hambledon. "How much of the wire would they take down at a time?"

"Not very much. Not more than they can finish in a day. They take the wire down and roll it up, for it must be used again. Then they pull out the old posts, put in new ones, unroll the wire again—has the Herr ever tried to unroll rusty barbed wire?—and strain it back on to the new posts. No, not a great length."

"I suppose not."

"I see what the Herr is thinking, but there were no shots that day. Not in this area at least. Besides, I remember that afternoon for another thing, the Russians had soldiers close up all along this frontier. We do not often see Russian soldiers, mein Herr—they keep them further back—but that day I suppose there was an exercise on. We see a Russian officer or two now and again but that is all as a rule. That day there were troops everywhere that side and the Vopos swarming like flies. But there were no shots fired so the Herr can assure himself that no one went across The Wire."

Hambledon thanked Schultz and walked back to Eckertal Station to catch the bus to Goslar. He was a little early; he stood and strolled about in the brilliant sunshine on the station forecourt with the weeds brushing his legs. It was very hot and there was nothing to sit down on, but Hambledon found himself preferring it to the platform side of the station, where the tall grass waved over the rusty lines and young bushes grew up between the points. Why such a big station in such a tiny place, with the town of Stapelburg only a couple of kilometres away? He could not imagine and there was no one to ask.

There were the deserted yard, the empty sheds, the road, and, beyond the road, the pine trees stretching for miles; it was very quiet but, instead of an air of peace, there hung over the whole scene a deep sense of brooding unease. He was glad when a distant rumble announced the arrival of his bus. It turned into the yard and stopped.

He looked round and there was Ritter, standing back on the perimeter of the station yard. A few people got out. Hambledon walked forward and looked round to give Ritter a farewell wave, but he had disappeared.

"I don't like this place at all," said Hambledon to himself. He entered the bus and sat down. A few minutes later three or four men arrived from nowhere in particular and also got into the bus and sat down. He wondered where they had come from and then mentally shook himself. Out of the station, of course, probably from the refreshment room; it was only that he had not seen them come out. It was completely ridiculous to picture this area as a sort of fourth-dimension country where people turned aside and were immediately not there. It was, certainly, the sort of place which might get on one's nerves, but one ought not to let it.

The bus turned in the yard and set off on the return journey to Bad Harzburg and Goslar. There were two more stops within the Eckertal boundaries—at a group of cottages and at a minor crossroads —and the bus began to fill up. People leaving work at the paper mill and the furniture factory and going home to sleep further away from The Wire.

After the first stop Hambledon noticed a man in the green uniform of the Frontier Police but could not see his face; at the second stop this man got out and Tommy saw to his surprise that it was Ritter. Hambledon lifted a hand in greeting and Ritter responded in friendly fashion, but he did look faintly sheepish. He might very well have had some errand at the crossroads, or was he merely making quite sure that Hambledon really had left the district, official police authorisation notwithstanding? A good fellow, Ritter, and they had become friends in the course of the long hot afternoon, but if it were his duty to see inquisitive strangers off his manor he would do it, and quite right too. The bus rolled on and Goslar, when they reached it, seemed like home.

the prisoner

GEORGE MICKLEJOHN was a healthy but studious youth who, having passed with credit all the previous trials with which the University of Oxford afflicts its young, was grimly determined to get a First in his finals. This involved, among other things, reading Roman law and this was not easy in a home which contained an hospitable mother, four cheerful sisters, and a generous allowance of the party spirit. George therefore departed for Goslar, in company with a congenial soul who also wished to work in peace. For a week they tramped long distances on walkers' trails, ate hugely, and read industriously until the friend slipped down a steep bank along with an angular boulder and broke his ankle. George bound up the ankle with their hand-kerchiefs, his scarf, and what he remembered of a course of first-aid lectures, hoisted the friend on his shoulders, and carried him as far as a road. Here they sat on a bank until a car came along and gave them a lift to Goslar and a surgeon. The friend left Hanover for England by air with his ankle in plaster and young Micklejohn carried on alone.

On the Tuesday before Hambledon came to Goslar, Micklejohn took the autobus from Goslar to Eckertal, since apparently the rail-way was not in operation now that there is a zonal boundary between East and West Germany. Micklejohn took no interest in politics, do-mestic or foreign, he heard too much of them at home. He alighted at Eckertal, armed only with a strong walking stick and a packet of sandwiches. He struck eastward along forest trails, for this country is heavily wooded, half expecting when he came to the zonal boundary to find a wire fence with notices hung upon it at intervals saying, in Gothic lettering, *Durchgäng Verboten.*

He did not find barbed wire or any other sort of fence. He walked sturdily on, enjoying the air, the theatrical effect of sunlight striking down through gaps in the foliage upon the red-brown trunks of pines, and the presence of twittering flocks of gold-crested wrens. He crossed a road and came to the bank of a mountain stream of the type which is either angrily in spate and quite impassable or else a string of clear brown pools joined together by rippling shallows, easily to be passed by anyone agile enough to hop from a boulder to a bank of flat water-worn pebbles and from there to a half-submerged shelf of rock. Micklejohn hopped across and sat down on a mossy bank to eat his sandwiches and commune with nature to the music of running water. Idyllic.

He got up and strolled on. The path he had been following had petered out and he was among bushes and undergrowth. However, there were pinewoods ahead and he made his way towards them, taking a childish pleasure in walking quietly without breaking branches or cracking sticks on the ground. Somewhere to his left he heard men's voices and circled round to avoid them; he was enjoying being alone and did not feel like talking to strangers.

A few minutes later he came upon a sort of track, as though some-one had ploughed a narrow strip; it came from his left and wound away to his right. He thought it a little odd but it conveyed no warning to his mind; the few Germans he had talked to had not discussed the frontier—it is not a popular subject in those parts—and it had never occurred to Micklejohn to ask about it. He looked carefully at the ploughed strip but no sort of crop appeared to be coming up in it so he walked across and entered more pinewoods. It was a perfectly beautiful day and the air was invigorating; he lengthened his stride and went on.

The working party replacing posts on The Wire consisted of three elderly labouring men and a guard of two young Volks-polizei. The Vopos were new to The Wire, having but just finished their training, and they were exceedingly conscientious. They had been told to watch the three labourers closely and the result was a practically unwinking Vopo stare, a thing which has to be seen to be believed and reminds the observer of stuffed owls. The labourers, who were old enough, given an early start, to be the Vopos' grandfathers, responded by ignoring them completely, but they did keep on working.

At about the time when George Micklejohn sat down on the river-bank to eat his sandwiches the senior workman glanced up at the sun, having no watch, threw down his pick, and turned away; the other workmen did the same.

The two Vopos shouted at them.

"What's all this? Why are you stopping?"

The senior workman threw the one word "Lunch" over his shoulder and they all repaired to a small clear space near by, where a pot was bubbling slowly upon embers. Three tin pannikins were charged with stew, three spoons were taken from pockets, and three workmen sat down in a row upon a low bank to eat.

After a momentary hesitation the two Vopos sat down opposite to them and continued their watch. The Vopos stared, three pairs of jaws moved rhythmically, the sun shone down, and silence lay over all.

Presently, with one accord, as at a given signal, the chewing stopped and the busy jaws were still. Through the trees behind the backs of the Vopo guard there passed the tall slim figure of an active young man.

There was no change of expression on the workmen's faces and no indication that they had seen anything unusual, only the slow chewing stopped and after a moment one of the Vopos commented.

"What's the matter? Food not good enough for you?"

The chewing started again and continued until the pannikins were empty, when the senior workman, addressing no one in particular, said that the food was all right but that there was not enough of it.

"You'd best be careful," snapped the Vopo. "That's enough from you."

The workmen sat still until the very last moment before the Vopos would tell them to get up and then rose slowly to their feet and plodded heavily back to work.

George Micklejohn walked on and presently came to the edge of the wood and looked across rolling agricultural country with a red-roofed town in the middle distance. There were people working in the fields but they took no notice of him. There was a path along the edge of the wood and he kept to it.

He heard suddenly the sound of a fallen branch cracking beneath someone's foot and turned to see two men in uniform with soft peaked caps on their heads. They carried arms; they were, in fact, soldiers. They came straight up to him, with no friendliness in face or manner, and addressed him in a language of which he did not understand one word.

"Nichts verstehe," he said, trying German first. "I'm sorry, I don't understand. *Je ne comprends pas,"* he added in French and then, having exhausted his repertoire, smiled at them.

They did not smile; on the contrary, they looked grimmer than before. One of them pointed down the path ahead and signalled to Micklejohn to proceed down it. By this time, of course, it had dawned upon him that he had somewhere crossed the zonal boundary and presumably these soldiers were Russians. In that case, the only thing to do was to apologise and retire. He stepped back.

"Frightfully sorry," he said. "Didn't know I was trespassing. I'll go back." Since he was plainly not understood, he pointed to himself, then back the way he had come, added: "Good afternoon," and turned to go, but one of the soldiers lunged forward and seized him by the left arm.

This was too much and Micklejohn reacted promptly. He uppercut the soldier as hard as he knew how and the fellow rolled over backwards into a heap of dead branches. Instantly the second man unslung his rifle, took it back and swung at Micklejohn's head with the butt. He saw it coming and dodged, but the blow fell upon his left shoulder, with paralysing effect. He staggered, caught his heel, and fell, and in a moment they were both on him, for the fallen man was more angry than hurt.

The next few minutes were a blazing kaleidoscope of pain, fury, and humiliation. They were both heavier and older than Micklejohn; they had never heard of Queensberry Rules and would not have cared if they had. When it was quite plain that he was no longer capable of resistance they dragged him to his feet, held him by both arms, and took him down the rough path at a pace which he could not maintain without stumbling continually.

Eventually they arrived at a small clearing in the forest, and stopped. Micklejohn, feeling more dead than alive, was dimly aware of a group of people. He pulled himself together and saw that they were more soldiers grouped about a table covered with maps and papers, there were some Army utility vehicles in the background and each of them bore the stencilled insignia of a red star.

One of the men in the group had the air of a high-ranking officer. He was a grey-haired man with a podgy red face. Micklejohn's captors talked, the officer evidently asked questions, and the soldiers answered. Finally they pushed Micklejohn forward and the officer addressed him personally.

Micklejohn shook his head and said that he was English. *Englander.* British.

The officer's face lit up, at last something had been said which had been understood, but if Micklejohn thought that his troubles were over he was wrong. He was taken back to the outskirts of the group and one of the soldiers, in obedience to some order, trotted off into the woods.

Micklejohn could hardly have chosen a worse moment to blunder into Russian Army activities. The Russians were in the acute stage of one of their periodical attacks of panic on the subject of an attack from the West; there was indeed a certain measure of poetic justice in Micklejohn's troubles, since it was largely his father's urging atomic weapons upon the West German Army which had set off the panic on this occasion. From the Russian point of view the Western Beast was crouching for a spring and the Smirnov Plan was being put into operation.

The Smirnov Plan involved a strong line of defence along the zonal boundary between East and West Germany. The Russian thinks that if there has to be a war it had much better be fought on somebody else's territory, not his, and a very sensible idea it is. General Vedovitch, the well-known expert on defence in depth, was making a close study of the Zonal Frontier, sector by sector, to co-ordinate, improve, and complete the layout of the land defence of Eastern Germany against attack from the West, which comprises the core of the Smirnov Plan. On the day when Micklejohn crossed the line, General Vedovitch was dealing personally with the Stapelburg sector; it was he before whom Micklejohn had been brought, and upon the table in the clearing lay the large-scale fully detailed maps covered with code markings and annotations about observation points, gun positions, fields of fire, concealed defences, ammunition dumps, lines of supply and communication, and all the rest of the Mystery of War.

Time passed. Micklejohn took out his handkerchief to wipe blood and dirt off his face and sat down to rest. He was aching in every limb, his left shoulder hurt him, his mouth was cut and bleeding and his head ached, but all these things were of no importance compared with the fury which possessed him. There is nothing like being contemptuously kicked by louts in heavy boots to rouse the primitive beast in the most cultured undergraduate. He muttered, "Wait, wait," to himself. He was so angry that his teeth chattered.

General Vedovitch did not even look at him. The maps on the table were closely studied and marks and marginal notes made upon them. The General seemed to be delivering a lecture to four or five officers gathered round the table; they looked at the maps and nodded from time to time. At last the General folded up the biggest map together with several sheets of paper and put them in a brief case. The table now being clear, an orderly came from one of the trucks and began to lay knives and forks. General Vedovitch was about to lunch.

The soldier who had trotted off upon some errand returned at this point with a young man in civilian clothes who was not much older than Micklejohn himself and not so tall, notably thin in the face and slender in build. He came to stand before the General, who looked at him with evident distaste and barked at him rather than spoke to him.

"The Big Boy doesn't like this one," said Micklejohn to himself. "Wonder why. Clean and tidy lad. Quite well dressed, too. A good suit and it fits him. Bit of a fop by the look of him."

The young man bowed to the General, turned on his heel, marched across to where Micklejohn sat on a mossy bank and said abruptly: "Get up!"

He spoke English.

Micklejohn looked up without attempting to rise and said: "Why?"

"The General will tell you."

George hesitated, the young Russian scowled, and two soldiers moved up. It would be merely idiotic to invite more punishment.

"I will hear the General's apology for this outrage," said Micklejohn, and got up slowly. The Russian's eyes snapped but he said nothing. Micklejohn ignored him and limped towards the table, for he had been kicked on the knee. General Vedovitch sat squarely on a camp chair with his fists on his knees, looked Micklejohn up and down, and said something.

The young man translated.

"Who are you?"

"George Micklejohn."

"What are you?"

"An undergraduate of Brasenose College, Oxford."

A few sentences were exchanged at this point, probably explanations.

"Your passport?"

George produced it and it was handed to the General, who examined it with the interpreter's help.

"Now," said Micklejohn firmly, "I am prepared to apologise for

41

having inadvertently trespassed across your frontier, provided that I first receive an apology from you"—he looked straight at the General—"for the insolent behaviour of your men and the brutal treatment I received at their hands."

He waited while the translation was made. As it ended, the General slapped his knee and laughed loudly, the other officers laughed with him, and even the interpreter looked faintly amused.

"How did you come here?"

Micklejohn was quite willing to answer this and did so fully.

"You expect we believe you merely stroll across without knowing where you go?"

"Certainly. The frontier is not marked in any way."

"It is the stream you cross."

"Indeed? It is still not marked."

"You could have asked."

"Asked whom? There was no one about."

"What are your political affiliations?"

"I have none," snapped George, for he considered the question an impertinence.

"We waste time," said the General impatiently, and that also was translated.

"I agree, we do," said George. "You will apologise and then I will go home."

"The cock thinks he is on his own dunghill," said the General contemptuously. "Andrey Lentov, take him down to my headquarters and lock him up. I will deal with him when I have time."

The young civilian received the order in silence.

"And do not take too much delight in airing your beautiful English on the way down. I do not trust you, Andrey Lentov, as you know. I would not send you if I could spare anyone else. Take an escort. Go!"

Lentov bowed again and stepped back.

"Wait," said General Vedovitch and addressed one of the other officers. "Vladimir, lend me your revolver."

Vladimir saluted and handed it over at once.

"Here," said the General, holding out the revolver to Lentov, "take this. Put it in your pocket," he added as Lentov stood holding the weapon in his hand. "Yes, I dare say it will drag your beautiful jacket out of shape but you will do what you're told. Pocket it, you fool, and take your hand out again. That's right. If the prisoner tries to escape, shoot him. No excuses now about not having a gun, eh? Now go. No, wait a minute."

Lentov, who had turned to go, spun round again and Micklejohn noticed that he was white round the nostrils and that his mouth was a thin hard line.

"You can take this brief case to Headquarters with you," continued the General. "It is to be locked in the safe. Be careful with it, the contents are valuable. Much more valuable than the life of a civilian liaison officer with the local civil authorities. Go. Oh, and our prisoner's passport, take it and hand it in with the prisoner. Go."

Lentov put the passport—it also contained George's few surviving travellers cheques—into his pocket and turned for the third time. This time he was not recalled. He said, "You come with me," to Micklejohn and shepherded him away from the table.

"Where are we going?" asked Micklejohn, but he received no answer.

andrey lentov

SINCE NO ONE had bothered to translate to Micklejohn anything but the questions he had been required to answer, he had no idea of what had been said, though the General's manner had been unmistakable. He did not like Lentov, he had made a fool of him in public; Lentov in consequence was in such a rage that his hands were trembling and he could not command his voice.

Micklejohn was conducted to a Russian version of a jeep and told to get into the front seat. Lentov took the wheel and a Russian private with a big machine pistol sat in the seat behind.

"Where are we going?" repeated Micklejohn as coolly as though he were being taken for a pleasant drive in the country.

"You will find out when you get there," snarled Lentov. "Sit down and keep still or I shoot you. This—" tapping the revolver in his right-hand pocket—"if fired into the stomach, it hurts."

He slipped his left arm through the handles of the brief case and pushed it up his arm, tucking it close to his side out of the way. Micklejohn looked round as they drove off. The group had scattered and the General's lunch was being served. George turned his head a little further and met the passionless gaze of the private in the back seat. The clumsy pistol he held wavered about as the car rocked on the rough track, but the muzzle was never more than a few inches from the back of George's head.

"No luck there," said Lentov coldly. "Stepan likes shooting."

Micklejohn looked straight ahead and made no answer.

For a few hundred yards they sidled and jolted down the forest track and then emerged upon a country lane, not a good road by any standards but yet a road. Lentov settled himself more easily and the car gathered speed.

About two miles further along the road the car's engine missed, spluttered, missed again, and stopped; Lentov coasted to the side of the road and brought the car to a halt. He gave some order to the private, who responded by practically resting the muzzle of his weapon upon Micklejohn's coat collar. If he leaned back he could feel it and if he moved forward it came with him.

Lentov raised the bonnet and examined the engine. He was, in fact, trying to flood the carburettor but without success. He went round to the back of the car and unscrewed the cap of the petrol tank. There followed a stream of remarks which were so unmistakably swear words that the fact of their being in an unknown tongue did not faze Micklejohn for a moment. Besides, he had already diagnosed the trouble. They had run out of petrol.

Lentov returned to his side of the car and threw himself into the driver's seat. He turned to the private in the back and led off a spluttering commentary which was certainly not praise. He banged the back of the seat with a clenched fist and uttered a series of single words which did not sound like endearments. Micklejohn could see the private's face reflected in the driving mirror above the windscreen and was interested to notice that its expression did not alter at all. The man merely stared straight ahead and made no attempt to answer. Finally Lentov issued an order, for the private laid down his gun, got out of the car, and walked off by the way they had come.

Lentov shouted one word after him and the man broke into a clumsy trot which lasted at least until he was out of sight round a bend.

Lentov uttered an exasperated sigh and pushed the General's brief case, still upon his arm, more comfortably against his side. He took a packet of cigarettes from his pocket, lit one, slewed round towards Micklejohn and spent the next five minutes trying to blow smoke into his prisoner's face. There was, however, a pleasantly fresh current of air blowing in on Micklejohn's side. The attempt was a failure and George gave not the faintest sign of having noticed it. Besides, he was engaged in thought.

Lentov's pistol was temptingly near at hand, since it was in the jacket pocket on the side nearest to Micklejohn. One might snatch the gun, shoot him, and run for it. George had read enough war memoirs to know that some men would do that at once and without turning a hair, but he could not imagine himself doing it. He was much too young to have served in the war and even his National Service had been postponed till he had finished at Oxford. Double-barrelled shotguns he had always known, but what was this weapon and how did it work?

"I know London," said Lentov suddenly. "A foul place full of sullen peoples. It is only of use to buy things in. You English are a nation of manufacturers."

Micklejohn took no notice. One could hardly shoot a man in cold blood. Besides, if he did so and ran for it he might well be caught and if he were—— If he was patient he might be taken to someone who had a little common sense.

"You make good suits, I admit," continued Lentov. "I myself have several I there bought. Good cloth, too. You should all be tailors. You would be more useful than trying to be clever at a university."

It occurred to George that perhaps the fellow was hoping to exasperate him into a quarrel in which he could be shot with a clear conscience. Patience, then, and take no notice. He looked up at the sky and saw a perfectly enormous bird very high up, it must be an eagle and a big one at that. It circled slowly in some rising current. George was so interested that he did not hear Lentov's next remarks. The bird sailed out of sight and Lentov said, "You are sulky, that is bad. We will cure you of sulks."

Micklejohn looked at his wrist watch, but the face had been smashed in the scrimmage and the hands were bent.

"Is your mother a good cook?" asked Lentov.

George was suddenly seized with the urge to answer "No, but my father keeps goldfish in his top hat." He resisted a desire to laugh; really, this was the most ludicrous little squirt. However, Lentov apparently decided that this game was not worth playing and they sat in silence until trudging steps on the gravel road brought them the private with a heavy petrol can in each hand. He unscrewed the petrol-tank cap and a refreshing glugging noise followed. The first can was set down empty, the second was brought into action, and Lentov leaned over his side of the car——

Micklejohn snatched the pistol out of Lentov's pocket, aimed it at Lentov about amidships and snapped: "Do what I tell you or I'll kill you. Start the car and drive on. Start the car——"

Lentov obeyed.

"Now drive on and keep going."

The car went off and left the private holding one tilted can with petrol running out of it on the road. He straightened it up, replaced the cap, and looked after the car till it was out of sight. He shook his head slowly, picked up the two cans, one empty, the other half full, and then went to sit on the bank at the side of the road until some-body should come and tell him what to do next. He lit a cigarette and leaned back. It was very pleasant to sit by the road and do nothing for a little while.

Lentov drove on. His face was a greenish-white and the sweat was running down his cheeks, for he was terrified, not so much of the Englishman, although he had suddenly turned into a demon, as of the Russians he had left behind. They would hear from the private that he, Lentov, had been alone with the Englishman for nearly half an hour and that as soon as there was petrol in the tank they had left the escort and driven off together, for the soldier could not see what had happened in front and would not have understood what had been said.

Lentov was under suspicion. He had been well educated and could speak several languages and his father was a man of some importance. Andrey had been appointed to the Soviet Embassy in London and the place had gone to his head.

Not the English way of life, for he thought that simply silly, nor the English people he met, whose politeness he mistook for servility and whose jokes he found incomprehensible. It was London which charmed him, the bustling colourful traffic—especially the scarlet omnibuses—the clean streets, the gracious houses, the bright flowers in Parliament Square, the busy shipping on London's river, but most of all the things in the shops—ah, the things in the shops! He would moon up Bond Street, flattening his nose against the windowpanes, for he knew enough to realise that much of what he saw was priceless. And the gadgets; tin openers, electric razors, potato peelers, bathroom fittings——

His colleagues were at first amused, then dubious, and finally dis-gusted. Andrey Lentov found himself being lectured, scolded, and finally sent back to Russia with a black mark against him.

"You are tainted," they said. "There is a weakness in your char-acter which has yielded to the false glamour of the decadent and self-indulgent West. Potato peelers, huh! You are politically suspect."

Then his father died and there was no one to back him. He ob-tained a dull post in the Civil Administration of Occupied Territory and was trying to re-establish himself, without much success.

Now it looked as though he had bolted with an Englishman.

"Keep going," said Micklejohn. His reactions to this wild ride were much simpler and not nearly so well founded. He merely thought that if he were in a Russian military vehicle being driven by a Russian, he was not very likely to be stopped. A little luck and he would find himself near enough to the boundary line to be able to slip across. It ought not to be difficult to get away from this fellow who, judging by the colour of his face, was not much of a hero. Besides, he was not armed. He could be, though, there was the submachine gun in the back. Micklejohn, still pointing Lentov's pistol at Lentov's middle, put his left arm over the back of the seat and a long stretch possessed him of the private's weapon. He brought it over with a steady swing and hurled it into a clump of bushes which they happened to be passing at the moment. That was that.

Now about finding the way. The zonal boundary runs approximately north and south, though it is anything but straight. On the map it is a series of unbelievable wriggles. However, generally speaking, it goes north and they were to the east of it, driving north. Let them, therefore, turn left and they would be going towards the line. Micklejohn, it will be remembered, knew nothing about Vopos.

Just ahead, the road forked.

"Take the left-hand road," said Micklejohn, "and step on it. I mean, accelerate. Drive faster."

There was a group of buildings up the right-hand road, with what looked like Army vehicles round them. They were Lentov's last hope and George realised it.

"This pistol, you said, when fired in the stomach, it hurts. You probably know."

Lentov took the left fork.

The road had deteriorated but was still passable; it did not appear to be much used, for there were no new tracks on the soft patches. Lentov became desperate. He would ditch the car and hope the Englishman would be flung out and hurt. Even, with luck, killed. But there was no ditch; the roadsides were low and soft. He drove on, two miles, three miles——

There was a dead tree lying by the side of the road. Lentov waited till he was almost upon it and then, without slackening speed, swung the car off the road and straight at the fallen trunk.

There was a hideous crash, the car stood on its head for a moment and then fell slowly over on its side in the soft ground.

When Micklejohn recovered consciousness he was first aware of gruff voices talking across him in a rather difficult brand of German. He opened his eyes and found two old men, one on either side of him; to his pleased surprise they spoke kindly to him, saying that the Herr was now feeling better, was he not?

Micklejohn agreed that he was, he sat up unsteadily and looked

48

about him. Andrey Lentov was a few feet away, lying on the ground in a careless attitude which suggested that he was either unconscious or dead. He looked dead and Micklejohn said so.

The two old men looked at Lentov with deep distaste. One said that no, unfortunately the —— a dialect word unfamiliar to Micklejohn, was still alive and the other suggested that it would perhaps be a good opportunity to finish him off, *nicht wahr?* He lifted a very adequate felling axe with a five-inch blade and a four-foot haft and turned it so that the back of the axehead was available for use as a hammer, but the other stopped him.

"No, Hans, no. There will only be reprisals, thou knowest."

"True," said Hans, and put down the axe. "A pity, though."

Micklejohn, who had shut his eyes, opened them again.

"But that is a very handsome bag he is carrying," continued Hans. "Real leather and practically new." He drew General Vedovitch's brief case off Lentov's arm and put it under his own. George Micklejohn, who had suffered many things in the last two hours, remembered the red-faced General and was seized with a fit of something very like giggles.

"The Herr is not yet himself," observed the other old man. "We had better get him away."

"You are right, Karl," said Hans. "To the hut first and to your house after dark. You have a loft. Can the Herr stand?"

"Quite well," said Micklejohn, and struggled to his feet. They supported him upon either hand, having gathered up their axes, and led him away through narrow twisting paths through a wood of mixed timber and thick undergrowth. After a little, Micklejohn could walk unaided and they went together into the depths of the wood at the deceptively slow forester's pace which yet eats up the miles.

"We are nearly there," said Karl. He turned round a clump of hazels and down a bank to a tiny shed so overgrown that it seemed impossible that anyone could ever find it. They went in. Hans threw down some not particularly clean sacks, and Micklejohn sank gratefully upon them. Karl drew out from a dark corner a black bottle and a chipped enamel mug, poured some of the contents of the bottle into the mug, and handed it to Micklejohn.

"Let the Herr drink, it will revive him."

Micklejohn thanked him and, remembering his manners, added *"Prosit!"* He took a pull at the contents of the mug and thought that the roof of his mouth had exploded into his brain; then the rest of the liquid ran down his throat and set fire to his gullet. He choked and Hans kindly patted him on the back.

"Not too fast," he said. "It is better drunk slowly. It is strong, eh?"

Micklejohn privately thought that this alarming liquid ought not to be drunk at all. It would, he decided, be fine as a paint stripper or for curing warts, but as a drink, no. However, in some unexpected way it seemed to be doing him good and the explosive effects were not so marked if taken in small sips. His colour came back and his legs ceased to tremble.

"Tell me," he said carefully, for his grasp of German seemed a little precarious, "you knew that fellow Lentov, did you?"

Karl spat, fortunately out through the doorway, and Hans answered the question.

"Ach, yes, we know the swine Lentov. The Herr also?"

Micklejohn gathered his thoughts, which seemed to be straying of their own accord.

"When you say 'know him,' I met him this afternoon. He was, I believe, taking me to prison or somewhere like that. What I wanted to ask was, why are you so kind to me when you didn't like him? I mean, we were together in the jeep and you might have thought we were comrades."

"Since the Herr was holding a pistol at that"—the dialect word again—"man's head and even after you both fell out the Herr was trying to strangle him——"

"What? Oh, was I? I don't remember that."

"No, no. The Herr was unconscious but still vigorous. But when we touched the Herr, he collapsed," explained Karl.

"Besides," added Hans a little apologetically, "the Herr has letters from England in his pocket."

"We looked at them," said Karl, "because we thought the Herr was English by his clothes and we wanted to see if we were right."

"Quite right," said Micklejohn drowsily, for his eyelids were suddenly and inexplicably heavy, "I am English."

"We were prisoners of war in England in the first war," said Hans, "so we know the English, how they look and how they dress."

"We are not ignorant men like those who have never travelled," said Karl, but Micklejohn's head fell back and instantly he was sound asleep. The two old woodcutters looked at him, at each other, and moved quietly out of the hut.

"He will sleep for eight hours," said Karl. The door of the hut was off its hinges and leaning against the wall. They propped it up in the doorway.

"When he wakes," said Hans, "he will be well again. Put that brushwood against the door."

"He has been beaten by those Russians," said Karl, "there are marks on his face."

"God curse them," said Hans mechanically, like a response in a litany. "If we look after him and help him, he will be grateful." They turned away from the hut, picked up their axes, and walked off towards the place where they had been working.

"That is so," agreed Karl. "He has plenty of money, good West marks. I am surprised They did not rob him."

"There is no knowing what They will do."

"What shall we do when we get back to the overturned car?"

"Nothing. We will work a little further off. We saw nothing, we heard nothing."

"That is right," agreed Karl. "Nothing at all."

Some time after Micklejohn and his elderly friends had gone away, Lentov had returned painfully to consciousness. His head ached violently and bright flashes tormented his eyes whenever he moved, but he dragged himself up to his knees and looked about him.

The jeep was a wreck.

The brief case, containing the Smirnov Plan, had disappeared.

The Englishman had gone.

Therefore the Englishman had taken the Smirnov Plan.

Lentov struggled to his feet, tottered to the overturned jeep and leaned against it. He would certainly be accused of having helped the Englishman. He looked about him for the revolver, but that had gone too. He could not even blow his brains out.

He felt in his pockets, vaguely, with no particular purpose, and found Micklejohn's passport and travellers cheques and with them an hotel card. Die Drei Bullochsen, Goslar-am-Harz, Room 32. Of course, of course, the Englishman had said that he was staying there. No doubt he was now on his way back there, taking the Smirnov Plan with him.

If it were possible to follow him and take the plan from him——

Lentov straightened himself, glanced up at the sun to get his bearings, and staggered off into the woods.

When Karl and Hans returned to the spot, there was nothing there but the overturned jeep slowly spreading an iridescent oily film upon the ground.

CHAPTER VI

in the attic

"But I must get back," said Micklejohn. "My family must be getting worried."

He was sitting on a mattress on the floor of the loft under the roof of Karl's house; it was twenty-four hours since the jeep had turned over. Apart from a loose tooth, cut and swollen lips, a stiff and painful knee, and a wonderful collection of ink-black bruises on various parts of his body, he was himself again and no worse than he had often been after a hard game of Rugby.

Otto Neumann looked at him mournfully and shook his head, a bald head with a fringe of grey hair round its perimeter and an intricately wrinkled scalp. These wrinkles fascinated Micklejohn because they reminded him of railway lines spreading and subdividing at the approach to a main-line terminus: Waterloo, for example. When Herr Neumann's expression changed, the wrinkles altered like points being reset on a railway, the Portsmouth line switched to Platform 5 while the Southampton line temporarily vanished. Micklejohn had to make continuous efforts not to watch them.

The two men were sitting on the floor because the loft was merely the space under Karl's roof, triangular in section and only high enough in the middle to allow the short figure of Neumann to stand upright. Micklejohn, who was five feet eleven in his socks, could not stand upright at all.

"I regret," said Neumann. "The anxiety of the Herr's relatives is never sufficiently to be deplored but, at the moment, impossible to be relieved." He spoke an educated German and Micklejohn found him very easy to understand.

"But why? It's only to slip back through the woods, avoiding the police, and——"

"Listen. I do not know what the Herr managed to do in the course of his passage over the frontier, but I tell you——"

"All I did was to walk straight on. You talk about The Wire; all I can say is that I never saw any."

"No. We know about that. There was a stretch of wire down that day while posts were being replaced and the Herr has to pick that one short length for his promenade, and by pure luck the Vopos were not looking his way. That is literally true, for the Herr passed behind their backs while they were watching the workers. The workers saw the Herr pass and said nothing."

"But why didn't they call to me and tell me I was trespassing? Then I could have apologised and gone back."

"They are decent men and they did not wish to see the Herr shot before their eyes. Nobody likes Vopos."

"Shot? For inadvertently crossing an unmarked frontier? But that's ridiculous, nobody would do a thing like that. Even the Russians let people into Russia itself now, ordinary tourists, you know, and you tell me the Vopos are Germans."

Neumann sighed. "The Herr must try to grasp this simple fact. Ever since the workers' rising over here, in the Soviet Zone four years ago, this frontier has been closed, closed, closed. Shut. Shut dead. Increasingly so. At one time refugees used to stream across that frontier in thousands; now, if seven try to go, three or four may succeed. The rest are shot. There used to be a number of official crossing places; at Eckertal, at Walkenried, and other places, now there is one only, at Helmstedt."

Micklejohn ran his hands through his hair.

"The Russian soldiers used to guard this frontier, but after a time they trained a special corps of the Volks-polizei to do the work under their supervision," continued Neumann. "Does the Herr now begin to understand?"

"But why shoot? If they arrested people——"

"Hear the Communist creed. Anyone trying to escape *to* the West is a traitor and therefore deserves to be shot. Anyone coming in *from* the West must be a spy and therefore deserves to be shot. Understood at last?"

"Perfectly. There is no difficulty in understanding your very clear explanation, Herr Neumann. It is the believing it which I find so difficult—please understand me. I do not doubt your word for a moment, it is just that—that it all sounds so completely mad! It's like a frightening fairy story."

"It is mad," said Otto Neumann soberly. "That is why it is frightening." There was a short pause and then the German went on: "All that is, however, normal now with us, we are becoming used to it. What is not normal is the extraordinary activity—upheaval—uproar—in the Russian Army along the frontier just now, which seems to date from the Herr's arrival. I said that we do not, now, see Russian troops on the frontier, but this last twenty-four hours there are thousands of them searching the woods and the houses and questioning people."

"You don't mean to tell me that the Russians have turned out a couple of regiments to hunt for me?"

"Not only the Herr. It seems that there is also a Russian missing, the man Lentov, who was also in the jeep."

"Oh? I don't know what has happened to him, then. The last time I saw him he was unconscious and Karl told me that when they went back to the wreck he had gone. I assumed that somebody had found him and taken him away."

"The Russians and their friends did not, for they are hunting for him. We true Germans would not, for he is hated. He is in charge of the Civil Administration in this sector, he sees to it that the civil authorities here carry out their orders and he is much more harsh and cruel than is necessary. It is said that he is in some sort of disgrace in Russia so I suppose that he is trying to earn his pardon."

"The General certainly did not like him," said Micklejohn thoughtfully. "Ordered him about like a dog. Go! Come back! Go! Come back!"

Otto Neumann smiled slowly and said that in all countries, so he had read, Army men despised the mere civilian.

"Except, I believe, in China, at least in the old days," said Micklejohn. "They considered that war was uncultured barbarism and that therefore only coarse and brutal men would stoop to become soldiers."

"It is at least a civilised point of view," said the German drily. "To return to whatever has exasperated the Russian Command, the thing that has stung them most sharply is the loss of the brief case and especially of the papers in it."

"Oh, indeed. Yes. What has become of the brief case?"

"It is no longer a brief case and therefore no longer recognisable. It is good soft leather and there is enough to make the uppers of a pair of shoes."

"Splendid," approved Micklejohn. "And the papers?"

54

"They are here," said Neumann, withdrawing flat folded papers from various pockets. "Can the Herr read Russian?"

"I'm sorry, no. Can you?"

"No. And I make no attempt to learn it. Before the war, Herr Micklejohn, I was a schoolmaster, it was always my profession, but now I am a labourer and work in the fields." He showed his hands, calloused with manual labour. "It is better so."

"For political reasons, I suppose."

"Precisely. Those entrusted with the education of the young must be politically reliable, that is, good Communists. I am not any sort of Communist and I am too old to learn. When I saw what happened to other teachers who also did not wish to learn communism I left my post, changed my name, and became a fieldworker. By this means I am still alive. It is very odd," said Neumann, in a faintly puzzled voice, "how one so naturally desires to go on living. I have often wondered why."

Micklejohn, who had not previously encountered deliberately inflicted human misery, said something incoherent about hope being innate in the human soul and Neumann said briskly that even when one was beyond hope there still remained innate damned obstinacy. "So," he concluded, "I have learned no communism nor Russian either. Please look over these papers. There is a large map, some smaller sketch plans, and a page of notes."

Micklejohn looked them over carefully. "This large map was on the General's table when I was first taken to him. I can't say I actually recognise the others but I saw him fold them all up together and put them in the brief case. They do look important, don't they? But I'm sorry to say I've no idea what they are all about. I suppose you could not borrow a Russian dictionary for me, could you? Or even a Russian-German primer of some sort? If one could make out even a few words here and there, it might give the gist of it."

"I will try," said Neumann, and got to his feet. "I must apologise for inflicting my company upon the Herr for so long, the delight of conversing once more with an educated man——"

"Please don't go, please sit down again. I also miss having someone to talk to. Karl is very kind and his wife is an old pet but she's nearly stone-deaf and they don't seem to have many interests. Besides, I wanted to ask you again about getting away. Do I gather that I must wait till all this excitement has died down?"

"That is so," said Neumann, settling down again. "I must explain that the Herr is reasonably safe here; he is outside the five-kilometre zone. That is, five kilometres from The Wire." Micklejohn mentally translated this into just over three miles and nodded. "Everyone in Soviet-occupied Germany carries identification papers, naturally. Within the five-kilometre zone he has also a special pass to live and work there. Within a half-kilometre zone, only the Vopos pass freely; anyone working there, like the fence-repairing party, has a temporary pass for a day at a time or less. The time for the work is estimated. If it will take three hours he will have a three-hour pass and if the work is not done in the time, he must leave it and come out. I tell the Herr all this not to depress him but to make clear what the difficulties are, even normally. Now, with the Russians swarming about it is not difficult, it is impossible."

"Yet I walked through——"

"*Herrgott!* And met the Russians. Also, the Herr must have been surrounded by a bright phalanx of guardian angels holding their wings about him, not to have been seen by the Vopos."

Micklejohn thought that he was far more likely to escape notice if he were not escorted by any bright phalanx however well-intentioned and also that this poor little man had got the wind up, and no wonder. However, things did seem to be extra difficult at the moment.

"I suppose," he said, "that there are, in fact, means of communication between you and friends in the Western Zone?"

Neumann fidgeted.

"There are, in fact, rare occasions when messages are passed across," he said evasively. "But it is desperately dangerous. If one is caught, there is an end."

Micklejohn took this with a large pinch of salt. If people made up their minds to pass messages, messages would pass, if they had to be tied round a stone and hurled across. The Vopos could not stand shoulder to shoulder along several hundred miles of wire. Neumann appeared to have read his thoughts.

"That is the whole point of the prohibited-zone system, you understand," he said. "People cannot get near The Wire except by permit and then they are closely watched all the time they are there."

Micklejohn still thought a good forester would get through if he chose his time and place, but it was no use arguing that now.

"I only thought," he said apologetically, "that I might get a note through to my people, saying I was quite well and would come——"

"No, no. It may be that the Russians think the English Herr slipped out again at once. If the note were intercepted they would know that he was still this side and then they would go on looking for him until they found him. No, no notes, Herr Micklejohn. Far too dangerous. I must go," said Neumann, getting to his feet more determinedly this time. "I have been here a long time and someone might wonder why. I will try to get a Russian-language primer of some kind for the Herr as quickly as possible and I will bring some identification papers for him, such as we all carry. Then the Herr will be able to go out a little, with care. That will make a pleasant change, *nicht wahr? Auf Wiedersehen,* Herr Micklejohn."

the road to walkenried

HAMBLEDON went again to see the Chief of Police at the *Polizeiamt* just behind the Markt-Kirche in Goslar.

"I am infinitely obliged to you for giving me that authorisation to show the Frontier Police," he said. "They tried to shoo me away before they saw it but afterwards no one could have been more helpful."

The Chief nodded casually and said that the Frontier Police were by way of being a *corps d'élite*; they were, as no doubt the Herr Hambledon knew, a body of men employed exclusively upon frontiers all round Germany.

Hambledon said yes, indeed, he had also seen them at Aachen and other frontier stations in the West. "And the Vopos? Are they to be described as a *corps d'élite* also?"

The Chief's face darkened and his voice became expressionless. "The Volks-polizei police the whole of Soviet-occupied Germany. Probably those who actually patrol the frontier are specially trained, but they are basically all one force."

"I gather that 'force' is the operative word," said Hambledon blandly. "I hope that, over the zone as a whole, they are not all equally trigger-happy, as I am given to understand that these men are?"

"The Herr," smiled the Chief, "has made good use of his time. I thought it better that you should see for yourself how things are rather than that I should attempt to describe it to you. Besides, I do not go up there, it is no pleasure. My hobby is model railways, not being glared at by armed hooligans through rusty barbed wire."

"Not a pleasant sight, no——"

"Particularly when it is one's own country," said the German angrily. "However, I do not wish to bore you with our troubles."

"I wish I could say that I found them merely boring, but it is plain that they are much more serious than that. I really went to try to find out whether young Micklejohn could inadvertently have strayed across the frontier——"

"I should say, quite impossible, 'inadvertently.'"

"And I learned that, on that day, there was a stretch where The Wire had been taken down for the posts to be replaced."

The Chief's eyebrows went up.

"I did not know that. The Herr will understand that the Frontier Police are not under my authority; they do not report to me. I was asked to make enquiries about this young man and I was told what I told you before, that he had been seen at Eckertal but that they—the Frontier Police—did not know which way he had gone from there."

"I found them very loth to admit that he was likely to have gone across."

"Naturally, since it is their duty to see that such incidents do not take place! What does the Herr wish to do now?"

Hambledon thought for a moment.

"Is there any undercover communication with sympathisers the other side of The Wire?"

"None," said the Chief sharply, and rather spoiled the effect by adding: "So far as we know."

Hambledon mentally translated that into: "Almost certainly there is, but they wouldn't tell the police about it." He dropped that line of enquiry and said that he felt he must know more about conditions before even beginning to make any sort of a plan. "I should like to hire a car with a reliable driver who knows the country and get him to drive me to all the places along the *Zonengrenze* where the line runs near the road. I see on the map that there are many such places. There are roads which used to cross, and so on. Perhaps you could recommend someone."

The Chief of Police stroked a rather bristly chin.

"Yes, there is a man—what is his name?—Britz, of course. Hugo Britz. He knows the frontier very well indeed, and he is an honest man and a good driver. He runs a taxi service in Goslar but there is not much scope for him in a small place like this. It will be a help to him financially to have even a short period of continuous employment."

"Is he a local man?"

"Not originally. He came in from the East about three years ago. He is quite reliable, he does not like the Communists. He has a girl in the Soviet Zone and they will not let him see her. He lives in the Schildergasse, I must make sure of the number, he has a room in the house of a widow. The Herr knows the Schildergasse? You turn off left, by the Jakobi-Kirche, from the road to the station."

"Thank you very much," said Hambledon, getting to his feet and taking the slip of paper on which the Chief had written Britz's address. "I will go there now and see if I can find him at home. I am so much obliged to you."

"Not at all," said the German. "A pleasure. You will find Britz very obliging, I believe. He will take you wherever you wish to go, and if you suddenly say to him: 'Turn the car and drive away like the devil,' he will do that too. He is afraid of the Vopos."

"People seem to be," said Hambledon thoughtfully.

"Yes," said the Chief of Police.

Hugo Britz was a square-faced young man in the early thirties, not tall but well built and strong. He had a quiet manner and was obviously pleased at Hambledon's suggestion.

"You wish me to drive you to wherever one may come close to The Wire. Certainly I will do that, it is quite easy. The Herr has, perhaps, a map, or shall I bring one?"

"I have one, here it is," said Hambledon, unfolding a highly coloured *Wanderkarte* of the West Harz, made for the use of walkers.

"Yes," said Britz, looking at it, "yes. It is not quite so easy as it appears on that map, some of those roads are closed, but there are many places where one can go to look. When does the Herr wish to go? Today?"

"I think so. It is not yet midday. We will have lunch and then start, if you have no other engagement?"

"No. We will at least see something," said Britz.

They drove out of Goslar by that one of the city's ancient gates which is called the Breite Tor, past the mines of Oker, where so many of the refugees live and work, to Bad Harzburg, and beyond that by a lovely road through pine forests.

On and on, past cleared stretches with the stumps of trees showing above the coarse grass.

"Quite a lot of the woods have been cleared here," said Hambledon. "I am glad to see that they are being replanted!"

The driver glanced about him indifferently. "The British had these trees felled," he said. "For pit props."

A notice against some tall fences a little back from the road: "The deer are fed here." But presumably it was not feeding time, for there was not an antler in sight. A tall slim radio mast with small buildings about it: the radio station which broadcasts to Eastern Germany. A high conspicuous hill upon the further side with what looked like a castle on the top: the Brocken: *Walpurgisnacht*, demons and witches and bale fires fading out in the dawn of May Day.

"That is an hotel on the top," said Britz. "The Russians hold conferences there sometimes; there is a ballroom for meetings. I myself have driven a West delegation there, via Helmstedt and back the same way."

On several occasions Britz turned off the main road to drive down a subsidiary lane towards the east, and at the end of it there was always the same thing: the road surface deteriorating to loose gravel, a pole across the road and, upon the further side, a pit dug and the earth out of it piled up into a bank, as at Eckertal, and, always, The Wire.

They passed through Braunlage, a small town with shops and people about the street, and on again until the road ran towards a pine wood and turned sharply to run beside it. At the corner the driver stopped the car.

"This is one of the best places to see The Wire. People come here quite a lot."

Hambledon got out and walked across the wide road margin towards the barbed-wire fence. The driver came after him and laid a hand upon his arm.

"Not too near, mein Herr. That line of stone posts is the actual frontier line. It is wiser not to overstep it." He dropped his voice. "There is a Vopo there watching the Herr. He is lying on the ground— no, not so far back. Just beyond the plough here. By this nearest tree."

Hambledon saw him suddenly, although he was only some ten yards away. There was The Wire, inside it the interminable narrow strip of plough, beyond the plough the trees, and, at the foot of one of them, a young man with a red face, flaming auburn hair, and staring brown eyes fixed on Hambledon. Under his hand there was a machine pistol. The sun struck down upon reddish-brown tree trunks, the brown carpet of pine needles and a red-haired young man in a brown uniform, all slightly differing shades of the same colour.

"I should not have noticed him if you had not told me," said Hambledon.

"They are like that," said Britz. "There are two more further back, standing up."

"Yes, I see them. There is another upon the watchtower," for there is one of the numerous tall lookouts at this point.

"I have never seen so many about as there are today," said Britz uneasily. "One may drive to these various points and hardly see one, but today they are everywhere."

There were two labourers digging a large hole just inside The Wire. They worked steadily on and never once glanced over their shoulders towards the road. One was an old man with sparse white hair round an almost bald head. Another car pulled up and four people got out. One was a girl with a camera slung round her neck. As she came forward one of the men in the party hurried after her, took the camera from her, and carried it back to the car.

"Are cameras forbidden here?" asked Hambledon, observing this.

"Not forbidden, no. But the Vopos don't like them."

"But surely one can do what one likes outside the Soviet Zone!"

"It is not advisable," said Britz, "to bring them so near."

Another car pulled up behind the last. The people in it got out and stood round the car, looking but coming no nearer.

"I know those people," said Britz. "Excuse me one moment."

He went away to speak to them and left Hambledon standing in the sunshine, looking up at the watchtower. It was difficult to see clearly the man silhouetted against the bright sky and Hambledon shaded his eyes. The man had binoculars and was looking at him, at closer range this time than from the other watchtower at Eckertal. What was really called for, Hambledon felt, was a thoroughly rude gesture.

Britz came back.

"Those people I know," he said, "that old man is their uncle. They heard that he was working here and they have come up to see him."

"Will they speak to him?"

"Oh, no. It is not allowed, but it is something to be able to say they have seen him. He had two sons but the Vopos shot them both."

"What——"

"They were escaping," explained Britz. "They got over The Wire but the Vopos got them before they could reach cover."

"When was this?"

"About three months ago, I think. Some little time ago."

The labourers went on working; the people in the road stood about watching them and talked in low tones. One of the Vopos lit a cigarette and the sense of brooding unease was nearly palpable.

"Let us go on," said Hambledon heavily.

"*Schön*," said the driver briskly, and led the way towards his car with long strides.

They visited several other such stretches where The Wire ran along close to the road, but they were all the same. The Wire, rusty in the sunshine, the ploughed strip six or seven feet wide snaking across the country without a break for mile after mile and, wherever they stopped, two brown uniforms—the Vopos are usually in pairs—somewhere lurking just within view.

There was one brighter interlude. Britz saw a party of men working in a field, hoeing turnips in fact. There were a dozen or so of them and a Vopo with the usual machine pistol in his hand was walking up and down in front of them. They were plainly not working any harder than they could help and every time the Vopo guard on his beat turned his back upon any of them they left off working at once and leaned upon their hoes. Britz broke into a laugh and pointed them out as the car swept past.

"Punishment party. All Vopos. Wonder what they've done. Punishment fatigue, the Herr knows?"

"In the British Army we call that 'jankers.' What a pity they are not all doing that."

A little later Hambledon said: "When I was at Eckertal one of the Frontier Police told me that there was one place where there is no Wire, somewhere beyond Walkenried, do you know the place?"

"Oh, yes. Between Walkenried and a little place called Neuhof. Nobody knows why there is no Wire there. There is the ploughed strip and that is all, but it is very closely watched."

"I should like to go there, please."

"As the Herr wishes, but there are many more beautiful and interesting places in our Harz than this melancholy *Zonengrenze*. At Walkenried there is a most interesting ruined abbey——"

"Some other day, perhaps."

"*Schön*," said Britz submissively and drove through Walkenried towards Neuhof. Here, at a point where the road bent sharply to the right, the ploughed strip swept up close to the road at the angle and there was no Wire. Britz stopped the car, Hambledon got out, and a couple of Volks-polizei who were leaning over a gate thirty yards off turned their binoculars upon him.

"If a car came along this road too fast and failed to take the turn," said Hambledon, "the driver would find himself in the Soviet Zone whether he wished it or not. Probably with his wheels in the air."

"It has been done," said Britz drily, "but not often."

"What happened?"

"The people were allowed out again after some delay. The car, usually, not."

"Oh. Britz, is there any way by which a man could travel to Walkenried from Goslar and not be noticed at this end?"

"Please?"

"I was wondering whether there were any place where a stranger might inadvertently stray across the frontier, and it seems to me that this is the only place."

"Ah. But here it is closely watched, as the Herr sees. There was a young Englishman who went missing the other day, when there was all that fuss and running about among the Vopos and the Russian Army, too. It was like upsetting a beehive, they say."

"Oh, really?"

"Yes. There was a lot of excitement. It was said on the other side that he went across to meet a Russian officer and steal some plans of the frontier defences."

"And what happened to him?"

"He was captured by the Russians but he got away from them, or so it is said on the other side, mein Herr. So now they are all looking for him and the Russian officer and, of course, the plans, or so they say on the other side."

Hambledon drew a long breath.

fear

BRITZ, who had been staring across into the Soviet Zone and speaking absent-mindedly, turned and looked at Hambledon.

"The Herr is evidently interested, perhaps he has heard about this Englishman? The affair has not been made public."

"I do know about him, Britz. I have come out from England for the express purpose of finding out what has happened to him."

Britz looked suddenly embarrassed.

"I talk too much—I, who should know better. The police recommended me to the Herr, he said so this morning. I beg the Herr not to tell the police that anything is known about what happens on the other side, especially not to tell them that I know anything. I beg the Herr, please. The police do not know anything about it, please——"

"So the Chief of Police told me this morning. I see no reason why I should inform them. They are quite capable of managing their own affairs and I am here to obtain information, not give it."

"Then the Herr will not tell them?"

"No."

"I thank the Herr. If the police knew that there was communication across The Wire——"

"They guess it, Britz. Any intelligent man would. There must be communication; it would be impossible to stop it completely."

"So long as they do not know how it is done or who knows about it——"

"Why are you so afraid of their knowing?"

Britz's eyes went to left and right.

"Let us get back in the car and drive away. We can be private in the car."

Hambledon agreed. He looked back as they drove off; the two Vopos who had been leaning on the gate had climbed over it and were walking slowly towards them. When the car had passed through Walkenried again Hambledon repeated his question.

"It is only because, if the police knew there were means of getting news out, they would be demanding it all the time. What is happening there—what is that new building for—can you get a message through to such a man? Then pressure would be applied. It would be insupportable, the Herr sees that. It is all far too dangerous."

Hambledon saw quite plainly that if it were the Soviet intention to establish a reign of fear along that frontier, they had succeeded admirably. The cameras which it was "inadvisable" to produce; the relatives who dared not speak to an unhappy old man; the hotels in Hohegeiss, Braunlage, and Walkenried, once tourist centres, now empty because German visitors will not sleep at night so near the Russians; the fieldworkers on the other side who kept their faces turned away from the West and would not even look——

What was even more revealing was the fact that it did not apparently enter the head of a single German to do a single thing about it. They were terrified and did not care who knew it. They cowered.

Hambledon averted his mind from the ugly picture and concentrated upon the task which he had come there to perform.

"I shall not tell the police anything about it," he said, "upon condition that you tell me everything you know. This young man, where is he now?"

"I have told the Herr all I know, I think. It is all vague, nobody knows anything definitely; and when stories are whispered from one to another they are not very reliable, the Herr knows? Some plans were stolen from, it is said, the Russian Army by an officer, and this young Englishman had them. He was captured and escaped again. The Russians were still looking for him yesterday so he must be in hiding somewhere but nobody knows where. If anyone were hiding him they would not talk, naturally."

"I suppose not. No."

"May I ask the Herr a question? Has he been up to The Wire before? Has he made himself, how shall I say it, conspicuous? Not wishing to appear inquisitive, but I have never seen so many Vopos about before. Wherever the Herr stopped and alighted, there they were. Often and often I have driven along here and seen one or two, no more, but today—— One would say they recognised the Herr."

"Recognised me? How the devil could they when I have never been along here before?"

"They might have photographs. On those watchtowers of theirs they have cameras with telephoto lenses and if anyone seems to be taking too much interest in The Wire and might be troublesome, a photograph is taken and circulated. Then they watch for that person to come again. They are very good photographs," added Britz, "if the light has been good. I have seen some of them."

"They can," said the irritated Hambledon, "take photographs of the backside of the road sweeper's female donkey if they like and I hope they go cross-eyed studying them. They are not civilised."

"They are subhuman," said Britz calmly.

"Britz. Is it possible for a man to pass into the Soviet Zone provided he knew where to go and what to avoid and had contacts warned to expect his——"

"No."

"But——"

"No. It is not possible. Listen, mein Herr. When I came across three years and more ago—three years and ten months—I left behind in Ilsenburg my fiancée. I begged her to come out with me, but her mother was ill and could not be left. Afterwards, when she was well again, it was too late. It is too difficult for a girl to get out; an active young man too often fails to do it. It is not The Wire itself, it is the control of movements on the other side, the restricted zones, the necessary passes, the—— Does not the Herr believe that if it were possible to go across I should do it? Not to see or speak to one's future wife for nearly four years, it is hard. I get news of her from time to time, yes. She is well, this and that happens, but to see her, no."

"Do people never come out, legally, by Helmstedt?"

"Oh, yes. Communists, with a job to do in the West. There are plenty of those about in the Western Zone, the Herr must know, but not my Elise, to join a man of military age who has skipped it to the West. Besides, if she could make the journey and evade the Vopos and pass The Wire and get clear away, they would take reprisals on her family, on her parents. One cannot have that. I tried to arrange something not so long ago but she would not come. The tears were running down her face as I begged her to listen, but she dared not. One does not know what they would do in revenge. They used to allow escorted parties of students to come across, under strict escort you understand, to join in our Jugendbund activities, camping and music and so on, but not now."

There was a short pause.

"So you do go across," said Hambledon quietly.

Britz uttered an angry expletive and slammed his hand against the steering wheel. The next moment he apologised.

"I beg the Herr's forgiveness, the word I used was meant for myself, not for him. It makes me angry every time I think of it, to be kept apart from my fiancée all these years, and when will it end? She and I should have been married before this and sharing our lives together, not wasting our best years in sterility. It preys on my mind; the Herr will please excuse me."

"Of course. It is abominable tyranny."

Britz forced a laugh. "The Herr is really not a safe companion for a man with secrets on his mind. The Herr is altogether too easy to talk to."

Hambledon had made his very considerable reputation largely by being "easy to talk to," but naturally did not admit it. He said merely that a strong emotion long suppressed was always liable to escape in speech in any unguarded moment; it was natural, it was understandable. But it could be inadvisable.

"The Herr is perfectly right," said Britz gloomily.

"Britz, will you try to get some news about the young Englishman for me?"

Britz looked doubtful.

"I do not believe one word," went on Hambledon, "of all this story about his going over to meet a Russian officer and steal confidential papers. Storybook stuff. Rubbish. He is a young student at the University of Oxford, of which you may have heard. He is of a quiet and retiring disposition and working hard for a degree in law. He is rather young for his age, takes no interest in politics and knows nothing about the Army. He has not even done his military service; that was postponed until he had finished his studies. I don't suppose he knows a multiple pom-pom from a regimental cooker. He is a babe in arms— especially in arms."

Britz laughed.

"I did tell the Herr that whispered rumours were apt to be unreliable. This one seems to be even wider of the mark than most. The poor young man, I am sorry for him. From the story I heard, I took him to be a man well able to look after himself, not a dreamy student with his head full of dusty law. I suppose there are not two Englishmen loose in the Soviet Zone? May I ask the student's name?"

"Micklejohn. I have not heard of another man being missing and I think I should have been told. It may be that there is a hunt on for the missing Russian and, possibly, for Micklejohn, too, if he was seen, and the two stories have got mixed together in people's minds."

"It is very possible. Micklejohn, I have it right? Micklejohn. I will see what I can do, mein Herr, not before Monday at earliest, but I will try. Today is Saturday and tomorrow Sunday, many people go up to The Wire on Sunday, their free day, and it is closely watched. May I offer the Herr, most respectfully, a word of advice?"

"What is it?"

"Let the Herr be careful of himself, even in Goslar as well as when he travels about. Yes, even in Goslar. There are plenty of Communists in Western Germany, as no doubt the Herr knows, and the Russians have many agents especially near the *Zonengrenze*. There are British troops stationed near by Goslar and they are a source of interest in themselves."

"Yes, no doubt they would be. What sort of thing had you in mind when you warned me?"

Britz shrugged his shoulders. "Anything. Strange things do happen."

"Abductions?"

"The police would say no."

"Of course they would," said Hambledon crisply. "I should, in their place. I am grateful to you for your warning and I will take precautions."

Herr Otto Neumann, once a schoolmaster and now a farm labourer in the Soviet Zone, came again, as promised, to visit George Micklejohn in his attic.

"I hope that the Herr has almost recovered from his injuries?"

"How kind of you to ask. The injuries are nothing, I have almost forgotten about them, but I shall fade away very soon if I have to stay here much longer. The heat is nearly insupportable, there is no window which opens, the air is full of dust, and I haven't stood upright for two days."

Neumann clucked sympathetically and said that he had brought identification papers for the Herr "such as we ordinary people carry. They will not pass the Herr within the five-kilometre zone—it is necessary to remember that—but they will serve for a little stroll in the evenings to take the air, especially if care is taken unostentatiously to avoid the Volks-polizei. The local ones are not such savages as those who patrol the frontier, but they are still police and should be avoided."

"Karl has promised to take me out this evening. I am, I believe, a nephew of his on holiday from Magdeburg."

"That is right, I have it here. You are Georg Melcher of 247 Bahnhof Strasse, Magdeburg. The Herr will remember to answer to that name? And the address, if asked for, but of course the Herr will memorise the details on this paper. The Herr has, perhaps, some money? I am ashamed, but I have not, myself, more than enough to buy food——"

"Oh, please," said George, and plunged his hands into his pockets. "I've only got West marks and that blighter Lentov went off with my travellers cheques in my passport, not that they would be any good over here, I suppose. Still, I cashed a cheque yesterday, so——"

"It is to obtain clothes and shoes, especially shoes. These the Herr is wearing are far too good, they will attract attention at once, and the English suit is most noticeable. Oh, no, that is far too much money. West marks are worth far more than East marks and the clothes will be cheap and not good, I fear. The Herr will not like them but it is necessary if he wishes to go out."

"My dear Herr Neumann, I would change clothes with a scarecrow, if necessary, to get a little fresh air and straighten my spine again."

"Yes, yes, I understand. I will go now and get something which will serve. I have here a German-Russian dictionary." Neumann dragged from his pocket a small fat book, dirty and dog-eared and with one cover hanging by threads. "It is to-the-last-degree dilapidated and I fear some of the pages are missing but it is the best I could get. The Herr can entertain himself with translating the late General Vedovitch's programme notes." Neumann smiled gently.

"The *late* General Vedovitch?"

"Even so. You see, it did not look well for him, did it? He has annotated maps and pages of notes about the reorganised frontier defences. Does he guard them with his life? No. He gives them to a Russian civilian who is already suspected of pro-British leanings——"

"Pro-British!" said George, with a shout of laughter. "I must say he concealed them very well!"

"He loathed the British, it is said, but he was not trusted, for all that. I was saying, General Vedovitch gave the plans to Lentov and let him drive away in a car with a British prisoner——"

"And an escort with a horrible-looking gun——"

"You rid yourselves of the escort, did you not, upon some pretext?

I argue as the Russian High Command are arguing. Lentov and the Englishman and, above all, the papers are missing, though it is true that the car was found, wrecked. It follows, therefore, that either Vedovitch connived at your escape to curry favour with the Western powers, or he was made a fool of by a simple trick. Fool or traitor, it does not matter, they come to arrest him and he blows his brains out."

Micklejohn was conscious of a certain degree of shock, it was the first time in his sheltered life that any man whom he had known personally had done himself to death, and so violently. Micklejohn was, as Hambledon had said, young for his age. The old schoolmaster watched the changing expressions cross George's face but said nothing, and eventually the boy summed up.

"Well, I expect he'd bumped off plenty of people in his time. So the Russians think that Lentov and I were working together, do they? How silly. By the way, you said that these papers are details of the frontier defences, didn't you? Are you sure——"

"No. That is why I want you to make an effort to check them. You have a young, active, and trained mind; my own is blunted with suffering. Besides, you have nothing to do at the moment and I have too much. Do you see what you can make of the papers and I will go out and get you some clothes. *Auf Wiedersehen.*"

Neumann went off with a sum of money so small in George's eyes as to be quite inadequate, but presumably the German knew his business. He came back in an hour's time with a shirt of some harsh material that scarified George's unaccustomed skin, workman's blue overalls of the bib-and-brace type; a pair of heavy shoes so stiff that they made Micklejohn feel like a Noah's Ark figure from the nursery at home—Shem, Ham, or Japheth standing immovable upon a round base; and a peaked cap such as German workmen wear.

"The overalls are secondhand but clean, it would not be wise to have all new clothes at once. The other things are new and here is the money left over."

Micklejohn, scarlet with embarrassment, tried to find an inoffensive phrase to beg the old man to keep the change and a little over, and was relieved to find that he was delighted to have it.

"For we are paid starvation rates and my clothes are what I stand up in. I thank the Herr most sincerely. Now, would he like to come downstairs? Karl waits below to take you out."

king charles

THE MOMENT WHEN Micklejohn stepped out of the stuffy airless cottage into the pine-scented evening air was one of the most delicious he had ever experienced. His own clothes were taken out of the house in case it should be searched. He refused to receive any money for them although apparently they were valuable merchandise, especially the shoes. They disappeared and he never asked what became of them, but Karl acquired a new pullover and his wife a new kettle and a blanket, for which they solemnly thanked him.

Two or three days passed. Micklejohn kept close to the cottage and obtained fresh air and exercise by digging Karl's potatoes. A few old and trusted friends, Hans among them, dropped in to see Karl's nephew from the great city of Magdeburg, but the nephew could only speak in a whisper. He had, it was said, been suffering from a throat infection and had come to the country for his health.

"Your German," explained Otto Neumann, "is far too good. It is the German of the old nobility and there are none left here. Can you stammer? No, better not speak at all, or as little as possible, a word at a time and the hand to the throat, you know? Yes."

George worked hard at General Vedovitch's papers and, considering that he had to start by teaching himself the Russian alphabet, he made good progress. He reported to Neumann.

"You were quite right. This is a thing called the Smirnov Plan for defence against attack from the West. These sheets are concerned with all the details and these signs on the top of the sheets refer to similar signs"—he pointed them out—"on the map here, and here. You see?"

Neumann nodded.

"I think the British should have these," finished Micklejohn. "I suppose that would be possible. Things are passed across The Wire as a matter of course, no doubt."

"Things are passed, but not as a matter of course and there is always considerable doubt about it," said Neumann a little sharply. "The Herr does not yet realise the state of affairs here."

George apologised and Neumann's expression softened.

"We have lived so many years as—let us face it—as prisoners," he said, "that it is as difficult for us to appreciate the point of view of the Herr, who has always been free, as it is for the Herr to realise what it is like to live in a concentration camp. However, there is an organisation which deals with such matters. I will get in touch with them and explain what is wanted to be done."

Micklejohn amused himself by making a neat parcel of the Smirnov Plan and sealing it with cobbler's wax. Neumann talked on and the deaf old woman pottered about attending to a stew simmering in a pot over the fire and occasionally interjecting a comment which had no bearing whatever upon what was being said. Karl's cottage was well outside the village and so close against the edge of the woods that on windy nights branches rubbed upon the roof like soft hands seeking entrance. Micklejohn, in his attic, had found this a little disconcerting until he found out what caused it.

"Karl is late," said his wife suddenly, in the toneless voice of the very deaf. "I say, Karl is late tonight."

"Something has delayed him," shouted Neumann in reply and got up to look out of the window. Before he reached it there came a sudden rush of flying feet and a boy of about twelve, Hans's son, put a terrified face in at the casement.

"They are coming," he said hoarsely, "searching the village—we are surrounded—Father says get out." The face vanished and the boy dived through a hole in the hedge.

Micklejohn sprang to his feet and Neumann thrust the parcel at him.

"Inside your shirt—go out by the back door—hide in the woods."

George pushed the parcel down the front of his shirt as he ran for the back door. A quick glance round the corner of the woodshed showed him a line of men in uniforms, spaced out like beaters, advancing from the village.

"Russians," gasped Neumann. "Run!"

Micklejohn leapt for the woods and ran, turning and twisting among the trees. He stopped for a moment to look and listen and there came a whistle ahead of him, and another.

"They are all round," he said to himself. "Now don't panic. Fatal to panic."

He leaned panting against the trunk of a big tree and the parcel under his shirt scraped his skin. To be caught with that on him——

The tree against which he was leaning was an oak; an automatic association of ideas leapt into his mind.

"King Charles," he said, half aloud, and sprang at a low branch.

Britz came to see Hambledon on Tuesday morning as promised; Micklejohn had then been missing for a full week.

"I have brought the car," said Britz. "If the Herr will be so good as to order me to drive him to, say, Hahnenklee, we can talk in the car without risk of being overheard, if the Herr pleases."

Hambledon played up.

"It is a nice day," he remarked as they strolled through the entrance hall of the hotel. "I should like to go somewhere, I think. Someone was telling me about Hahnenklee, though I've forgotten exactly what there is about the place—is it far?"

"Oh, no, mein Herr, half an hour, less than that. There is the Miners' Church there, very interesting. All built of wood and not a nail in the whole structure."

There were people standing about in the hall, as people always do in hotels; some of them were staying there and Hambledon nodded to them in passing.

"I shall be interested," said Tommy unblushingly.

"The scenery also," said Britz, "is delightful."

They got into the car and drove away; two men strolling on the pavement opposite to the hotel glanced into the car in passing. As soon as Britz had disentangled himself from the municipal dust cart, a local bus, and a waggon drawn by two horses, Hambledon said: "Well?"

"Not very well. The Herr Micklejohn was being hidden in a woodman's cottage, but the Russians encircled that area yesterday and entered and searched all the houses."

"Did they catch him?"

"It is not known, mein Herr. At least, he was not seen to be led away, but he might have been and my friends not have seen it. The news comes from the perimeter of the operation, the Herr understands, the Russians were about there a long time and it was not safe to go in."

"I see. No one overheard anything that was said——"

"They were all speaking Russian and very few understand it."

"No. What happened to the people who were sheltering him?"

"I do not know, mein Herr."

"I suppose that he may have got away."

"It is possible," said Britz noncommittally.

"I wonder why the Russians suddenly searched that area."

"I do not know, mein Herr. It may be that they are searching every-where and came to that place in its turn, or it may be that someone talked."

"Where is this place?"

"A small village just south of Ilsenburg. My informant did not know its name."

"It does not sound too good," said Hambledon.

"No, mein Herr. But there is always hope."

Hambledon grunted and there was a short silence.

"If the Herr is interested," said Britz, in the tone of one who is happy to introduce a more cheerful subject, "there is news of the Russian who disappeared with the papers."

"Oh?"

"His name is Lentov, Andrey Lentov. He was not an Army officer but a civilian in charge of that area, an official of the Civil Administra-tion of Occupied Territories."

"Indeed."

"They gave me a photograph of him," said Britz, fumbling in his pocket for his wallet. "They thought the authorities here might like to have it in case he had got across to this side, and I thought the Herr might be so good as to pass it on." Britz stopped the car while he took a small print out of his wallet. "Here it is."

Hambledon glanced casually at it, looked again more closely, and gave no sign of any particular interest.

"Andrey Lentov, you said. An official in the organisation for the control of Occupied Territories. Very well. I shall be seeing the Chief of Police in Goslar today and I will give it to him. He will know to whom it should be passed on if he does not want the information himself."

"And if he should ask where the Herr obtained it——"

"It will be in vain."

"*Schön*," said Britz contentedly.

"You will do all that you can to get further news of the Herr Mickle-john, please."

"I will do what I can, certainly, but it is very difficult just now. The disturbance on the other side is not yet at an end and it is still necessary to be extra careful about where one goes and to whom one is seen talking."

"Did you, then, go across on Monday night?"

"What, with the frontier in that uproar? Heaven forbid!"

Hambledon thought to himself that Britz would certainly forbid it if Heaven did not, but it would be useless to ask questions to which he would certainly not receive answers. He assumed that there was probably a hidden telephone working somewhere, but the passing of a photograph implied personal contact. He tried another line of approach.

"Is there any smuggling across The Wire? I have had a good deal of experience of frontiers in one place and another and I have never known one where smugglers did not operate if it were really worth their while. I remember hearing about a case of smuggling brandy from France into Belgium, the operators laid down a pipe across the frontier, just underground you understand; they simply poured cognac into the pipe on the French side and their friends on the Belgian side merely turned on a tap and collected the outcome."

Britz laughed.

"How long did this continue?"

"Until there was very clearly far more cognac in Belgium than was covered by the customs duty receipts. Then there was a real search made and the source was discovered."

It is only human nature to cap one story with another.

"There used to be a great deal of smuggling across our Zonal Frontier before it was tightened up," said Britz. "Clothes and boots mainly; for some reason they cannot make boots in the Soviet Zone. It is said that they have no leather but I cannot understand that, since they have cattle and horses in large numbers and they all have hides."

"One would think so. What did they exchange for these things, or did they pay money for them?"

"Hams, mein Herr, principally. The East mark is worth much less than ours so for them to pay in money would come very dear to them."

"I can't see anyone staggering up to The Wire with a load of hams."

"Not now, no. All that trade is at an end, but there was good money made out of it while it lasted."

No doubt, but where a photograph can be passed other things can be passed also. However, Britz was plainly not going to talk about it. He changed the subject with some decision and Hambledon did not persist.

When they returned to Goslar, Hambledon went to see the Chief of Police.

"I have something to show you," said Tommy. "I fear it has not helped me to find Micklejohn but I thought it might interest you." He laid the photograph of Lentov upon the desk and the Chief picked it up.

"I have seen this man—of course! It is the man whom you found dead in your room. Who is he, do you know?"

"Andrey Lentov, a Russian civilian administrator of Occupied Territories——"

"I have heard of him. He is—was—in control of the sector opposite to us here. He was much disliked."

"I rather gathered that somebody didn't like him."

"Do you know who shot him?"

"I have not the faintest idea."

"Nor why he was shot in your room?"

"Nor that, either. Since he was in Micklejohn's room with Micklejohn's passport, there is a connection somewhere but I have no idea of what it is."

The Chief of Police grunted and looked again at the photograph.

"It is the same man, there is no doubt at all. Where the devil did you get this, eh?"

"Just came across it," said Hambledon blandly.

"I see," said the German, and asked no more.

"Tell me," said Hambledon, "is there no means at all of getting into the Soviet Zone legally?"

"There is, such as it is. If you are a member of a family resident in the Soviet Zone and there is really important business to be settled —family business—perhaps someone has died and there is property to be divided—it is possible to apply for a permit to visit the place. If you are very lucky the permit may be granted after a lapse of three months or so. The permit will allow you to enter the zone at Helmstedt, travel to the place you want to visit by a specified route, stay a specified number of days, and return by the same route, not diverging from it. While you are at the town or village you may walk about within its boundaries but you will not go outside them until you leave again for Helmstedt. And, of course, if the Russians have anything against you, such as having illegally fled the country, you would be very silly indeed to go back at all."

"That is no good. Three months hence is far too long to help Micklejohn."

"The Herr had some idea of finding out where he was and arranging a good excuse for a journey there? It would be a great risk but it might be possible, apart from the delay."

"Is it always three months?"

"Or longer. Or they do not answer at all."

Hambledon shook his head.

"There are, no doubt, cases where a man has successfully crossed The Wire and made his way into the interior without being caught."

"Herr Hambledon, if you are tired of life I recommend the attempt."

"I asked you——"

"I know you did. I have heard stories of men who have done it but I would not vouch for their truth. The five-kilometre zone inside The Wire—let me explain that——"

"I have heard about it."

"Very well, then. Even if by some miracle you passed that you would still be under surveillance. Papers would be necessary and a proof that you had a right to be there doing whatever you were doing, and a background for your life, relatives, previous employment, and so on. Any police officer can demand your credentials and you would have to supply them."

"I believe there is a song or an oratorio or something," said Hambledon, getting to his feet, "called 'Oh, for the Wings of a Dove.' How I sympathise."

"Not a dove, Herr Hambledon. She would not be safe."

Hambledon left the police station. Twenty yards along the street two men were looking into a shopwindow, they did not look round as Hambledon passed, but he recognised them. They were the two who had watched him drive off from his hotel that morning.

Micklejohn climbed high into his oak tree, selected a comfortable crotch, and settled down to wait. The short summer night passed, the dawn broke, and the sun rose; with the returning light the search was resumed and Micklejohn, peering between leaves, saw the uniformed men still diligently searching the hedgerows, beating the coverts, and going into barns. Voices and footsteps below froze him to immobility and passed him by.

"'And far below the Roundhead rode,'" quoted Micklejohn, "'and humm'd a surly hymn.' I wish they'd go away, I want my breakfast. Now I come to think of it, I didn't have any supper, either." He laid a hand over the area of gnawing emptiness and added: "Curse the Russians."

banger and bacon

AT ABOUT MIDDAY there came a hopeful change of scene. The soldiers could be seen to be gathering together in groups; Micklejohn climbed higher up the tree to a point from which he could see the road. Whistles were blown, presumably to recall stragglers.

"'Trumpeter,'" said Micklejohn, who had a regrettable habit of quotation, "'what are you sounding now? Is it the call I'm seeking?'"

Lorries came up the road in convoy and the soldiers climbed in, a few belated arrivals came, running, and scrambled in as the vehicles moved off. The village street was left silent and deserted.

"I wonder if they've all gone or is it a trick to get me out of hiding? Nobody moving yet; they think there's a catch in it. Yes, there's young Erich Meyer from the sawmill. And his father, and the old woman from the post office. Ha."

He began to climb down quickly, but lack of food and sleep and too much excitement took hold of him and suddenly his head swam. He crawled down with painful care to the crotch where he had spent the night, sat down, and put his head between his knees. The giddiness passed and presently he heard someone moving about below. He stiffened and waited, listening intently. The man below was whistling. The tune was vaguely familiar without being quite recognisable, it reminded him of something—ah!

The whistling noise was Hans trying to remember "Tipperary."

Micklejohn swung and slithered from one branch to another and dropped from the last branch to the ground. Hans rushed up and shook him warmly by the hand.

"*Gott sei Dank*, you are safe!"

"But starving," said Micklejohn. "My stomach is sticking to my backbone."

79

"Naturally. It would be. Come with me."

"Are they all gone? Karl and his wife, are they all right?"

"Yes, the Russians are gone. They searched Karl's house. You had left your cigarette case on the table but the old lady saw it and dropped it in the stew, yes, even as the soldiers came through the door she did that."

"Good job it was empty. Can I go back there now?"

"For something to eat, yes, but not to stay. The Russians asked Karl where was his nephew and he said you went back to Magdeburg yesterday, so you must not be seen there again. Someone has told them about you and may tell them again if you stay there. We will find somewhere else for you to go."

Micklejohn was fed and banished to the attic again until after dark, when he was taken to Neumann's cottage.

"They say it is safest under the lamp," said Neumann. "I hope it is true. The house next door"—he pointed—"it is the Volkspolizeiamt."

"Good gracious! But——"

"On the other side"—the long finger swivelled round—"the sausage factory. Herr Muller is short of labour. He had engaged a new man from Ilsenburg but the man has had an accident and cannot come. You are the new man from Ilsenburg. I have your papers here."

"Does Herr Muller know——?"

"He does, but he will pretend not to. You will go to work like the others and do what you are told."

"Certainly. I only hope I give satisfaction."

Neumann smiled slowly. "To work the big mincing machine it is not necessary to have had a college education, but I expect you will make good. You will live here with me, you can go to work by the back door and never appear in the street. It may be the Vopos will never see you, but, if they do, you are working the mincing machine. Yes? Good."

"It is you who are good," stammered Micklejohn. "I—I cannot begin to thank you, you take all this trouble, you run these frightful risks for a total stranger, it is unbelievable—Karl and his wife too——"

"Herr Micklejohn," said the old man, "we are poor and in misery, but we are still Christians."

George was infuriated to find that he could not speak.

"Besides," went on Neumann, in a lighter tone, "we lead wearisomely dull lives here. We work, we eat and then we sleep and tomorrow is like today and so the months pass. To have a secret, to make plans, to foresee difficulties, it is a little excitement, you know? It will be something to talk about among ourselves when the dark evenings come and you are safely at home in England again. Let us not get emotional about it. Emotion clouds the judgement."

"Tell me," said George, "something about this man whom I am to impersonate."

"Here are his identity papers," said Neumann, fumbling in an inner pocket. "You may as well take them at once, you will have to carry them always. Give me the other papers I made out for you. I will put them away, they may come in useful for some other unfortunate. So."

" 'Gustav Ehrlich,' " read Micklejohn aloud, " 'born at Stettin on April 6, 1932'—I've grown three years older all in a moment—'grey eyes,' that's lucky; 'brown hair,' that's all right, mine's getting browner every day; 'height 175.5 c.m.,' that's"—— George engaged in mathematics with the help of his fingers. "Oh well, I shall have to slouch along with my knees bent. 'No distinguishing characteristics,' that's a good thing. Be a bit awkward if he'd had a wooden leg, wouldn't it? But what happens if he turns up?"

"He will not," said Neumann cheerfully, "for he is dead and buried deep. He was—he was very much disliked. He was a tool of the Russians. When there was trouble among the workers at Breslau he wormed his way into their confidence and then betrayed them. When their leaders were executed some of their friends took an oath to execute Ehrlich, so he left Breslau very quickly. The Russians sent him into West Germany, to Dortmund, I think—it does not matter. He got into trouble again there, a police matter, I believe, and again had to run for it. He came in secretly over the frontier because the West German police would have stopped him at Helmstedt. But we who are not Communist were looking out for him, you understand. He had not been forgotten, no. But his Russian masters were not pleased with him either. He was in disgrace with them too, so he said he would take a job somewhere and live quietly for a little. His nerves had been affected, he said. His nerves!" said Neumann, with an angry snort. "He was coming to Ilsenburg but he did not reach it, he is dead and buried and here are his papers."

"But," objected Micklejohn, "quite apart from one's natural objection to taking over the identity of that—that infernal scoundrel, is it a good idea? Because plenty of people must know him personally. I gather that he was quite well known."

"Ach no! A very minor devilkin. Soviet Germany is full of two-mark Ehrlichs. And he was not known in these parts at all, only in

Breslau in Silesia and that is a long way off. No, there is no risk of that, and those who tracked down Ehrlich and killed him will not speak. No, what we thought was this. The Russians will let him alone for a time and then it may be they will send him orders to go back to the Western Zone. That would suit you very well, would it not? To be ordered into the West Zone?"

George said it sounded almost too good to be true. An ideal arrangement if it came off. "But tell me, was it in fact this Ehrlich whom Herr Muller had engaged to work his sausage machine?"

"Ach, no. That is only the story he tells. It is true that he wants another man, but if Ehrlich had come I think he would have gone into the mincing machine. There are always dogs to be fed," added Neumann savagely. Young Micklejohn shuddered; the old man saw it and changed the subject. "Now then, I have something here to show you."

He opened a book which lay on the table and took out a photograph, an unmounted print, small but very clear. It showed a broad-shouldered man against a background of pine trees. He held a pair of binoculars in his hands and appeared to be looking up straight at the camera.

"Do you know this man?"

Micklejohn studied the print and shook his head.

"I don't know him at all, never seen him before to my knowledge. An Englishman, by his clothes. Who is he?"

"He is an Englishman staying at Goslar in order, it is said, to enquire about you."

"Oh, really? Indeed. I suppose he is someone my father has sent out to look for me. What is his name?"

"Hambledon."

George shook his head again. "No. But can one get a message through to him? My people must be getting anxious."

"I am trying to arrange for that, but it is not easy."

"No, I know. I am beginning"—George smiled apologetically—"to realise the state of affairs over here. You told me that I did not and you were quite right, but I am learning fast. I tell you what I think: this man would be a good person to send these papers to, if one could." He fumbled inside his shirt. "Ouch! That cobbler's wax has got warm and stuck to my skin. This man, Hamilton or whatever his name is, if my father has sent him out he will be a good chap. Capable, you know. Where did this photograph come from? How did you get it?"

"The Vopos took it, they have telephoto lenses on their cameras. This man was seen repeatedly along The Wire, examining it and looking across. So they took the photograph and circulated it so that he could be recognised, you know. One of the prints went astray, as it were, and came to me. The name is Hambledon, you had it not quite right."

"Hambledon, yes. I have torn the covering paper on this packet getting it off my skin, and the Smirnov Plan is falling out."

"One moment, I have paper and string here."

"There ought to be a covering note," said Micklejohn, "don't you agree? It's a thousand to one this man Hambledon cannot read Russian and he will not have any idea what it is. Too bad if he only used it to wrap up sandwiches, after all our trouble."

"The Herr is quite right——"

"I will write a note on the back of one of these sheets."

"No, no. English handwriting is very unlike German. If this packet is intercepted it will announce that you are still within the zone. I will write it."

"But suppose Hamil—Hambledon cannot read German either?"

"He must know German or your father would not have sent him out to make enquiries. But if it is in German anyone here would be able to read it; you are right, it should be in English—I have it. Do you write the message in English and I will copy it in German script. Thus we shall have the best of both worlds. How refreshingly unusual!"

Micklejohn wrote a short message in block capitals. Neumann copied it out, the draft was burnt, and the message enclosed in the package.

"There," said George, "all neat and clean again, what an improvement! I seem to have come off a bit on the other wrapping, what a horrid idea. Can I possibly, do you think, need a bath?"

"You English and your baths, they are famous! You shall have a wash in a hand basin before you retire. Tell me, you speak of your father, is he connected with the Herr Augustus Micklejohn of your British Foreign Affairs?"

"The Foreign Secretary. Yes, that's him. I mean, he is my father."

Neumann's jaw dropped. "But this is very serious."

"Why? Does it matter?"

"You are very young," said Neumann severely, "but there is no necessity to be childish."

Micklejohn thought this was a little much and threw his chin up.

"No doubt I am excessively stupid," he began, but Neumann's hand closed upon his arm.

"Do not be offended with me, I only mean that you are evidently an innocent in these matters. Your father is now in Bonn endeavouring to persuade the West German Government to arm themselves with atomic weapons."

Micklejohn nodded. "He is going all round Western Europe offering people atomic missiles," he said. "I don't take any interest in politics, myself. I've had them talked over my head ever since I was in the nursery and I'm bored stiff with them. I have trained myself not to listen, but I did read something about it in the *Hanoversche Presse* at Goslar——"

"Listen," said Neumann impressively. "The Russians are very angry with your father. They do not want the nations armed with atomic weapons——"

"I don't blame them."

"If they had you in their hands they could bring pressure to bear on your father."

"What do you mean? Threaten to bump me off if he didn't give up the idea? That's ridiculous, it wouldn't work. Why, even if my father resigned his post—which he wouldn't—some other man would take it on. It is the policy of the Government, not a private scheme of my father's."

"But such pressure would cause a great deal of trouble and probably delay. You must not be discovered, whatever the cost."

Micklejohn thought this over for a moment and a slow smile spread widely across his face.

"Poor old Dad," he said, "would be livid."

Britz came to the Drei Bullochsen a few days later.

"There is news," he said. "The Herr Micklejohn escaped the Russian search and is now being hidden elsewhere."

"I am delighted to hear it. Where is he?"

"In the same village but in a different house. Formerly he was in a woodman's hut at the edge of the forest, outside the village. Now he is in a house in the village itself. It is said that he has obtained employment of some kind, but I do not know what, mein Herr."

"Good lad. What is the name of the village?"

"Waldecke, a little south of Ilsenburg. It is very small and unimportant, but the Herr will find it on a good map."

"Do you know what name he goes by?"

"No, mein Herr."

"Or the name of the people who are sheltering him?"

"No, mein Herr."

"Find out for me, will you? The name he goes by, whose house he lives in, where he works."

"I will do my best," said Britz dubiously, "but it is all very difficult, as the Herr knows."

"I should know by now," said Hambledon to himself, "you have said so often enough. Would it be possible to get a message to him, if necessary?" he added aloud.

"I will try to find out. A verbal message, perhaps, not a written note."

The two men who had appeared to be taking an interest in Hambledon were still in evidence. He continued to see them at increasingly frequent intervals, though he told himself that the increased frequency might be due to the fact that he was now looking for them. It seemed that whenever he went out he saw them at some time or other; if he went into a café for a drink, they dropped in for a glass of beer. If he strolled about the town, they also would be deciphering Gothic inscriptions on mediaeval houses or admiring ties in Karstadt's windows, but they never appeared to look at him or display the slightest interest in him. Only, they were always there.

One was lean and saturnine, the other stouter, fair-haired and rubicund, and both were well dressed. Hambledon asked about them from a café proprietor whom he knew, a policeman, and one or two others, but no one knew who they were or where they lived. "They speak good German," said the café proprietor, "not a local dialect, mein Herr. I thought myself that one of them came from the Rhineland."

The policeman shook his head and said that they were strangers to Goslar, not local residents, but the town was full of visitors, as the Herr knew; these men might come from anywhere, being on holiday.

One evening Hambledon decided to turn the tables and trail them. He was good at trailing people, having had much practice at that most difficult art, but they seemed to have a sixth sense in such things. They turned down a side street; when Hambledon reached the corner they were not there but when he returned to his hotel for dinner they were there before him, having soup at a small table in the window. Why not? The restaurant was open to the public.

Hambledon sat down to his own dinner and a little later a Swede who was also staying in the hotel came to his table. His name was

Petersen, a cheerful and friendly soul though not, perhaps, quite so abstemious as his best friends might have wished. He was on holiday and intended to enjoy himself in his own way; if this involved getting tipsy every evening, at least he was never noisy or tiresome and Germans are notably broad-minded about drink. The hotel staff used to help him to bed at night and send him up strong coffee in the morning. Hambledon rather liked him. He was refreshingly carefree in a town where everyone seemed to be apprehensive and uneasy. The people of Goslar, one feels, do not sleep soundly at night.

Petersen asked if Hambledon was coming up to the Zwinger. "There is what they call an International Evening laid on tonight, it's quite good fun. Parties, you know, from the various nationalities staying in Goslar; Norwegians and Danes and Dutchmen and even some English people, and lots from my own country. This town must be packed out with visitors. Oh, and a lot of the locals, of course. It's quite a place, the Zwinger, you ought to see it."

"Oh, really? Where is it?"

"Down near the—what is it—something Chapel. It's all that is left of the old cathedral which was pulled down before it fell down. Don't you know? Oh, well, you go across the Markt-Platz and down by the side of the Kaiserwerth Hotel—you know that, I've seen you there. Yes, you go down that street and on and bear left and there you are. It's a round tower, there's a sort of park and a lake. Very pretty, I've been there in daylight."

"I know whereabouts you mean," said Hambledon. "It's quite a hike."

"Oh, we're having a bus affair, one of those little ones. That fellow who drives you about, you know, it's his. He's coming here for us at about nine. Besides, there's going to be a storm, it's raining already. Oh, come on, it will be fun. The proprietor is a great character, huge fellow with a face like a full moon, everybody calls him Onkel Otto."

Hambledon was rather tempted; it would be a pleasant change to see people enjoying themselves even if they were only passing visitors who did not "realise the state of affairs" in that region.

"I expect you've got a busload already, have you?"

"I don't know," said Petersen vaguely. "Always squeeze one more in, can't you?"

"I'd like to come," said Hambledon. "I will if I can. Don't wait for me if I'm not here when the bus comes."

Petersen nodded and took himself off.

Hambledon decided to go if he could shake off his shadowers. They

86

had finished their dinner and gone out. In any case they could not have heard what was being said at Hambledon's table. But it would be better to go in the bus and not walk alone in the narrow, winding, and ill-lit streets which are so picturesque at night and so empty. The centre of Goslar from the Markt-Platz up to the station is cheerful and thronged with visitors, but away in the maze of ancient streets behind the bright lights, the shopping centre and the cinemas, it is very different. The streets are empty but for an occasional passer-by in a hurry; the windows are curtained; all the corners are full of shadows and all the doors are shut. When night falls, Goslar takes cover.

When the bus came to take the hotel party to the Zwinger, Hambledon's two followers were nowhere to be seen. The rain was coming down heavily, so he slipped into his raincoat.

"Perhaps they've turned a sharp corner too quickly and both fallen down a well. I hope there's a dead cat in it," said Tommy viciously, and climbed into the bus with the others.

As he did so Britz turned in the driving seat and handed him an envelope. "Excuse me, please. The Herr asked for his account."

"Oh, thank you, yes," said Hambledon, and put the envelope into his wallet. As soon as he could do so without being overlooked, he opened the envelope and drew out the slip of paper it contained; on it was written simply: "Gustav Ehrlich. Otto Neumann's house. Sausage factory."

Hambledon put it away carefully in the innermost compartment of his wallet.

The Zwinger is a massive round tower built in about the year 1500 as part of the defences of the city wall and is as good as new to this day, which is not surprising since it is immensely strongly built, with walls twenty feet thick. In these degenerate days it is what the Germans call a *Gaststätte*, which is a restaurant-beer-hall-café all in one. Instead of defensive earthworks it has a coffee garden; instead of gun emplacements a parking place for cars, and its dungeons contain the landlord's stores of wine and beer instead of prisoners mouldering in chains. Otherwise it is very little altered and indeed it is difficult to see how anyone could alter it unless he were to blow it up with dynamite and even then it probably would not be blown. One can more easily imagine the baffled dynamite bursting downwards to disrupt, severally and collectively, the entire sewage-disposal system of Goslar while the massive Zwinger still sat calmly in its place, unruffled and unmoved.

Petersen had evidently started his usual evening celebrations before the expedition started and some of the ladies in the party eyed him distrustfully, but he did no more than talk a good deal and laugh rather too loudly. There is a modern ramp which now leads up to the main door of the Zwinger. Probably in the old days there was merely a ladder which could be pulled up as the enemy approached and the door slammed in their ugly faces. Petersen made rather heavy weather of the steep ramp and Hambledon gave him a helping hand up the flight of stairs inside the door.

The great room at the head of the stairs is round to conform with the curve of the walls, but there are long narrow rooms leading off it at intervals so that the floor plan resembles the steering wheel of a ship with the hand grips projecting from the rim. There is a window at the far end of each of the narrow barrel-roofed rooms. It was a moment or two before Hambledon realised that they were merely window embrasures tunnelled through the thickness of the walls to provide air and light to the central space. It would not do to jump out of those windows; they must be fifty feet above the ground.

The place was filling up. There was an orchestra of four playing a truly international medley of dance tunes from "O My Papa" and "Loch Lomond" to "Einmal am Rhein" and the middle of the floor was kaleidoscopic with whirling couples. Hambledon and his party edged their way between long narrow tables and past the bar to the cloakroom, rows of pegs in one of the alcoves; having hung up coats and hats, they were ushered to óne of the narrow tables opposite the bar.

"Jolly, isn't it?" said Petersen. "Look at the chandelier. It's as old as—as the Ark. I like old things, don't you?"

Hambledon assented; the great wrought-iron chandelier, if not quite as old as the Ark, was well worth looking at, but what he was looking for at the moment was two familiar figures. However, they were not to be seen. Splendid!

"Let's have a drink," said Petersen. "There's Onkel Otto over by the bar. Picturesque figure, isn't he?"

He was an enormous elderly man with the *Kellner's* traditional leather apron girt about his substantial form. The orchestra stopped playing, the floor cleared, and Onkel Otto held up his hand for silence for an announcement. They were to be privileged to hear the two finest yodellers in all the Harz, they had won prizes in many places, they were justly famous——

Hambledon averted his mind from the two men who went up to the platform. They were not the two in whom he was interested and yodelling was not one of his enthusiasms. He shifted his chair a little, the more easily to watch the door. The wine waiter came to serve their wine, an odd little man with a large head, a skinny agile figure, and a green baize apron.

"Funny little chap," said Petersen, leaning across the table, for he was sitting opposite to Hambledon. "I say he's just like a kobold. It is a kobold I mean, isn't it?"

Hambledon agreed amiably. "He only wants a pointed cap and he would be one of the Seven Dwarfs in person."

The door swung open and two men sidled in. Since most of the company were sitting down to hear the singing, these men were plainly visible and Hambledon recognised them at once.

"Banger and Bacon," he said, half aloud, and Petersen caught the words.

"Banger, what is that?" he said, turning to see what Hambledon was looking at. "Those two who have just come in? They were in the hotel this evening, do you know them?"

"Only by sight," said Tommy with exact truth. "Banger is a sausage and bacon is thin and stringy—sometimes."

"Very good," said Petersen, and laughed heartily. The singing ended, the orchestra started again, people stood up to dance, and Banger and Bacon found themselves seats from which they could watch Thomas Elphinstone Hambledon.

CHAPTER XI

the zwinger

SOME TIME LATER the kobold waiter came wriggling through the press of dancers in his own inimitable eel-like manner—it is an education to see him do this with a tray of full glasses—bringing a flat parcel in his hand. He came to a stop by Tommy's chair and said: "Excuse, please. The Herr Hambledon?"

"That is my name."

"I have been told to bring this parcel to the Herr Hambledon and to give it into his own hand."

He did so. Hambledon took the parcel, a flat cardboard box with the name of Karstadt, Gentlemen's Outfitters, on the lid.

"But," said Hambledon, detaining him by the baize apron, "what is this? I——"

"Presumably the Herr left a parcel behind him at Karstadt's and someone, having been told that the Herr is here, has brought it after him."

"But I have not bought anything at Karstadt's. Who gave you this parcel?"

"A gentleman, I did not know him," said the waiter, detaching his apron from Hambledon's fingers. "He did but point out the Herr to me and tell me what I was to do."

"Wait a minute," said Hambledon peremptorily. "This gentleman, can you point him out to me?"

The kobold looked steadily round the room, a survey which included the table where Banger and Bacon were sitting in full view.

"No, mein Herr, I cannot see him and, indeed, after he had given me the parcel, he made his way towards the door."

"When was this?"

"But just now, mein Herr, three minutes ago, no more."

"Thank you," said Hambledon, and let the man go. Banger and Bacon had not moved from their table for half an hour at least, though, if the parcel were from them, they could have employed a messenger. The box was tied up with string and, under cover of fumbling with the knot, Hambledon glanced across at them. They were sitting up on the edges of their chairs and their eyes were protuberant. When they saw that he was watching them they both looked away.

"Incompetent oafs," said Hambledon to himself and went on disentangling the knot under a fire of comments from other members of his party.

"What is it, Mr. Hambledon? A birthday present?"

"From a lady, I guess. Look, he's blushing."

"That's right. It's his blue eyes that's done it."

Petersen stood up, wavering, and leaned heavily on the table. "Practical joke?" he suggested. "Look out something doesn't hop out and bite you."

Hambledon laughed and opened the box; inside was a flat packet wrapped in poor-quality brown paper tied with twine. He slipped off the twine; the adjacent members of the party, with natural good manners, immediately turned away to watch the dancing, and Petersen sat down with a bump.

Inside the wrapping were a number of papers folded together; one at least was a map and some others looked like sketch plans. On the top there was a slip of paper bearing a message which puzzled him for a moment till it dawned upon him that though the writing was German script, the words were English.

> Mr. Hambledon. Goslar.
> This is the Smirnov Plan which was
> stolen. Please deliver to British
> authorities immediately. Highly
> valuable, take care, look out for
> trouble.

Hambledon was in the act of folding up the note when someone brushed against the back of his chair. He looked round quickly and saw that it was Bacon, who, with an aloof air of distant purpose, was making his way across the room. He could have seen, if only vaguely, what sort of contents were in the package. He strolled across the room and passed through a swing door opposite. Banger sat still where he was and Hambledon, making no attempt to conceal what he was doing, put the packet back into Karstadt's box and tied it up again.

"That fellow," said Petersen disgustedly, "was peering over your shoulder."

"Odd manners some people have," said Hambledon. "Perhaps he thought it was feelthy postcards. Interesting but not exciting," he added, to his tactful neighbours at table. "I was talking to an archaeologist fellow today about that"—what had Britz called it?—"abbey ruin at Walkenried, and he promised to send me a lot of details about it and other places within reach. I am a little overpowered," he added, with a laugh. "He seems to have sent me enough stuff here to keep me quiet for months and, what's worse, he wants it all back." He tapped the box under his arm. Bacon, carefully not looking his way, returned to the waiting Banger.

"Will he put you through an examination to find out how much you've seen, Mr. Hambledon?"

"Not if I can help it," he said, rising, and made his way between tables and round the perimeter of the dance floor into the place of seclusion from which Bacon had just returned. Here, having locked himself in, he reopened the packet and rapidly stowed away the contents in his inside pockets. The printed map was large and on stiff paper. He glanced at it and saw that it covered the western edges of the Soviet Zone from Helmstedt in the north to the borders of the Schwarzburg in the south. He looked more closely at some of the added markings upon it and whistled tunelessly between his teeth. The map was too stiff to go unobserved in any pocket. He undid his shirt buttons and slid it inside, against his chest. If the map could have expressed its emotions it would have sighed deeply and said: "What, again?"

The next step was to find something to pad out the packet to its former solidity and weight. Hambledon, choosing a moment when the place was his alone, robbed cabinets of most of their amenities until he was satisfied that Karstadt's box did not feel empty. He hurriedly tied it up again and returned to his table. Bacon, looking really anxious, was standing against the wall watching for him.

There was a rather messy game in progress with a sausage, tied to a string, dangling from the great chandelier. Half a dozen young men, with their hands clasped behind their backs, were leaping at the sausage with open mouths while Onkel Otto, holding the other end of the string, made matters more difficult by jerking it occasionally. By degrees the sausage was bitten away and the last inch fell to the floor amid cheers and laughter.

"Revolting," said an English lady next to Hambledon at the table, "quite revolting."

"I absolutely agree," said Hambledon. "What's the matter, Petersen?"

"I don't feel very well," said Petersen. "I think I'll go home."

Hambledon was not surprised; he had been expecting this.

"I'll help you find your coat," he said, and steered the sufferer across to the cloakroom.

"I don't feel sick or anything," explained Petersen carefully. "I've just had quite enough to drink and I don't want any more. Hot in here, isn't it?" He staggered and clutched Hambledon's arm.

"Hold up. You'll be all right when you're out in the air."

"That's right," said Petersen vaguely. They were at the back of the cloakroom where it was rather dark and he took no notice when he was helped into Hambledon's raincoat and crowned with Hambledon's hat. They were almost exactly the same height.

"You'll be all right," repeated Hambledon. "A nice quiet stroll back to the hotel will clear your head. Do you want to walk across the big room?"

"Not if there's another way out. Certainly not. Is there?"

"At the back here," said Hambledon, who had noticed the stairs when they first arrived. "Can you manage? I'll come down with you. Hang on to the handrail."

The winding stairway, burrowing down in the thickness of the wall, was steep and worn, but a cool draught blew up it and Petersen drew long breaths.

"That's better."

"You know your way, don't you?"

"Oh, yes. Along by the lake and turn right at that memorial affair. I say, Hambledon, you're a good chap. Ah, that's fine, it's left off raining."

"Would you do something for me?"

"Course I will, what?"

"Take this box back to the hotel for me? It's rather a nuisance here. Give it to the porter. He'll keep it for me."

Petersen tucked the box under his arm and started off, walking up the ramp to pass the main door. Hambledon stood back in the doorway to watch him out of sight and then slipped across in the shadows to hide behind the trees. He could see the main door at the top of the ramp from where he stood; as he had expected, a long lean figure came out of the doorway, looked after Petersen, and beckoned to someone behind him on the stair. Bacon, of course, summoning Banger. The stout figure also emerged and they both ran down the other side of the ramp by the way Petersen had gone.

"That's right," murmured Hambledon. "You go and snitch the box and we'll all be happy. Petersen probably won't notice it's gone."

He walked out from under the trees towards the tower, intending to rejoin his party, but there came from the way Petersen had gone a yell of rage and fury followed by Scandinavian curses. Hambledon ran like a hare up the ramp, down the further side, and round the curving path towards the lake; before he reached it there was a splash and ripples spread across the water. The path was ill-lit and embowered in trees, but he caught a glimpse of two running figures disappearing in the distance.

There was no difficulty in locating Petersen. There was a commotion in the water such as might be caused by a grampus coming ashore—if they do—accompanied by a string of remarks such as no delicate-minded grampus would think of using. Hambledon cantered up to the spot and helped Petersen to climb out.

"What the devil happened?"

"I don't know—two men came up behind and barged me into the —ugh—lake. Ugh—ugh! I've lost my hat. I'm absolutely dripping. I've swallowed lake water—oh, Lord, I'm going to be sick."

He was, and Hambledon supported him.

"Now," said Tommy, when the crisis was over, "we're going back to the hotel and I'm coming with you. If you keep walking you won't catch cold."

"I never catch cold," said Petersen with dignity. "Let me wring some of the water out of my trousers, they do cling so. Was I very tight?"

"Oh, just nicely."

"Well, I'm stone-cold sober now," said Petersen, and it was quite true, for he set off towards their hotel at a good four miles an hour. "I suppose those two fellows were a bit screwed too and just staggered into me. Where did they go?"

"I don't know. I saw you in the water and didn't worry about them."

Hambledon waited for some enquiry about the cardboard box, but Petersen had evidently forgotten all about it. He had probably never realised that he had it in the first place. When they got back to the hotel Petersen dripped on the marble floor of the entrance hall and the night porter dashed out with pitying cries.

94

"We have been to the Zwinger," said Hambledon. "When we came out, the Herr fell in the lake."

The porter nodded understandingly, but Petersen was pulling off his raincoat and looking at it.

"I've got somebody else's coat, this isn't mine. I'd better take it back."

Hambledon made a surprised noise and said: "But that's mine. My fault entirely, I took it off the peg. My mistake."

"Then mine is still at the Zwinger and tomorrow will do for that," said Petersen, taking his key and starting off up the stairs. "Oh, here's your coat, Hambledon. Sorry I got it so wet and, by the way, whose hat did I lose? Yours or mine?"

"I don't care if it was mine, I never liked that hat."

"If the Herr," said the porter, pursuing Petersen, "will put his clothes outside the door, they shall be dried."

"I'll toss them out," said Petersen. "My goodness, I'm sleepy. Early to bed for once. See you tomorrow, Hambledon, and many thanks."

He trailed wetly round the curve of the staircase and rose out of sight.

"The poor Herr," said the porter, and laughed quietly.

"That unfenced path by the lake is, actually, a little dangerous," said Hambledon severely. "It is quite easy to wander over the edge."

"That is so. The Herr Petersen is not the first to fall in there."

"I daresay not. Could you," said Hambledon, who had been doing some intensive thinking during the walk home, "could you oblige me with a large envelope?"

"Willingly," said the porter, rummaging in a cupboard beneath the desk while Hambledon looked round the office. There was a safe in the corner which seemed to be quite a good one. It would be foolish to keep the Smirnov Plan in an hotel bedroom with one flimsy lock on the door; he would put the plan in an envelope when the porter could find one—he was now frantically hunting through the desk drawers—seal it up, bring it down again, and ask to have it locked up for the night. It ought to be secure in a good safe with a night porter watching over it.

The porter abandoned the drawers, looked wildly round, and said ah, perhaps there were some in there. Before Hambledon had time to wonder where "there" was, the porter took a key off a nail above the desk, opened the safe and produced from it a large, stout Manila envelope.

"We put stationery in here sometimes when the desk is overfull," explained the porter, "as now. Will this one suit?"

Hambledon said, with thanks, that it would do admirably; the porter said that he was happy in being able to serve the Herr. He then locked up the safe again and returned the key to its nail; Hambledon wished him an undisturbed night and went upstairs to his own room.

Here he locked himself in and examined the papers, comparing the small sketch plans with the large map and looking through the sheets of notes which accompanied each of them. They were plainly originals; if they had been stolen before fair copies of them had been made, no wonder the Russians were buzzing like mad bees round an overset hive, no one could write out all those details from memory.

"All that work to be done all over again," said Tommy, and bounced gently upon the edge of his bed. If Micklejohn had accomplished that he was a lad worth knowing.

Even if these were only the rough drafts of plans subsequently copied out and duplicated, they would still be of enthralling interest to the British High Command. Certainly not to be entrusted even for one night to a safe of which the key was helpfully hung upon an adjacent nail.

Hambledon folded the papers again with the map and the covering note—had Micklejohn written it? No means of telling—and put them all into the envelope. He sat looking at it for a moment and then, in clear block capitals, addressed it to himself and sealed it down. After a moment's thought he carefully inked his right thumb and impressed a beautifully clear thumbprint upon the left-hand top corner.

He took his Luger from his locked suitcase, left the room and walked down to the Norddeutsche Bank in Fischmaker Strasse. There were plenty of people about; the cinemas were just closing. Hambledon pushed open the stiff flap of the bank's night safe and dropped his bulging envelope through the slot.

"There," said Hambledon inaudibly, "that will defeat you, I think."

He turned away and strolled comfortably home.

CHAPTER XII

some elementary trigonometry

HAMBLEDON UNDRESSED and went to bed but for some reason could not go to sleep. There was a party in progress in one of the ground-floor rooms. There was a piano and an accordion and choruses and the clock in the Jakobi-Kirche struck one. Eventually Hambledon cursed the noisemakers, got up and shut the window. Normally the *Lays of Ancient Rome* would send him to sleep but on this occasion they failed him; for one thing, the room was hot and stuffy. He got up again after a time and reopened the window. The party seemed to be petering out, the choruses were intermittent and not sustained by so many voices; also the pianist had gone home to bed. The last chorus died on the night air, the Jakobi-Kirche clock struck the three-quarters, and all was quiet, but still Hambledon could not go to sleep and he had nothing to read. He had, increasingly, a sense of waiting for something to happen.

He turned over, thumped his pillow, and started upon his second string, the *Ballad of the Revenge*. His mother used to read it to him when he was a little boy in the rectory garden, to keep him quiet when his father was writing his sermons. Bumblebees in the holly-hocks.

> At Flores in the Azores Sir Richard Grenville lay,
> And a pinnace, like a fluttered bird, came flying from far away:
> "Spanish ships of war at sea! We have sighted fifty-three!"

Then there would have been a scramble. Look out, make haste, the enemy is coming——

The clock in the Jakobi-Kirche struck two.

Hambledon got out of bed, put on his soft bedroom slippers and his dressing gown, dropped his Luger in the pocket, and opened his bedroom door inaudibly. Outside in the passage the sense of tension was keener. He moved silently along the passage to the head of the stairs and the sound of a voice came faintly to his ears. It was followed by another voice speaking not louder but more sharply. "Hold your tongue!" it said peremptorily in German.

Tommy glided down the stairs and looked over the banisters at the turn. There was no one in the passage leading to the front hall; the speakers must be in the office which opened off the passage. The door of it was standing wide. He went on, down the stairs, along the passage, and looked in at the office door.

The porter was facing him with his hands above his head, a man in a mask was threatening him with an automatic. A second man, also masked, had the safe door open and was snatching out the contents.

Hambledon jabbed the muzzle of his Luger against the spine of the man nearest to him and said: "Drop that gun or I'll kill you! Drop it. On the floor."

Before he finished speaking the man at the safe was up on his feet, out through the further door into the front hall, out of the front door and away. The man with the gun dropped it obediently.

"Schatz," said Hambledon to the porter, "pick up that gun and telephone the police. You—" prodding his captive—"hands up and walk forward."

The man obeyed, walking forward till his nose bumped the opposite wall.

"Clasp your hands behind your head," said Hambledon sharply. "That's right. If you move your fingers I will shoot you, here," and he prodded him again while Schatz at the telephone howled for the police, *schnell, schnell,* armed robbery, attempted murder, and then sat staring and shaking until the police car whirled up to the door.

When the man had been seized and handcuffed and the mask taken from his face, Hambledon looked at him and laughed.

"Banger," he said. "I thought so. Your svelte curves, you know."

Ludwig Kirsch lived in a small modern house a mile or more outside the city boundaries on the road to Oker. It was not his own house; he had rented it furnished because Goslar was not to him an abiding city. He had lived there a little over a year, having come from Hamburg. He was, by his own assertion, an author of books upon mathematics for the use and torment of boys in the upper-school age groups.

He lived alone, being waited upon during certain hours of the day by the wife of a railway worker, a simple-minded hard-working woman who regarded with deep respect amounting to veneration anyone who could understand, let alone produce, such sheets of complicated trigonometrical calculations as those which could be seen, neatly sorted into piles under paperweights, upon the table in his study.

"Be very careful, Hanna," he said, "in dusting my table, not to disturb my sheets of calculations in any way. If they got into the wrong order——"

"With respect," said Hanna, turning pale at the bare idea, "would it not be better if I did not dust the table at all?"

"Perhaps it would, perhaps it would. My books also, if their place in my bookcases were altered it would seriously annoy me."

"I had better not touch the books——"

"I agree. Do not touch the books. I have a stupid habit, Hanna, of putting odd notes behind the clock. If by ill chance they swirled into the fire——"

"May I, then, leave the mantelpiece untouched? If I were to confine my attention to the floor?"

Kirsch considered this.

"I think it might be better if the room were left for occasions when I have time to oversee your efforts. There will then be no danger of your disturbing my work."

Hanna looked relieved.

"If the Herr will tell me when he wishes me to clean the room, I will come at once."

Kirsch nodded approvingly.

"And at other times——"

"I will not enter without the Herr's permission."

"Thank you, Hanna. That will be best."

"*Schön*," said Hanna, and scuttled away. Kirsch, to make doubly sure that there was no mistake, made a habit of keeping the study door locked and the key in his pocket. The study was only a small room opening off the main sitting room. It would not matter if it were sometimes a little dusty. It would matter much more if a thoroughly industrious cleaner turned out cupboards and drawers, or even wondered why they were all kept locked.

On the evening when Hambledon went to the Zwinger and Petersen fell in the lake Kirsch was in his sitting room waiting for two men to come and report. It was late in the evening and Kirsch was alone in the house.

Presently two sets of footsteps sounded on the gravel path and someone knocked at the front door. Kirsch opened it to admit two men whom Hambledon would instantly have recognised. The tall lean one whom he called Bacon entered first, followed by the short rotund Banger, and both were plainly pleased with themselves.

"Come in, Dittmar," said Kirsch, "and you, Tosen, also."

They came in, grinning. Even the lean saturnine Dittmar laughed as he spoke. "We have good news for the Herr."

"We have a little something to show the Herr," said fat laughing Tosen, undoing his raincoat to take a flat parcel from a pocket inside it. "The missing papers. They were passed to the Englander this evening at the Zwinger. Dittmar here saw what was inside the parcel when it was opened, so we waited until the Englander left, sprang upon him in the dark, took this package, and threw him in the lake."

"We have been watching the Englander for days, ever since the Herr told us that the papers would probably come across this side and that someone like that Englander would have been sent here to receive them," said Dittmar.

"As soon as I saw him," exulted Tosen, "I said to myself that here was the type of man the English would send."

"Aided in your perspicacity by the fact that I pointed him out to you myself," said Kirsch sarcastically, and Dittmar was mildly annoyed. He and Tosen, after all, had done all the work while Kirsch had done nothing but sit in a comfortable armchair and pretend to write sums for boys.

"The Herr," said Dittmar, with excessive meekness, "was quite inspired when he drew the right conclusion from the facts that this Englander had Micklejohn's room, spent days examining and asking questions about the frontier, and was openly in league with the police."

Tosen looked a little nervous, for he feared Kirsch's explosive temper, but the mathematician merely tapped the Karstadt box affectionately and said quite mildly that there were also other factors involved. "Anyone might have had Micklejohn's room, the English are always nosy about the frontier, and as for the police, any man would call them in who found a dead man in his bedroom and you know what I think about that." He treated Dittmar to a long cold stare and added: "Wait here while I check these papers against the list. You may sit down." He went into his study, leaving the door ajar, and Dittmar muttered: "Sez you," under his breath, for he was a cinema addict.

"There are two spare glasses on the table," said Tosen in a soothing voice, "and I am thirsty after hurrying all this way. Do you think——"

He was interrupted by a roar of rage from the further room and Kirsch charged out, spluttering and quite incoherent with fury; he was trailing crumpled white streamers behind him. "Look—look—look," he stammered, "you—you——"

He gathered up the toilet paper, seized Dittmar by the collar, and made frantic attempts to cram it into his mouth and down his neck, finishing by scrubbing his face with it. Tosen dodged round the table and went to ground behind Kirsch's big armchair. Dittmar made feeble attempts to push off the attack, but Kirsch in a rage had the strength of madness. He ended by slapping Dittmar savagely across the face and then dropped into a chair as one exhausted. There was a long silence and Tosen rose carefully to his feet.

Eventually Kirsch lifted his head.

"You see what happened—where is Tosen?"

"Here, mein Herr," said Tosen, and walked round the chair into view.

"This Englander made a fool of you—it would not be difficult. *Sakrament da lekts mir*, what it is to have to make use of wooden-heads like you!"

Kirsch swept his hands through his hair and struggled for self-control.

"You—— Let me think. He took the papers out of the box so he still has them. He——"

"With respect, mein Herr," said Tosen nervously, "it may be that he is drowned."

"What, in that duckpond? Fool, hold your tongue. Or did you kill him before he went in?"

"No—the Herr was so angry when Dittmar shot the Russian, Lentov, in the hotel——"

"I did not shoot him," stormed Dittmar, exploding suddenly. "You did!"

Kirsch cursed them both into silence.

"The Herr said," persisted Tosen, " 'no more killing.' "

Kirsch looked at him and he backed away.

"I am trying to put myself in his place," said Kirsch, as though talking to himself. "I should take them back to the hotel. I should not keep them in my bedroom even for a single night; that bedroom has been visited before. I should put them in the hotel safe, of course.

It is in the office and there is a night porter on duty with a telephone at his elbow. Yes, that is what I should do."

He sat up with a jerk.

"Now I tell you what you will do. You will wait until all the lights are out in the hotel except the hall light, you understand? Sometimes there are parties there and it is late before they finish. When all the ground-floor windows are dark and the bedroom windows also, you will walk quietly but quickly up the street and turn without hesitation in at the door of the hotel. If you are seen to go in, you are belated guests, that is all. Open the door quietly; it may be that the porter is asleep in his chair. Seize him, hold a gun to his head, and he will give you the key of the safe. Tosen, you will continue to hold a gun at the porter's head while you, Dittmar, search the safe for these papers. Take them out, stun the porter but do not kill him, and bring the papers back here. I shall be waiting."

Dittmar looked at the clock, the time was half-past midnight.

"You are right," said Kirsch, answering the unspoken thought, "it is too early yet. I should think, about two o'clock, but you must use your discretion, if you have any. If you cannot tell the time, you can listen for the chimes from the Jakobi-Kirche. Any questions?"

They shook their heads and turned to go.

"Stop," said Kirsch. "How do you propose to prevent the porter from giving your descriptions to the police, since I have told you not to kill him?"

"Scarves round our faces," said Dittmar.

"Scarves slip," said Kirsch. He got up and went into the study, returning at once with something black in his hands. "Here are two masks, you will put them on the moment before you enter the hotel. Now go, and remember that if you fail me this time I will throw you over into the Soviet Zone. You know what they do to failures there, don't you? Now go."

"Since we are such fools," said Dittmar, "would it not be better if the Herr did this errand himself?"

"It would. Much better. It would at least be properly done. But you are perfectly well aware that the whole strength of my position here depends upon the fact that I am seldom seen out and that only in the mornings with a shopping basket. I am never seen out at night and I never will be. I am too important to risk, whereas you are expendable. Now go."

He closed the front door after them, took up a book, and sat down to read and wait. When the clock struck two he laid down his book to look up at the dial for a moment before taking up the book again.

He was still waiting when the dawn broke and when the sun rose he was still there, waiting.

When the daily woman let herself in at seven, Kirsch was in bed, but he had not been to sleep.

The police squad who arrested Tosen at the hotel were led by an inspector who knew Hambledon and had seen him with the Chief of Police. Hambledon drew him aside.

"A word in your ear, Inspector."

"Certainly, mein Herr."

"This affair here is not a mere matter of robbery for gain. In the words of a great English poet," said Hambledon, who was rather enjoying himself, "'Things are seldom what they seem.'"

"I imagine—if I may say so without presumption—that where the Herr is concerned they seldom are."

"Thank you. Your chief knows that the purpose of my visit here is not entirely to take a holiday. That dangerous-looking criminal there is somehow involved in that purpose."

The Inspector looked across at Tosen, who was wilting in a corner. His fair hair was standing in tufts like the crest of a cockatoo; his normally red complexion was pale and the corners of his curiously small mouth were turned down like a baby about to howl. Even his fat face looked flabby and drooping and his fat hands plucked aimlessly at the handcuffs.

"He does not look particularly dangerous," said the Inspector, "but if he is really concerned in the purpose to which the Herr refers, appearances are no doubt deceptive. I have seen killers who looked like that."

"So have I."

"Excuse me one moment," said the Inspector. "A little adjustment, perhaps."

He called up one of his men and handcuffed Tosen to him with a word of warning.

"His interrogation——" began Hambledon when the Inspector returned.

"Will begin at once. My chief will himself wish to interrogate him in the morning, but in the meantime we can worry him a little. The Herr would not wish to be present?"

"Heaven forbid that I should intrude upon your communings with any prisoner. Besides, I want to go to bed. This man, by the way, is one of the two who have been shadowing me for the past week or more. The other one was going through the safe here but I could not hold him, he ran too fast. Never mind, I have a feeling that we shall meet again."

"Did he get away with anything from the safe, did the Herr see?"

"I have reason to think not. My compliments to your chief and if he can spare me a few moments in the morning, I have something to tell him. Good night."

"The Herr's message shall be delivered," said the Inspector.

Hambledon went back to bed and fell asleep at once with no assistance from Tennyson or Macaulay. In the morning he was finishing his last cup of coffee when he was called to the telephone. The Chief of Police would be delighted to see him as soon as was reasonably convenient.

"I come at once," said Hambledon.

He was shown into the Chief's office and found him going through his correspondence. At sight of Hambledon he dropped the whole pile into a tray and said: "That fellow won't talk."

"Dear me. Did you ask him what they hoped to find in the safe?"

"He says money. What do you think he was looking for?"

"You remember the story we heard," said Hambledon, "about some papers having been stolen from the Russians at the time when Micklejohn disappeared? That fellow Lentov was supposed to have had a hand in it."

"I heard that from various sources," said the Chief of Police. "I suppose there was some truth in it."

"Certainly there was. It was those papers which were being looked for in the hotel safe."

"*Himmel!* Why?"

"Because I had them," said Hambledon, and told the whole story of what had happened at the Zwinger the night before. "This fellow, whom I called Banger, not knowing his name——"

"Tosen."

"Tosen, is not a principal. He is not the type to be, neither he nor Bacon, whose name also I do not know. He was the man who was searching the safe. What we want to know is: Who gives them their orders?"

"He will not talk," said the Chief gloomily. "Except for saying that they were looking for money, he answers only, 'I do not know,' or 'Nobody' to all questions."

"What have you charged him with?"

"Armed robbery. Safebreaking. Menaces," said the Chief rather helplessly. "He does not seem to mind."

"It follows, then, that he is more afraid of what someone else will do to him than he is of a term of imprisonment," suggested Hambledon.

"It would seem so. Particularly as, in fact, nothing was stolen and technically a safe is not 'broken' if it is opened with its key. He can be charged with 'attempting' this and that, but all he actually did was to terrify the night porter."

"Charge him with something more serious, then."

"What? There is nothing against him previously."

Hambledon thought for a moment.

"Charge him with the murder of Lentov in my bedroom, then. A murder charge will make most people talk."

"But there is no shadow of a—wait a minute. There were finger-prints in your room. Two men's prints."

"So there were. If the charge produces any results, you can compare those prints with his, can you not?"

"If we compare them first and they are his, we should have something definite to back the charge."

"Certainly. But if you compare them first and they are not his, your accusation will, I feel, lack that fire and energy which are so convincing. Charges can always be withdrawn."

A slow smile spread across the German's face.

"It is plainly to be seen," he said, "that the Herr is not a policeman." He touched a bell upon his desk, when a constable answered it he was told to bring in the prisoner Tosen.

CHAPTER XIII

the man in the dressing gown

THE CHIEF OF THE GOSLAR POLICE, a square and solid man, sat behind his big desk; Hambledon sat in a chair at one end of it; at a small table in the corner a shorthand clerk waited with pencil at the ready. Tosen was brought in and set before them.

"Tosen," began the Chief, "since you were before me earlier this morning, further evidence has come in."

Tosen's gaze was fixed on the carpet at his feet. His eyelids flickered but his expression did not change.

"Interesting," said the Chief, observing this. He looked at Hambledon. "The Herr agrees with me?"

Tommy realized that he was supposed to ask what was particularly interesting, and did so.

"The prisoner's reaction," explained the Chief. "If a man who knows himself to be innocent is told that further evidence has become available his face lights up, his shoulders are thrown back, his chin rises. Hope nerves his sinews and uplifts his heart—no?"

"Not on this occasion, it would seem."

"No. The guilty prisoner knows only too well that further evidence can only tell against him."

The Chief of Police paused for this remark to sink in.

"Tosen. You are now charged with the murder of a Russian named Andrey Lentov in Room 32 of——"

Tosen leapt as though he had been jabbed with a pin.

"I did not! I am not guilty, I tell you, I was not even carrying a gun that day, I——"

"Carrying a gun," repeated the Chief of Police thoughtfully. "Who told you that Lentov was shot?"

"Who told you I shot him?" demanded Tosen, turning at bay.

"Who could tell us?"

"Any liar who wanted to cover himself! It was all over Goslar that a man had been shot at the Drei Bullochsen and that he was a Russian. I don't believe anybody told you I shot him. You are trying to pin it on me because you can't find out who did it! It is only," babbled Tosen, who, once his silence had been broken, was like a cask of Hanover beer with the bung knocked out, "because I was caught there with a gun tonight that you conclude I was the man there with a gun ten days ago! It's ridiculous. I've never carried a gun before except in war against the enemies of my country," said Tosen magnificently, "and I've never been inside the Drei Bullochsen in my life before tonight. I swear it."

At this point the Inspector who had arrested Tosen stepped forward and laid a slip of paper on the desk before his chief, who glanced at it and then at Hambledon.

"Now I come to think back," went on Tosen, "on that day I was not in Goslar at all. I was in Hanover, spending a couple of days with an old comrade I had not seen since the Battle of the Reichswald at the end of the war. He and I——"

He met the eye of the Chief of Police, who was looking so amused that Tosen's voice faltered and came to a stop.

"That must have been most gratifying," said the Chief. "We must have his name and address, must we not? I should like to ask him how you managed to get along without your fingers."

"My——"

"Fingers. The things you leave prints with. How dare you tell these fairy tales to me? Your fingerprints were in Room 32 of the Drei Bullochsen when we found Lentov dead."

Tosen staggered and one of the police escort kindly supported him.

"So you see," added the Chief, "our informant was speaking the truth after all. Wasn't he?"

Tosen jumped, as it was hoped that he would, to the natural conclusion that Dittmar was also in custody and had been talking.

"That swine Dittmar," he raved, "the biggest liar the devil ever made. He'd sell his mother for two marks. It was he who shot Lentov, not I. I wasn't even armed, I told you that. We ought to have made some excuse about the wrong room and got out. Kirsch said——" he stopped abruptly.

"Kirsch! Who is he?"

"Nobody. I don't know."

"But you said——"

"I was going to say that Dittmar had been drinking, that's all. Kirsch is a drink, you know. Dittmar always drinks kirsch."

"Then why did you stop suddenly?"

"Because I did not think you would be interested in what Dittmar drinks."

"You are lying," said the Chief contemptuously. "Your words were 'Kirsch said.' Listen, Tosen. You are involved up to the neck in the murder of Lentov and I mean your neck. Do you really want to hang for it while the man who sent you there goes free? Because you will."

Tosen hesitated.

"Can I have a cigarette?"

"No."

"Can I have a drink, then, please?"

"Give him a glass of water."

The water was brought and Tosen drank thirstily.

"*Danke*," he said, and put down the glass. "If I tell you all I know, will you swear to send me back to the Rhineland and tell no one—no one at all—where I have gone?"

"You are proposing to bargain with us," said the Chief, in a menacing voice.

"Yes, mein Herr, please. The Herr will understand that if I tell all I know it will save the Herr a great deal of trouble, whereas if I do not talk I shall only be imprisoned or hanged and both are preferable to what I have already been promised if I should fail—as I did."

"Fail to get the papers, you mean," said Hambledon, speaking for the first time.

"That is so, mein Herr," said Tosen, looking at him with plain curiosity. "May I apologise now for having thrown the Herr into the lake?"

"No need," said Hambledon, lighting a cigarette. "You didn't."

Tosen blinked. The Chief of Police said that they were straying from the subject and Hambledon apologised.

"Go on," said the Chief to Tosen.

"I am a Rhinelander, mein Herr, and the Rhine is a pleasantly long way from the Soviet Zone. Even if I am in prison——"

"You will be."

"—so long as it is in the Rhineland I shall be safe, not here, where one may be abducted into the Soviet Zone and——" Tosen shuddered.

"Was that what you were promised as a reward for failure?"

Tosen nodded.

"You are a scoundrel," said the Chief thoughtfully. "You are a traitor, which is worse. You are probably a murderer too." Tosen shook his head violently. "You are also a fool for putting a weapon into my hand. If you do not tell all you know, I myself will have you put across the frontier."

He paused a moment and then continued:

"But if you tell me frankly and fully all you know, I will do my best for you, since, although you are a man of no importance whatever, it is in your power to save us some time and trouble. Understand this," he went on, as Tosen tried to thank him, "if it is proved that you murdered Lentov you will hang like anybody else."

"I did not murder Lentov," said Tosen steadily. "Here is the truth, then. My employer is Ludwig Kirsch." Tosen added particulars of Kirsch's address and ostensible occupation. "He comes from Hamburg and has been a Communist for years. He ran a Communist cell there and taught in a school. He has a violent temper and was dismissed for half killing a boy who angered him. So he came here and organises the Soviet espionage and—and other activities for them here. He——"

"Just a moment," said the Chief. He wrote a message upon a slip of paper and handed it to the Inspector, who immediately left the room. "Now, go on."

Tosen talked, incidentally clearing up a number of small mysteries which had been puzzling the police, and went on: "When the Smirnov Plan papers were stolen from General Vedovitch, it was not known whether Lentov had them or the Englander Michel—Machel——"

"I know whom you mean. Go on."

"Or even if they were in it together. They both disappeared and there was no trace of where they had gone, it was thought likely that the Englander at least had slipped back over the frontier to Goslar. Kirsch ordered Dittmar and me to find out if he had returned to Goslar but there seemed to be no news of him. Then we were ordered to search his room at the Drei Bullochsen. We got in without being observed, choosing our time, there was no one in the room but it was occupied, clothes and things in the room. So, we were searching when there was a step outside and the door handle turned. Dittmar was behind the door when it opened. I went down behind the bed, on the floor. Somebody came in—I could not see who—and cried out something and there was a shot and someone fell. Dittmar spoke to me and I got up. There was a man dead on the floor. He wore English clothes and the passport in his pocket was the English one of Michel

—that Englander." Tosen picked up the glass and drank the rest of the water.

"Go on."

"Dittmar said: 'This is good, this is that Englander who stole the papers. It may be that he has them on him.' So we searched his pockets and found not the Smirnov Plan papers but the identity papers of Andrey Lentov, Under-Commissar for Civil Administration of Occupied Territories. So then, mein Herr, we did not know which man had been shot."

"Very awkward," said the Chief of Police. "Go on."

"I said, 'It is the Englander, look at the clothes,' but Dittmar said, 'It is the Russian, look at the photographs.' So we propped him up in the armchair, mein Herr, out of respect, took his Russian identity papers and his gun, and came away. Kirsch was very angry with us for having shot Lentov, but Dittmar said that Lentov had drawn his gun and were we to stand there and let ourselves be shot? But Dittmar said that I had shot the man, not he."

"I see. Now tell me about Dittmar."

Tosen embarked willingly upon a picturesque survey of Dittmar's personal character, morals, habits, and tastes, but the Chief of Police stopped him.

"No, no. We will take all that as read. Do you know anything about his history, where he was born, what he is by trade, where he has lived, that sort of thing?"

If one could believe a single word that Dittmar said, it appeared that he had been born and brought up at Glogau on the Oder, that he was trained as an engineer and worked in a factory at Frankfurt-am-Oder until the war, when he went into the Army and served on the Western Front and in North Africa; "that is how he knows French," explained Tosen. After the war he had worked in Hamburg and it was there that he met Kirsch in the Communist organisation. "But his home is in the Soviet Zone and he still keeps in touch with his people there."

Tosen was removed to a cell and the Chief of Police turned to Hambledon and was about to speak when another note was brought in.

"Kirsch," said the Chief. "He was arrested and brought here, just like that. He has not spoken since he was arrested. My friend, you provided a key to unlock the tongue of Tosen; have you any suggestion as to how we may induce confidences from Kirsch?"

Hambledon said that he was sorry he had not, never having heard of the man until half an hour earlier. "But some help might be obtained from a study of his private papers," he added. "What accommodation did he have, a couple of rooms in a house?"

"A house all to himself with a small room kept locked. It has cupboards, locked, and a desk, locked, a safe and numerous drawers, all locked. Sounds interesting, does it not?"

"You make my mouth water. If I were a spaniel I should be dribbling visibly. Kirsch must have a bunch of keys the size of a prison warder's."

"Herr Hambledon, this part of Germany is in the British Zone of Occupation and this is a Security matter. You will wish to go through Kirsch's papers yourself and I will postpone his examination until you are able to be present."

"You are more than correct, you are generous," said Hambledon gratefully, for, though what the Chief had said was quite true, it is much pleasanter to be offered facilities than to have to insist on them. "I am very much obliged to you and I will go there at once if you will kindly give orders for me to be admitted."

"Certainly. And, thank you. In return," said the German, with a laugh, "do you feel that you could satisfy a curiosity which is burning me to the point of pain? Where are those famous Smirnov Plans now, in your pocket?"

"Oh, no. They are in that bank in Fischmaker Strasse, the Norddeutsche Bank is it? I dropped them into the night safe last night, addressed to myself. There was also with the Smirnov Plan a covering note addressed to me by name, rather odd, it was written in English in German script—unsigned. I have no means of knowing whether Micklejohn wrote it or not. I should say it was written by a German but it is in idiomatic English and ends by telling me to look out for trouble. How right he was. Now tell me, Herr Chief of Police, have you yet sent up your detectives to search that house?"

"Not yet. My police are there but I have not yet given the other order."

"May I suggest that it might be as well to withhold your detectives for the moment? If you will agree, I should like to spend two or three days there on the chance that someone may come or the telephone may ring. I am not really interested in the Smirnov Plan for its own sake, though now it is in my possession I shall be happy to send it on to those interested and if the Russians are running round in small circles tearing each other's hair over it I am filled with fiendish delight. But Micklejohn is my job, not the Smirnov Plan, and I am only interested in it to the limited extent that Micklejohn seems to have come across it somewhere. However, one can't miss possible chances. By the way, did Kirsch have any domestic staff or did he wash up and make his own bed?"

The Chief of Police looked at the Inspector, who had returned after arresting Kirsch.

"He had a woman in by the day, mein Herr, the wife of a man on the railway, but she has been called away to keep house for a married daughter at Hameln who has just been confined."

"Are you sure she did not provide a substitute?" said Hambledon. "I don't want someone letting themselves in with the back-door key at seven tomorrow morning and sending for the police because there's the wrong man in the house."

"There was another woman. She came to the house just after Kirsch had gone. I told her that the Herr had gone away unexpectedly and that I was waiting for her to ask her for the key, I have it here. I said that the Herr would let her know when he was coming back." The Inspector smiled. "She said that she did not mind how long it was before the Herr came back, so I do not think she will give any trouble."

"It almost sounds as though she did not like him."

"It appears, mein Herr, that the Herr Kirsch looked at her over his glasses, and——"

"No one could possibly like that."

"No, indeed, mein Herr. And that he went about the house unshaven and in a dressing gown all day. She said it was not respectable."

The Chief laughed, but Hambledon asked interestedly whether Kirsch had any other peculiarities.

"Only a tendency to draw the blinds at the earliest possible moment. He said it was an invasion of privacy if people could look in at him."

"I rather sympathise," said Hambledon. "By the way, may I use your telephone to ring my department in London?"

The message was to tell his department that young Micklejohn was alive and well and being sheltered by sympathisers in the Soviet Zone.

CHAPTER XIV

do not forget us

"I WILL DRIVE you out there myself," said the Chief of Police, "and you shall tell me what you want my police to do. No, it is no trouble, indeed, I have to go to Oker about something."

"What I should really like the police to do is to keep watch on the house but keep out of sight. I should like them to notice anyone who comes to the house and to follow him when he leaves. Not to arrest him but to find out where he goes."

"You shall hear me give the orders."

Goslar, like most ancient towns which once were walled, has its houses closely packed within the old perimeter; outside it the houses are immediately more widely spaced. Kirsch's house stood alone in a garden. A drive came up to the front door and past it to a garage containing his car. A lane between hedges ran down the side of the garden to cross a stream called simply *Die Abzucht* and so on towards the railway.

When the Chief's car came up to the front door a uniformed man came out of the house, saluted, and said that they had made another arrest.

"Get back in the house," said the Chief abruptly, and followed him in with Hambledon. "Who is it and where is he?"

"In the scullery, mein Herr, he is handcuffed and there are bars on the window. We locked up the house after the prisoner was taken away and Mulder and I were talking just within the entrance to the lane, when this man came down the road and turned in at the gate, so we kept observation through the hedge. He knocked several times at the front door and again at the back door but, of course, the house is empty. Then we saw him working on the catch of one of the windows and preparing to climb in. We accordingly apprehended him, mein Herr."

The Chief looked closely at his constable and said that something seemed to have happened to his left eye.

"Yes, mein Herr," said the man woodenly. "Mulder also was kicked in the stomach. That is why we handcuffed the prisoner. Mulder is being sick outside."

"I see."

"The prisoner's papers are not in order but, according to them, his name appears to be Bauer."

"Just a moment," said the Chief of Police, and took Hambledon into the sitting room, shutting the door behind them. "You were right, someone did come."

"Yes," said Hambledon, "yes," and took a turn up and down the room. "A pity he came so soon, but it can't be helped. He seems to have reacted rather violently when asked to explain why he was climbing in at a window and, when you come to think of it, that is rather an odd thing to do in broad daylight even if he did not know there were two constables behind the hedge. I mean, why not go quietly away and come back later?"

"It may be that his errand was urgent, perhaps? A message to be delivered at a time when Kirsch ought to have been at home? I wonder if he is carrying a letter."

"I should think not," said Hambledon, but the Chief put his head out at the door and asked if the prisoner had anything on him in the way of a letter, besides his personal papers.

"No, mein Herr, only the usual things a man carries in his pockets, though it is true that we have not searched his clothing. There might be a letter sewn in somewhere. Does the Herr wish such a search to be made? Mulder has left off being sick now."

"No, it can wait till we get him down to the station," said the Chief, and shut the door again. "You were thinking——"

"That if this man disappears without trace they will send someone else if the message is really urgent. You have enough against this man to hold him?"

"Plenty. Housebreaking, papers not in order, assaulting the police, ach, yes. I will take him away at once, shall I?"

"If you please. I think it would be as well if he did not see me. I don't really know why; just my natural caution breaking out. I will stay on here, I think. No doubt there is food in the house."

"We will look; if not I will send some up. I will send two other

114

men up also. This fellow outside is not our brightest specimen and I imagine that Mulder ought to go off duty for the rest of the day. Ring me up at least four times a day, will you? And, of course, at any time you want anything. *Auf Wiedersehen*."

Hambledon, armed with Kirsch's keys, entered Kirsch's study, shut the door behind him and opened the window, which protested that it was not accustomed to being opened. He then started upon a search of the various locked containers which were not, thank Heaven, nearly so numerous as the Chief of Police had suggested. There was a safe and a writing table of the type which has four small drawers at either side acting as pillars to support the leather-covered top. There was a sizable table in the middle of the room bearing a typewriter and the neat piles of trigonometrical calculations which had so impressed the simple mind of Hanna. Hambledon looked over the sheets and recoiled, for mathematics was not his subject; when it occurred to him that they might conceivably be an innocent-seeming series of keys to codes, he backed away until he bumped against the opposite wall. He had not the crossword-puzzle type of mind and regarded codes much as the average man regards nuclear science—a wonderful thing worked out by marvellous minds, but they can have it.

There were two long shallow drawers under this table. He unlocked and opened these first, to discover that Ludwig Kirsch was, actually, in the last stages of preparing a textbook on *Trigonometry for Higher Forms*. There were the pages carefully laid out with incredibly neat footnotes. So Kirsch really was doing what he said he was doing, and why not? Even a Soviet agent must have his hobbies.

Hambledon abandoned the trigonometry and turned to the safe. Even as he inserted the key he thought of booby traps and stood at one side when the door swung open. However, nothing squirted vitriol at him or even tried to shoot him, and he came round to the front and looked in.

"Not even a cobra poised to strike," he remarked, for one of his fellow guests at the hotel had lent him a really blood-curdling thriller into which politeness had compelled him to dip.

The safe was reasonably full, mainly of information about the British Occupation Forces in the area. Hambledon looked through them and marvelled for the thousandth time at the German passion for detail. Kirsch had complete particulars of the strength of the British forces, the units concerned, their arms and equipment, their guns and their transport, the exact position of all the units, and even the layout of their barracks and posts. There were complete lists of all the officers in order of seniority; their names, ages, war records, decorations; the part of the country from which they came, and even the schools which had nurtured their formative years, though why it should interest the Russians to know that the Colonel was at Winchester and the Adjutant at Rugby, only Heaven knows.

"Perhaps it enables them to show off," said Hambledon. " 'To us, your lives are an open book; from us, there is nothing hid.' Blast them." He looked more closely at the typewritten pages, they were carbon copies, kept in case the top copies went missing in transit, no doubt.

He stacked them on the floor in a space by themselves—the British should have those—and turned to the next shelf. Here were reports about individual Germans in that area of the Western Zone, with their full names and addresses and comments about their characters and capabilities. "Accurate and thorough, this man is commendable." "Conscientious but has not the technical knowledge required for his post." "Unreliable, drinks to excess. Should be dropped." "Brilliant but careless, lacks application."

Hambledon sat back on his heels, there was an old, familiar ring about these comments—of course! End-of-term reports. Once a school-master, always a schoolmaster.

"I wonder how often I give myself away," said Hambledon, who had been a schoolmaster himself.

There were further details about German Communist agents, with brief notes about information which they had supplied and useful work which they had done.

Another set of papers were copies of suggestions sent across by Kirsch himself. Would it not be a good idea, subject to approval, of course, to work up ill-feeling between the British Occupation Forces and the German people? Incidents involving the troops, such as assault and rape, robbery at lonely houses, scenes of violence in cafés. It would be possible to produce most convincing evidence, it did not really matter if it did not convince the British Army authorities so long as the Germans believed it.

The next discovery was a series of bright ideas about sabotage, particularly of the kind which causes accidents.

" 'Don't blow up the barracks,' " commented Tommy, " 'tamper with the steering gear.' One must admit that this fellow is capable. The Russians are going to miss their Ludwig, aren't they?"

There was a locked drawer at the bottom of the safe, which contained one stout envelope, unsealed. Hambledon slid out the contents.

They comprised a set of personal papers of a kind which he had never seen before, for they were Soviet-issued passes to enter the Soviet Zone at Helmstedt. That is, there were a number of passes but they all referred to Ludwig Kirsch. There was a German passport complete with photograph and visaed for entry into Soviet-occupied territory at Helmstedt only, not anywhere else. There was a grey card authorising him to travel by railway from Helmstedt direct to Magdeburg and a white one permitting him to move about within the city limits of Magdeburg for a period not exceeding seven days. This must be taken to the police by the bearer in person *within* three hours of arriving in the city. There was a short list of names and addresses of "permitted" hotels; a note at the foot of this said that ration cards were obtainable at the office of the Rationed Food Distribution Controller and identity papers must be produced at the time of application. There was a further card, blue this time, giving the name and address of the particular *Volksbank* authorised to exchange West marks into East marks; Hambledon, who had heard from Britz, his driver, that there was a thriving black market in the Soviet Zone for the more valuable West marks, guessed that this bank was not nearly so busy as it ought to be.

"Dear me," said Hambledon. "I wonder whether you were in the habit of running across to see your little playmates every so often." He took up Kirsch's passport again and examined it closely. It had been issued in 1954 and was therefore three years old. It bore exit and entry stamps into Holland and back in 1954 and again in 1955 and these were the only entries before the Soviet visa dated January of the current year. Kirsch's address was given as Hamburg.

Hambledon looked at the passport and the beginning of an idea began to germinate in his mind. Of course, this passport only said that Kirsch had not entered Russian territory since 1954. He might have made a habit of it before that, not so long ago. Besides, it was practically certain that Kirsch would have had visitors from the Soviet Zone. Russian Intelligence Services would not conduct their business through the post. Hambledon's idea, always a little misty, thinned out almost to vanishing point. There would be no sense in entering Soviet-occupied territory on these papers, only to be confronted with rows of hard-faced autocrats all looking coldly at him and saying with one voice: "This ain't our Ludwig." Then, moving as one man, they would all draw out their Army-issue revolvers. No, no future in that. None at all.

Hambledon sighed and returned the papers to the safe for the moment.

The drawers of the writing table, although as scrupulously locked as the rest, contained only such innocent and homely things as blotting paper, writing paper, envelopes, paper clips, pencils, and boxes of nibs. The bottom left-hand drawer alone contained something not strictly utilitarian, a box of chessmen and a folding board. The man kept no letters—there were a few tradesmen's receipts—he seemed to have neither family nor friends. No "Lieb' Ludwig, could you lend me fifty marks till the end of the month"; no "Lieber Onkel, there is great news, Gretchen has a son and the little Lottchen has cut a tooth." Nothing human.

Hambledon went over the rest of the house. Downstairs there was also a kitchen and the small scullery in which Bauer had been confined. Here there was a back door leading to a neglected garden and a secretive-looking little path between currant bushes to an inconspicuous gate in the side lane. A quiet route for shy visitors.

Upstairs there were two bedrooms and a small box room, unused. One bedroom was kept under dust sheets by the careful Hanna; the other was Ludwig Kirsch's. The grey dressing gown which had so much affronted Hanna's deputy had been flung across the foot of the bed. Presumably Kirsch had changed into more formal attire when he was taken to police headquarters. There were clothes in a hanging cupboard, underwear and handkerchiefs in the dressing-table drawers, shaving kit and so forth on the fixed wash-hand basin. Everything that should be in a man's bedroom was there and nothing more. Had Kirsch no gun, then? Oh, probably on him when he was arrested, and taken away, with him, by the police.

Hambledon reckoned that he was not likely to be approached by anyone from Soviet Intelligence until it became obvious that Bauer was missing; not, probably, for two days. In the meantime it would be idiotic as well as intensely boring to sit indoors continuously at this stage. Dull and stuffy, even with the windows open. Besides, he was getting hungry.

He reopened the safe, took out Kirsch's careful details about the British Army, and put them in a large envelope with a covering note for transmission to the British Army of Occupation, Security Branch. Kirsch's passport and various passes for the Soviet Zone went into Hambledon's own inside pocket; it was painfully unlikely that he would ever be able to use them, but one never knows. The fact was that he could not bear to part with them.

He rang up the Chief of Police on the telephone.

"I have found a lot of stuff in Kirsch's safe which will interest you. In fact, it won't matter in the least if Kirsch never speaks another word as long as he lives; it's all here. I'll bring it along to you. I think it would be wiser if your detectives were not seen to be buzzing round this house at the moment . . . What? . . . No, no trouble at all, I'm going out to lunch. There's no sense in my sticking close to this place until it becomes obvious to those who sent him that Bauer has got lost. I wish Bauer would talk, but . . . Yes, I agree. I've often thought so . . . Yes, but one couldn't rely on what he said and there's no means of checking it. I assume that he did come in from the Soviet Zone . . . Oh, have you? Well done. Through Helmstedt yesterday, I see. Probably stayed the night at Brunswick. Yes . . . Well now, I have also found some stuff the British authorities ought to have, not that it will do them much good, it's all carbon copies but it will make nice bedtime reading . . . Oh, would you? How kind, I'll bring that along too, then. Very well, I'll have some lunch, it's getting late, and then come on to you. I beg your pardon?"

"I said," repeated the Chief of Police, "that I have a message for you from London. Here it is. 'Your message received. Please arrange get Micklejohn out earliest possible moment.' Message ends."

Hambledon caught a bus into Goslar and stood himself lunch at the Schwartzer Adler. If he were going to spend two or three days—or even more—immured in Kirsch's house with a choice between cooking for himself or living upon sausage, he would at least have a nice lunch to remember. Besides, if he were to go about with two or three days' beard upon his face none of the better hotels would admit him, and rightly.

He emerged, pleasantly replete, from the Schwartzer Adler and stood outside the door while he lit a cigar. Apparently Adolf Hitler used to stay at the Schwartzer Adler when he came to Goslar, though why anyone should think it recommended an hotel to have had among its clients a man who ate boiled cabbage and cream buns and drank *Apfelsaft* it is hard to understand. If it could be said that Goering had approved the place, there would have been much more sense in it.

He walked up the path to the road and turned right to go into the town. The side wall of the Schwartzer Adler's decorative forecourt ends in a square stone pillar and on this pillar there is a bronze plaque. Hambledon stopped to look.

It is about two feet high by eighteen inches wide and depicts, in low relief, a barbed-wire fence such as are placed round prisoner-of-war camps. Against this fence there is the figure of a man, seen from behind, drooping against the wire in an attitude of the most heartbroken despair. One hand drags at a strand as though his legs will scarcely support him, his body sags sideways, and his face is hidden in the crook of his arm. An inscription across the top reads *Vergesst Uns Nicht*—do not forget us.

It is a memorial to the eighty thousand German prisoners whom the Russians still refuse to release. Quite recently, in fact, the Russians have said that these prisoners cannot now be returned because they are all dead.

He turned away and walked on, wondering whether or not the irony was intentional which had set this plaque outside the one place in Goslar most associated with Adolf Hitler.

the smirnov plan

HAMBLEDON WENT ON down the road and angled across the square which contains the Jakobi-Kirche to reach the Police Headquarters by footways and narrow side streets. The Chief of Police received him at once.

"These will interest you," said Tommy, and gave him Kirsch's lists of Communist agents in that area—the end-of-term reports—and the further list of what these men had done.

"I am interested," said the Chief grimly, running his eyes down the lists. "So will they be when I bring them here before me. I will give them something to occupy their minds, yes, yes. I——"

"These," said Hambledon, "I think you should see and then, if you will, pass them on to the British authorities. I really don't know whether you or they are the more concerned."

These last were Kirsch's suggestions for stirring up trouble between the British Occupation Forces and the German people, and also for sabotage.

"These, I think, will form an important part of the case against him, but I will send copies at once to the British authorities, do you agree? Good. Anything else?"

"Only this rather fat envelope for the Army Security people. You said that you would kindly send them up."

"I will send a police car out at once. There is no message with them? No. They shall have them in an hour," said the Chief. "Anything else?"

"Only an enquiry, a complete shot in the dark. The man may not even exist but it would be foolish to neglect the most outside chance—

Gustav Ehrlich is the name. Do you know anything whatever about a man named Ehrlich, Gustav?"

"Ehrlich. I have heard the name and that quite recently. One moment." The Chief of Police went to a tall card index, pulled out the drawer labelled EB–EN, and flicked over the cards. "Yes, here he is. 'Ehrlich, Gustav, born at Stettin 1932, engineer, employed at Breslau 1952–54, went to Dortmund October '54, Communist. Suspected on good evidence of embezzling firm's money, complaint laid with police May 27, this year. Evaded arrest and is thought to be making for Soviet Zone.' That is right, we were looking out for him but we have not caught him. That is quite recent, you see, but I expect he has got across by now. I have no photograph but here is his description: 'Eyes, grey; hair, brown; round face; long nose; cleft chin; ears flat, no lobes; height 175.5 centimetres, no distinguishing marks.' That, mein Herr, is all I have."

"Thank you very much," said Hambledon.

The Chief looked at him, but, as it was evident that there was nothing more forthcoming, he put back the card, shut the drawer again, and asked what Hambledon proposed to do now.

"Dispense with shaving, trail about in Kirsch's old dressing gown, and hope that someone may come who does not know him personally."

Two days later, in the evening as the light was going, a knock came at Ludwig Kirsch's front door. Hambledon, with the grey dressing gown on over his shirt sleeves, no collar, a two-day stubble on his face, a spare pair of Kirsch's glasses on his nose and bedroom slippers on his feet, opened the door cautiously. A small neat man stood on the mat outside and said, in an enquiring tone: "Herr Ludwig Kirsch?"

Kirsch's glasses were very strong and Hambledon could not see through them at all; he let them slip down his nose and peered at his visitor over the top of them.

"That is my name," he said, not attempting to move.

"Lorenz Grober," said the small man, introducing himself. "May I come in?"

"I suppose so," said Hambledon grumpily. He showed Grober into the sitting room and waited to lock and bolt the door before following him. "Please sit down."

"Thank you. You do not know me, Herr Kirsch——"

"You are perfectly right, I do not."

"Perhaps I might show you my passport," said Grober, and opened it to display the stamp of entry into Western Germany from the Soviet

Zone at Helmstedt, dated that day. Hambledon dropped his glasses and managed to steal a glance at the page before putting them on again. He stared owlishly at the passport and then at his visitor.

"I do not like dealing with strangers," he said abruptly. "Where is Bauer?"

"Has the Herr not seen Bauer?"

"Of course I've seen him. Repeatedly." Hambledon knew that Bauer's passport showed frequent transits across the frontier at Helmstedt. "I do not like this at all. Who are you to be asking me questions about Bauer? I was expecting him. One moment. That curtain gapes a little." Hambledon got up and arranged, with meticulous care, one of the window curtains which did not quite meet its fellow. "I detest gaping curtains when I have lights on in the rooms. Now tell me why Bauer has not come. I was expecting him before this."

"We greatly fear," said Grober, "that something has happened to Bauer. He crossed at Helmstedt three days ago with the intention of calling upon you the following day, but he has not returned to us and now you say that he did not come here. It does look as though something has hap——"

"Nothing irritates me more," said Hambledon, so energetically that his glasses fell off his nose into his lap, "than this stupid and inaccurate habit of using a vaguely harmless circumlocution in place of a definite statement. If you mean that you think Bauer has been picked up by the police, why not say so in plain terms? Accuracy, accuracy."

"But he may not have been arrested," pleaded Grober. "He may have been taken ill—met with an accident—been run over in the street."

"It is possible. These are all possible suggestions, now that you have applied your mind to formulating your ideas. Well, at least it is clear that Bauer was on his way here and has failed to arrive."

"Yes. That being so, I have had the honour to be sent in his place, and the substance of my message concerns the Smirnov Plan, which, as you know, was stolen from the late General Vedovitch. The papers have not been found on our side and it is thought increasingly likely that they were brought across the frontier here. I am to urge——"

"Quite right. They were."

Grober sat up. "You know that, for a fact?"

Hambledon replaced his spectacles—Kirsch's spectacles—firmly on his nose. The effect was to make Grober's face look like a large, pink bath sponge, but that could not be helped.

"Have I, then, a reputation for making inaccurate statements?"

"Heaven forbid, Herr Kirsch! Quite the reverse. My remark was more in the nature of an exclamation of pleased surprise."

Hambledon sneered and Grober went on hastily:

"That being so, I am to urge upon you the imperative necessity for locating them and securing possession of them at the earliest possible moment. The Soviet Army authorities lay the greatest possible stress upon the importance of their being regained at once, as the utmost inconvenience and damage would be caused if they fell into West German or British hands."

Hambledon sat with his hands lightly folded in his lap, waiting patiently until Grober should have completed his sentence. When it was quite clear that there was no more to come he moved his head just enough to make his spectacles flash like the eyes of the witch in "Hänsel und Gretel" and remarked:

"I already have them."

Grober bounced in his chair.

"You—already—have—them?"

"I wish Bauer had come instead of you. He at least did not expect me to repeat even my simplest statements twice."

Grober also wished that Bauer had come; presumably, long acquaintance had taught him how to deal with this peppery old horror. He himself was not enjoying the interview at all.

"I beg your pardon. I was surprised, that is——"

"Surprised? That I was told to regain possession of certain plans and have actually done so? Why should that surprise you?"

Grober drew out his handkerchief to wipe his brow.

"Gnä' Herr, I beg——"

"Go on. What do you beg?"

"Permission to say that whatever may be the case with an inexperienced young man like myself, my superiors at least will not be surprised. The Herr has no idea—can have no idea of the extraordinarily high value which Russian Intelligence places upon his services. The Herr's reputation is unsurpassed."

Hambledon was not surprised; he had himself formed a high opinion of Kirsch's capabilities. He thought it time to unbend a little.

"'I use only the best butter,'" he murmured, and allowed his grim expression to relax slightly.

"Indeed, indeed, it is not flattery," protested Grober. "Would the Herr care to tell me something of how the plans were recovered? My superiors will be so eager——"

"It was nothing. Perfectly simple. That fellow Andrey Lentov brought them across and I took them from him. That is all. It was, surely, known from the outset that Lentov had them?"

"Of course, yes. General Vedovitch was so ill-advised as himself to give Lentov the plans to take to headquarters, and the young man was not seen again."

Hambledon made a shocked noise and added: "Imbecile. Criminally imbecile. I take it that General Vedovitch has been suitably dealt with?"

"He committed suicide, mein Herr."

"Good. Most suitable for a high-ranking Army officer."

"Yes, indeed. And where is Lentov now?"

Hambledon raised his eyebrows.

"In Hell, presumably, if the theologians have their facts right."

"Then he——"

"I shot him myself, as a matter of fact," said Hambledon casually. "He was a traitor."

He took his glasses off to rub his eyes. The strong lenses were straining his sight. "Be so good as to report that also to your superiors," he added. "And apologise on my behalf for depriving them of the pleasure, but circumstances were a little pressing at that moment."

"Certainly, certainly. And the Smirnov Plan—you have it here?"

"What? In this house? *Himmel*, no! I do not consider this house altogether safe. I think the police take a little interest in it sometimes." He replaced the spectacles and peered at Grober over the frame. "One cannot be too careful. One of my assistants was arrested and the other has taken fright and run away."

Grober seemed to grow smaller where he sat.

"Then you think—do you think——"

"Frequently," snapped Hambledon. "And, if I may say so, intelligently. On this occasion I think I want a new assistant."

"But the man who was arrested, will he not talk?"

"Do dead men talk?"

"Oh, he is dead. You did not say that, you only said he had been arrested and——"

"Blistering nincompoop," roared Hambledon, "do even you suppose that I should be sitting here quietly in my own house if my late assistant were wagging his tongue off at Police Headquarters? You are a fool."

"Evidently," said Grober faintly, "evidently. But the Russians are very eager to have the plans back."

"I do not insult them by suggesting that they would expect me to hand them over to you—a man I have never seen before in my life. If Bauer had come——"

"But you do not know any of us except Bauer, now that Groenfeld is dead," said Grober desperately. "I applaud—we all applaud—your extreme caution in never crossing to our side, in having no dealings with the usual Communist clubs, in never attending meetings, in never having people at your house here except the occasional visitor like Bauer, even your care with the drawn curtains—all admirable. But I am sent to beg you to come over so that we may see what manner of man has served us so well. Bauer brought you the passes, did he not?"

Hambledon got up and took a turn up and down the room, waving his glasses in his hand. Grober, of course, had to stand also.

"He did, yes, and I still have them. I am gratified at this courteous desire to make a fuss over me, but I have always refused to come across for the simple reason that once I was noted as having crossed your frontier I should be marked down as being in touch with the Soviet Zone, whereas at present I am not tainted with any political affiliation. I think that is quite simple and clear."

"Perfectly, and we——"

"But the present emergency is quite serious. The Smirnov Plan papers are of the greatest importance—I am aware of that—and the Russians should have them back at the earliest possible moment, but to hand them over to a total stranger! No, no, I cannot bring myself to do it."

Grober had enough tact to hold his tongue and wait.

"I see no help for it," said Hambledon finally. "It seems that this course of action is forced upon me. I only hope that I shall not have to regret it," he added, from the bottom of his heart.

Grober, in fluent phrases, expressed himself as being overjoyed at the prospect of being able to take back with him such good news as that the famous, nay, the illustrious Herr Ludwig Kirsch was actually——

"Make sure that you do get back with it and do not fall into oblivion on the road like poor Bauer," said Hambledon. "Now, the passes Bauer brought me provide for a train journey to Magdeburg and back to Helmstedt. That will not do at all because I shall be travelling by car. My car. And I cannot be confined to any particular route. I must be able to choose any road which I think best."

"But——"

"Triple-damned idiot," snarled Hambledon, "do you seriously suppose that there is no anti-Communist organisation on your side?"

Grober knew very well that such organisations did exist and was obliged to admit it.

"Very well, then," said Hambledon. "I drive my own car——"

"I shall be asked," said Grober timidly, "your excellent reasons for not wishing to travel by train."

"Because I shall be carrying the Smirnov Plan."

Grober's face lit up. "It will, of course, be concealed in the car?"

"You have your brighter moments."

"Thank you, indeed. The necessary passes shall reach you within twenty-four hours."

"I shall not be ready to come across for a couple of days. I told you the plan is not here, it is hidden. I must go and get it and I may have to watch my moment for taking it from where it lies hid. Let us say two clear days to be on the safe side—I have a mania for being on the safe side——"

"How wise! How right!"

"How true. Well, now, today is Tuesday, is it not?"

"Certainly, gnä' Herr."

"Wednesday, Thursday. I will cross the frontier at Helmstedt between fourteen and fifteen hours on Friday and you will be there to meet me, Grober. Understand? If you are not waiting at the Soviet Zone barrier when I drive up, I turn straight round and drive back again. It is still true that I do not know nearly enough about you but at least I shall recognise your face. I absolutely refuse to be landed with an unknown escort who may be a member of your subversive underground movement only waiting for a lonely stretch of road to cut my throat."

Grober made clucking noises.

"Do you realise," said Hambledon, with his most terrifying scowl above the spectacles, "that even now you may be a member of that organisation who has wormed himself in here—having cut Bauer's throat on the way—to penetrate my obscurity and betray my secrets?"

"Herr Kirsch," said Grober, in a voice trembling with sincerity, "believe me, if I were not perfectly genuine I should have fled long ago."

"If I had not believed you genuine you would never have left the house. Let us before all things be accurate: you would never have left the garden. Why are we standing up? Sit down."

Grober sat down with a bump and Hambledon sank slowly into his chair, settling his dressing gown about him. One of the pockets bulged and a weight inside dragged it down, it contained Hambledon's Luger, and Grober's eyes had been nervously upon it.

"I think that is all, is it not?" said his terrifying host. "Unless you have anything further to tell me, I need not detain you."

Grober sprang up again.

"Only the car number, mein Herr, for the pass, the number and make and colour of your car."

"Oh. Yes. Well, the number is GS 13579, you had better make a note of that. As for the make, that is a little more difficult. You see, it was built—you had better come out and look at it."

Hambledon took a small electric torch from a drawer and led the way into the entrance hall, where he unlocked and unbolted the door and switched the ceiling light out before opening the door.

"It is not really dark outside," he said, stepping out confidently. "It is a strange thing, but in the dark I can see better without my spect—— What have you done? Please do not make so much noise."

"I fell over—I think, the scraper," said Grober, getting up painfully and rubbing his shin, but Hambledon had not waited for him and could dimly be seen at the garage door. A key turned in a lock, the door swung open, and the light of Hambledon's little torch could be seen inside. Grober limped after him.

"This car was constructed by a local mechanic at a time when cars were hard to come by. Long before I came here, of course. I am not a specialist in automobile construction but I understand that the—the underframing and the engine are of one make, the bonnet and the radiator are of another, a Renault radiator, is it? And the body is an extremely comfortable coupé. I like it."

Grober looked at the car and blinked, for he did know something about automobiles. The original chassis had belonged to a full-length saloon car of some sort. The coupé body was much too short to cover it and the rear end of the frame members with the transmission shaft, differential, back axle, and what Hambledon in his own mind called "all the rest of the gubbins" stuck out behind in naked majesty. The general effect was of a sedan chair perched upon a secondhand bedstead, but the car was clean and well cared for and the paint in reasonably good condition. Hambledon patted the bonnet affectionately.

"It goes very well," he said casually. "Now you have seen it do you think you will recognise it again?"

He gave Grober full marks for keeping every trace of emphasis out of his voice when he said that he would.

"Now," added Grober, "I think I need not inflict my company upon you any longer." He stepped back while Hambledon shut and locked the garage door. "Your valuable time—I have taken up too much already. In taking my leave——"

"Be quiet!" hissed Hambledon, and listened intently. "Back in the house."

He hustled Grober into the dark hall and took some pains to close and fasten the door silently.

"What——" breathed Grober. "Police?"

"Yes, but the fellow on duty tonight is hard of hearing. I think he may not have heard you. It will be better to wait a little. Come in and sit down."

Grober would have given much for a drink, but probably the Herr Kirsch only drank at breakfast time or when the moon changed. In any case, he did not suggest it. Grober's head was beginning to ache and his shin was abominably painful, but he eased the trouser leg away from it and composed himself to listen while Herr Kirsch talked about the car, which appeared to be his one human weakness.

"You will understand," he said eventually, "that, since I am passing here as nothing more than a retired teacher of mathematics, I cannot afford to appear well-to-do. Quite the reverse. So when I saw this car pushed away into the back of a garage with an absurdly low price upon it, I seized the opportunity. The car——"

But Grober really felt as though he could not stand any more car.

"I must, finally, refer once more to my boundless admiration for your farseeing caution," he said. "Your cover is so good, this artistic simulation of a quiet student writing a book of algebra for boys——"

Herr Kirsch sprang from his chair. He was not a tall man, but to Grober's alarmed eyes he appeared to tower like the tall Agrippa in the *Struwelpeter* his grandmother used to show him on Sundays.

"Simulation?" he stormed. "You suggest I am pretending? Come with me."

He seized Grober by the ear and dragged him into the further room, the little study.

"Look," he said, releasing Grober in order to switch on the light, "look upon that table. Behold a small part of years of work. Those are the examples and the exercises for my *Trigonometry for Higher Forms*, every one deliberately selected to display some fresh facet of— of trigonometry. Look at my pages here." Hambledon dragged open a table drawer and thrust a handful of Kirsch's careful layouts under Grober's terrified nose.

"I—I am overcome," said Grober, backing away to the door. "I am incapable of appreciating—I never understood mathematics. In any case, esteemed Herr Kirsch, I must go now. I have detained you too long from your for-the-instruction-of-youth-indispensable labours." He picked up his hat in the sitting room. "I shall look forward with joy to meeting you at Helmstedt on Friday." He laid his hand upon the front door. "*Auf Wiedersehen*, gnä' Herr."

"Not that way," said Hambledon, and steered him through the kitchen to the scullery. "Here is the back door. There is a path through the garden to a small gate in the lane. When you reach it, turn right and the lane will lead you back to the town. *Auf Wiedersehen*, Grober."

He closed and locked the door almost before the young man was clear of the doorstep, and listened with pleasure through the scullery window to rustling noises and smothered yelps, for some of the bushes were gooseberry. "And I hope you fall in *Die Abzucht*," he added unkindly.

Now, *Die Abzucht* means The Drain.

CHAPTER XVI

a meal with wine

HAMBLEDON TOOK OFF Kirsch's glasses and looked at them.

"That was a mistake," he said to himself. "If I go on wearing those things I shall be cross-eyed in six hours." But Grober had seen the thick pebble lenses and would notice at once if they were replaced by plain glass. Besides, the frames did not fit him. Of course, the answer was simple; plain glass with tinted glare-proof glasses clipped over them. Simple. See about it tomorrow. He crossed the room to Kirsch's sideboard, took out a bottle and a glass, poured himself some wine, and sat down again to enjoy it.

Ten minutes later someone tapped on the windowpane. Hambledon got up and went to the door to speak to the police officer outside.

"Well?"

"He didn't go down the lane, mein Herr. He came back up to the main road and a car picked him up. They went off towards Oker, mein Herr, but I've got a man trailing the car."

"Thank you very much. I expect he'll turn off north. He's bound for Helmstedt. Is your chief still at the office, do you know?"

"When he heard that this man had come, he said that he would wait until he heard from the Herr."

"Very good, I'll ring him. Thank you very much. Good night."

Hambledon telephoned to the Chief of Police.

"He has been and gone again and all's well. He did not know Kirsch, so there was no trouble. I meant to ask you before, I want to ring up my department in London, will it be all right to use this phone?"

The Chief hesitated. "A long-distance call, you would have to give your number to the exchange—come and take your call from here. Do you want to do it tonight or will tomorrow morning do?"

"I would rather do it tonight, I think."

"Sit tight and I will send a police car for you. No, no trouble at all, they are only patrolling round and getting bored. Any immediate news for me?"

"Not immediate, no, it will keep till the morning."

"Very good indeed; then I go to bed and you can have my office all to yourself. I am tired. There is nothing which tires me more than asking questions and getting no answers. That Kirsch and that Bauer, they will not even say yes or no."

"Very sensible of them," said Hambledon.

"I hate sensible criminals," said the Chief tartly. "Never mind. I send the car for you and then I go to bed. *Auf Wiedersehen Morgen, ja?* Good night."

Hambledon's message to his department was to ask them to send out, as early as possible next day, by air to Hanover, a man with gear for photographing documents. He was to stop in Hanover and Hambledon would come there to meet him with the documents to be photographed. Yes, tomorrow without fail. What? Yes, of course it would be later today since it was past midnight, sorry. Today, then. Very important indeed, there must be no hitch. Good.

After which Hambledon, yawning his head off, went back to Kirsch's house and to bed.

On the following morning, having had a nice clean shave, he slipped out by the back door in case someone—besides the police—might be keeping an eye upon the house of the illustrious Herr Kirsch. He went down the lane and by devious ways to the town. Here he straightened his back, held up his head, and walked about like a free man, for was he not once more the English visitor staying at the Drei Bullochsen? His first errand was to a photographer's for a passport photograph, his second to the bank in Fischmaker Strasse for the envelope which he had dropped into their night safe. Here he was prepared for a little trouble in establishing his identity, but his passport and a detailed description of the envelope with a black thumbprint in the left-hand top corner served to convince the bank officials. Perhaps the Chief of Police had smoothed his path.

With the Smirnov Plan in his pocket he went to look for Britz and found him washing and polishing the small bus in which the party from the Drei Bullochsen had travelled to the Zwinger. Britz straightened himself when he heard a step behind him and his face lit up at sight of Hambledon.

"*Gott sei dank*, I feared that something might have befallen the Herr. I saw the Herr Petersen yesterday and he told me that the Herr was away from the hotel, and I feared——"

"Thank you," said Hambledon. "I am sorry to have caused you anxiety, but I have been spending a few nights at the house of a friend. I want to speak to you. Are we private here?"

"Let us get into the bus," said Britz, opening the door for him, "thus we may be private enough. There are some fresh people on the ground floor of this house. I do not know anything about them." He got in beside Hambledon, shut the door, and took a large road map out of the cubbyhole. "If we are observed," he said, opening it out, "we are planning the route for a drive."

"There is," said Hambledon, leaning across to point out a place on the map, "a face behind that muslin blind, but I think it is only a child."

"One cannot be too careful," said Britz gloomily.

"No. I wanted to ask you to get a message across to the Herr Micklejohn, Gustav Ehrlich, you know."

"I will do my best, but the Herr knows that it——"

"I know it is difficult, but this one is very important. Say to him that if he hears that Ludwig Kirsch is asking for him, to go to him without fear, for Ludwig Kirsch is a trustworthy friend."

"Ludwig Kirsch," said Britz, running his finger along the road to Clausthal-Zellerfeld. "I will remember that name."

"Thank you. The other thing I want you to do for me is a great deal simpler. I want you to go to a certain house"—he gave Britz the full address of Kirsch's house—"and look over an extraordinary old car you will find in the garage there. Here is the key of the garage. I don't want an elaborate overhaul and in any case I shall want her in the morning of the day after tomorrow—Friday. I only want her to start when required, continue to proceed and stop when I want to stop. That's all."

"General checkup," said Britz cheerfully. "Petrol, oil, you want me to fill her up? Tyres, brakes, steering, running—certainly, mein Herr. I will go out there at once."

"If the police should ask you what you are doing there," said Tommy, scribbling a message upon one of his cards, "show them this."

"Very good. And if anyone else should ask me?"

"Tell them to go to hell."

"*Schön*. What make is the car?"

"Oh. That is rather difficult. It's a composite affair with a coupé body on a long chassis. It's got a Renault radiator, but what the engine is I really don't know."

"*Ach*, that is the car which my friend Ernst Krueger made up soon after the war out of what scraps he could salvage when he came home. He used to drive her about, she goes very well, it is a good engine, but she looks so odd that the girls used to laugh at him and say that the body was once the porch of Noah's Ark. Ernst, he does not like girls to laugh at him, so, as soon as he could, he bought a Volkswagen and pushed the old car out of the way. Then one day he told me that he had sold it to a Herr Kir——"

He stopped.

"Herr Kirsch, that's right. I have been staying in his house," said Hambledon. "The Herr is away from home at the moment and the police are keeping an eye on the house, that is why I gave you that card."

Britz looked up with eyes full of questions, but Hambledon merely smiled and the questions remained unasked.

"I may take it, Britz, may I not, that you are not a man who talks?"

"*Herrgott*," said Britz violently, "I have had enough practice in not talking."

"*Schön*," said Hambledon. "Well, I must go, I have an engagement." He turned to get out of the car, but Britz said: "Excuse me, please. The Herr reached his hotel safely the other night from the Zwinger?"

"Safe and unmolested," said Hambledon with emphasis. He looked Britz squarely in the eyes and added: "I did not even have my pockets picked."

Britz said with what was, for him, a broad grin, that he was delighted to hear it, and Hambledon went off to catch his train for Hanover.

"Though why in the name of common sense," he said to himself, "Britz could not simply have come to the hotel quietly and handed the Smirnov Plan to me personally, I cannot understand. All that business about the waiter bringing me that box from Karstadt's——"

He came level with the Schwartzer Adler and glanced over his shoulder at the *Vergesst Uns Nicht* plaque.

"Perhaps if I lived only ten miles from the Russian Army," he concluded, "I should become tortuous and complicated too."

He returned from Hanover in the evening, called in at the photographer's, and went on to see the Chief of Police.

"Will you be so good as to take charge of this for me? Put it in your safe, if you will. It is the Smirnov Plan."

"That almost fabulous document," said the Chief, taking the envelope. "You wish me to guard it for you until your return to England?"

"Oh, no. Only until Friday morning. I'll pick it up on my way to Helmstedt. You see, I thought it would be a nice gesture to let the Russians have it back. They will be pleased, don't you think?"

"But——"

"It has spent the afternoon in Hanover," said Hambledon, gently flicking the envelope, "having its photographs taken."

"Ach! I begin to see. And the photographs?"

"Are on their way to London. If the plane should fail to arrive, there is still time to have them photographed again tomorrow. That is why I am not going until Friday."

"You are going, you said, to Helmstedt?"

"I am going by Helmstedt into the Soviet Zone to deliver these precious papers personally to the Russian Army authorities. They ought to be pleased, don't you think? They will probably lay on a banquet. Fortunately I like vodka."

"But, my poor friend, you are mad! You have allowed yourself to become mentally deranged! Because you managed to pass yourself off as Ludwig Kirsch to one man who did not know him——"

"Nobody knows him," said Hambledon, and explained Kirsch's elaborate security precautions. "Only two men from that side knew him. One is Bauer—don't lose him, will you?—and the other is dead."

"But they may have a photograph of him and you do not resemble him in the least."

A sudden memory flicked up from the recesses of Hambledon's mind: Britz, on that first drive along the frontier, saying that there were cameras with telephoto lenses in those watchtowers. They take very clear photographs when the light is good. Hambledon put the thought away for future consideration.

"If they produce a portrait of Kirsch and point out that it is nothing like me, I shall proclaim in the ringing accents of unmistakable sincerity that they have got the wrong photograph. Then they can take another look at me and see that it is so."

The Chief of Police appealed to his Maker.

"No filing system," added Hambledon, "is completely watertight.

Especially, I imagine, the Russians'. The human element, you know."

"But why are you putting your head in the lion's mouth like this? Do you hope to be able to find young Micklejohn?"

"I shall tell them that I want a new assistant. My man Tosen was arrested, though I managed to kill him before he could talk, and the other man, Dittmar, took fright and ran away. I know the man I want, he has worked on this side before. His name is Gustav Ehrlich. I am telling you this in advance, Herr Chief of Police, in case it may happen that Gustav Ehrlich gets across the frontier separately, alone, before I do. If he does, you will take great care of him, won't you?"

"Micklejohn," said the Chief, in a voice so low as to be barely audible. "Tell me," he added, "what do you think has happened to the real Ehrlich?"

"I don't know at all but I should think that he is probably dead, since he doesn't seem to be using his identity papers any more. Well, I think that is all at the moment. Are there any special formalities about leaving this zone at Helmstedt?"

"You will need a Russian visa and——"

"Ah, yes. That brings me to my next point. Here is Kirsch's passport complete with Russian visa as required. The only thing the matter with it is that it carries Kirsch's photograph instead of mine and, as you so truly remarked just now, there is little or no resemblance between us." Hambledon laid the passport on the Chief's desk and took a small photographic print out of his wallet. "Here also is a passport photograph of me and no one can say it is not up to date, because it was taken today. Now, if Kirsch's photograph were carefully removed from his passport and mine substituted, the thing would be complete. Wouldn't it?"

He sat back and beamed upon the Chief of Police, who spluttered. "But—but—but this is——"

"Oh, come," said Hambledon kindly. "You can't tell me that you have reached your present deservedly exalted rank without ever having heard of a cooked passport? In a good cause, of course. Besides, it isn't as though Kirsch will want his passport again in what politicians call the foreseeable future. Consider the issues involved. Consider the practically tearful gratitude of Britain's Secretary of State for Foreign Affairs, the Right Honourable Augustus Micklejohn, Member of Parliament. I shouldn't be surprised if you received a ceremonial visit from the British Ambassador in person. Besides, consider yourself; how refreshing, how ennobling it is occasionally to take a strong line against pettifogging restrictions. One must above all things refuse to allow oneself to become hidebound."

The Chief's face slowly turned deep red and appeared to swell and for a moment Hambledon thought that he had gone too far, but the big man's shoulders began to shake and it became plain that he was amused.

"Herr Hambledon," he gurgled, "I am sure that that is an accusation which will never be brought against you." He wiped his eyes and picked up Kirsch's passport. "The difficulty, of course, is the official stamp here, which is partly on the photograph and partly on the page. It will need very careful reproducing upon yours so as to fit in."

"That is so," said Hambledon cheerfully. "I used to know a man in Paris who did that sort of work quite beautifully, but it is a long way to Paris and he may not be with us now."

"No need," said the Chief firmly. "Germany also is not without her artists. There is a man now serving a long term in the convict prison at Hanover who will be happy to do it for a box of cigarettes and a good meal with wine. Leave it with me and I will arrange it."

"You are extremely good——"

"Not at all. I spend my days trying to stop this sort of thing, it will be a pleasant change to encourage it for once. Besides, it will help me not to become hidebound."

"I do apologise——" began Hambledon.

"Ach, please! Your other passes for travel inside the Soviet Zone? There are many needed, as I once told you."

"I have them, all except the passes for the car, which may arrive this evening, so I had better get back to my house—Kirsch's house. By the way, I asked London to ring through to you to report the safe arrival of those photographs. I hope you will excuse me. I thought they had better not ring me direct. About leaving this zone?"

"No, there is nothing extra you will need but I will make sure that you are not held up."

"Tell them to clear the road for me when I come back," grinned Hambledon. "I may be in more of a hurry then."

He walked through the streets of Goslar, through the great gate called the Breite Tor and out upon the road to Oker, recalling what Britz had said that day they drove to Walkenried. Britz had said that he had never seen so many Vopos about on any occasion before, and certainly, wherever they had stopped, there were the brown uniforms and the clumsy intent faces somewhere near by if one looked carefully. At Neuhof, where the country was more open, there were two of them leaning over a gate studying him through field glasses. "One would say they recognised the Herr."

Well, it could not be helped and probably the risk was slight. Hambledon had no intention of going anywhere near The Wire and copies of the photograph would only be circulated to patrols along the frontier. No doubt a further copy would find its way into some filing cabinet where no one but a filing clerk would ever see it; there must be a good many photographs taken along The Wire if it were worth while installing telephoto cameras, and what is one among so many? Not worth bothering about.

He turned in at Ludwig Kirsch's gate and found Britz working on the car. He said it was in good condition; he had had it out on the road and it appeared to be suffering mainly from insufficient use. The Herr Kirsch, it would seem, was not an indefatigable motorist. Hambledon thought that, judging Kirsch's eyesight by the type of glasses he wore, the roads of Goslar and district would be a great deal safer if he never drove again. Well, he would not in any case, since he was in gaol and likely to stay there for some considerable time.

Hambledon encouraged Britz with a few kind remarks and went into the house to cook himself some supper. The telephone rang: a message from Police Headquarters to say that a packet had reached an address in London. Good. He finished his supper and went upstairs to hunt through Ludwig Kirsch's wardrobe for a suit which would approximately fit him; there was one which would serve reasonably well. Continental suits do not fit as do those of English cut and Kirsch was notoriously not a dressy man.

Hambledon ran over in his mind the various arrangements he had made. The only thing left to do tomorrow was to get some glasses which would not blind him as Kirsch's did. The passes for the car had not arrived but there was all tomorrow.

He poured himself a glass of wine and looked through Kirsch's bookcase for something to read and at this point it occurred to him that as an expert on trigonometry he should at least know something about its field of operations, if only in order to dodge the subject if it looked like coming up. He selected a book from the shelf and sat down to study it.

Trigonometry is a means of working out, in figures, calculations which, in geometry, are expressed in diagrams drawn accurately to scale.

Trigonometry is particularly useful in gunnery for calculating the range on targets.

"I shall avoid gunners," said Hambledon aloud.

Trigonometry is indispensable in the work of surveyors. The Smirnov Plan was largely the work of surveyors. He was to take the Smirnov Plan to those who, of all men, were most interested in it. Probably they worked out trigonometrical problems in their heads over breakfast. Plane trigonometry. Spherical trigonometry.

"Curse Kirsch!" said Hambledon violently. "This is much more dangerous than all their cockeyed photographs. Why the hell couldn't the fool take up Chinese hieroglyphics if he wanted a hobby? Nobody knows about Chinese hieroglyphics."

He hurled the book across the room and went to bed.

smoke screen

WHEN HAMBLEDON CAME DOWN to get his breakfast on the following morning he found inside the front door an envelope which had been dropped through the letter slot; it had not come through the post. It contained a frontier pass for the grey coupé valid for Helmstedt and an open pass to authorise the driver, Ludwig Kirsch, to travel freely upon the roads of the Soviet-occupied zone of Germany.

Evidently Britz and his friends were not the only people who communicated through The Wire. Well, nobody supposed that they were.

Hambledon went into the town to buy a pair of horn-rimmed spectacles with plain glass instead of lenses, to the mild surprise of the optician, to whom Hambledon explained that they were for use in private theatricals. He added a pair of sunglasses of the type which clip on over the lenses and walked out wearing spectacles for the first time in his life. It fidgeted him to wear them but he was reassured when he saw himself in a mirror and wondered momentarily who was the man staring at him.

Britz had finished work on the car by lunch time and Hambledon took her out for a trial run. She steered a little front-heavy but presumably one would get used to that. The day seemed rather long but, like all other days, came to an end at last.

On Friday morning Hambledon picked up the Smirnov Plan and the passport from the police station and drove away in the direction of Helmstedt. He admired the passport, which was a thoroughly artistic production, at least as regards the photograph; the personal description had had to stand but at least the eyes were the right colour and there was nothing outstanding about Kirsch's appearance. It is very difficult to tamper with the personal-description page because it is printed upon a special kind of paper which reacts violently to any attempt to alter the written word.

Hambledon drove some five miles out from Goslar and pulled the car in to the side of the road. He lifted up one of the floor boards in the boot, took it inside the car with him, and tucked the Smirnov Plan away in an ingenious cavity in the board. Britz had found it because this board was a little thicker than the others. Hambledon put in the two little screws which kept the thin lid in place, put the board back where it belonged, and screwed that down also.

He drove on towards Helmstedt and found that the car, though noisy, went extremely well considering its age. He stopped for lunch at a roadside inn and considered various possibilities; before he drove on he went to a garage and bought a litre can of lubricating oil, which he took into the car with him.

He had arranged to meet Lorenz Grober at the Soviet frontier post at Helmstedt between two and three o'clock that afternoon and he did not wish to get there too early. It was nearly half-past two before he came in sight of the red and white barrier which marked the West German post and was pleased to see that there did not appear to be much traffic passing at that time. This is the main road to Berlin, the only road through the Soviet Zone, there might have been a long queue of lorries; in point of fact there were only six or eight and they were not being long delayed. Probably the process would take longer on the Russian side. He drove to the tail of the queue and stopped, got out and emptied the can of oil into the sump which Britz had filled the day before.

Hambledon turned to the carburettor. He had watched Britz delicately adjusting the carburettor setting the day before; it had appeared to be a case of "the little more and how much it is." After all, most carburettors are like that.

When it came to his turn he drove up to the officer on duty and it was clear at once that the Goslar Chief of Police had been as good as his word, for no difficulties were made, inspection of the car was perfunctory, and his papers were stamped without any delay. He drove on the short distance to the East German post and noticed in his driving mirror that the smoke from his exhaust was a public offence.

He drew up behind the last lorry in the line and kept his engine running. A blue malodorous haze spread across the road and an official shouted to him to stop the engine. Hambledon took no notice and merely lit a cigar while he was waiting. Drivers alighted to look back at him and other drivers emerging from the office with their papers called official attention to him, pointing. Two lorries behind him stopped a respectful distance away.

A frontier official came, running, and said that he was making a nuisance of himself with all that smoke. Hambledon smiled amiably and said ah, he had been told before that his mixture was too rich, "if I have the phrase correctly. I am not, myself, an automobile mechanic."

The official said that that was reasonably evident and called him on out of turn to get rid of him. Hambledon drew up at the office door with a flourish and went in with his papers. The moment he was inside, someone switched off his engine for him.

"Dear me," said Hambledon in a pained voice, "someone has stopped my engine. I only hope that it will start again. I have had trouble already this morning."

"If it won't, it will be towed away," said the official briefly. "Papers, please."

Almost at once an argument started because the space on the car's papers headed "Make of Car" had been filled in "Composite." What was meant by "composite"?

Hambledon tapped irritably with his fingers on the counter and said composite meant composite, that he had understood that this office was a Frontier Control & Customs Post and not an elementary school, though, as a retired schoolmaster, he would be happy to give instruction upon the meaning of such ordinary words as might puzzle the class as and when required. In the meantime, why not go out and look at the vehicle?

The official said sharply that impudence would not help him and information had to be supplied to the office. The staff were not supposed to fill up travellers' forms for them. Hambledon agreed that filling up forms did indeed demand a certain minimum standard of education and intelligence and a deadlock was rapidly forming when there was a swirl in the interested group in the doorway and Grober rushed in to the rescue.

"Ah," said Hambledon, relaxing, "here is my courier at last. He will deal with the matter."

There was a hurried consultation in low tones during which Hambledon absent-mindedly strolled out of the door and had to be brought back to have his passport stamped.

He returned to the driver's seat; Grober, nervously asking permission which was graciously accorded, sat beside him. Rather to Hambledon's surprise—for he was beginning to think that he had overdone the oil—the engine started at once and the car moved off under the lifted barrier into what starry-eyed optimists call the German Democratic Republic and tactless realists the Soviet Zone.

"I have been instructed to guide you," said Grober, "direct to Magdeburg, where the Army High Command are waiting to receive the Smirnov Plan from your own hands."

"Excellent," said Hambledon. "I shall be interested——"

His voice was drowned in the roar of six powerful motorcycles which formed up round the car as it went, two in front and four behind. They were ridden by six highly polished soldiers smartly dressed in glossy black leather uniforms. Their faces were pink with cleanliness and their expressions conveyed that earnest devotion to duty seen only in official escorts under the eye of authority.

Hambledon slowed down to a walking pace.

"Is anything the matter?" asked Grober.

"I am only waiting till that noisy cluster of mechanised blackbirds has passed on," yelled Hambledon, above the din. "I cannot hear myself speak. Why are they stopping?"

"They are your escort, mein Herr. No further risks are to be taken with the Smirnov Plan, by order of the High Command."

"What? Am I expected to tolerate this nuisance all the way to Magdeburg?"

"It is only about fifty kilometres," shouted Grober, so apologetically that his voice went up into a squeak. "By express order of the High Command."

Hambledon said something about the High Command which Grober thought it tactful not to hear, changed into second gear, and stamped on the accelerator pedal. The result was a loud bang in the exhaust which spattered the two front men of the rear guard with a mixture of oil and carbon and filled their eyes with smoke while the car leapt forward so briskly that the vanguard, paddling along with their toes on the road to keep upright, had the nearest possible escapes from being run down. They roared off ahead while those behind, cursing aloud, mopped their blackened faces and followed after some distance behind.

"That," said Hambledon with what he hoped was a fiendish grin, "will teach the escort to keep its distance. I cannot endure to be crowded on the road."

Grober said nothing and some miles passed before the car showed signs of resenting its condition. One and sometimes two of the six cylinders began missing and there was that sickening intermittent hesitation which all drivers have experienced at some sad time. The vanguard looked back over its shoulders and slowed down and the rear guard closed up. A little later a third cylinder also gave up the struggle, the engine stopped and Hambledon coasted in to the side of the road.

He leaned back in his seat and lit a cigar and the sergeant in charge of the escort came up to the driver's window.

"There appears to be something the matter," said Hambledon, waving him towards the bonnet. "Tell me," he added, turning amiably to Grober, "something about the organisation of agriculture in these parts. These large agricultural machines which I see at work in the fields, are they the property of individual farmers?"

Grober had been born and brought up in Magdeburg and worked in an office ever since he left school. He knew nothing whatever about the country and regarded it as a muddy place inhabited by rude people who kept pigs, but he did know something about Soviet organisation in general.

"Oh, no, I think not. They would be the property of some sort of farmers' association. Collectivisation, you know. There would be a certain number of the—the necessary machines allotted to each area and they would be taken from place to place as required."

"I see. So many haymaking machines to so many square miles, I suppose."

"Exactly. Precisely."

"And what happens if all the hay in an area wants cutting at once? As it probably would, you know. They would all have the same weather, presumably."

Grober was spared answering by the sergeant, who came to the window with a plug in his hand, showed it to Hambledon, and said it was oiled up.

"Well, you know what to do, I am sure. I have the utmost confidence in you," said Hambledon blandly. The sergeant looked pained and went away. Hambledon leaned back in his seat and closed his eyes.

Ten minutes later the sergeant came back to the window and said that if the Herr would try her now——

Hambledon woke up with a start and said that he supposed they ought to be getting on to Magdeburg before long. He then switched on, started the engine and drove off rapidly, leaving the escort hastily gathering up tools in the road and transferring streaks of black grease from their dirty hands to their overheated faces. The sergeant looked from one to another of what had been an impeccably smart patrol.

"You look like greasers off a tug," he said bitterly. "You look like chimney sweeps who've lost their top hats. You look like charcoal burners. Get cracking."

"Did someone say, Sergeant, that we are to escort that—that—that——"

"All right. I know what you mean."

"—wherever he goes for a fortnight?"

"Not if I can get out of it," said the sergeant desperately. "Ready? Mount!"

Hambledon was out of sight by this time, but the escort had no difficulty in following the smoke trail which he laid behind him.

He drove on until Magdeburg lay before them; as they entered the outskirts of the city, the escort formed up once more round the car. The cortège attracted a certain amount of public notice; people looked first at the odd-looking car and then, more interestedly, at the embarrassed motorcycle escort, who, with one accord, bent their heads and fiddled with some unnecessary adjustment.

"Look," said Hambledon to Grober, "we attract attention, it seems to me. They take me for the Emperor of Senegal in a homemade car with an imperial Negro escort." He sounded a cheerful fanfare upon the horn.

Grober said something Hambledon did not catch and then: "Slow here, if you please. We turn off before entering the city. If the Herr will kindly follow the leading escort, here, on the right."

There, on the right, was the imposing entrance to what had once been a large country house outside the city boundaries but was now an Army headquarters standing in a few acres of severely disciplined grounds. There were sentries stiffly on duty at the entrance, but even discipline could not entirely suppress amusement as the motorcycle patrol swept past. Hambledon followed up the drive and came to a stop at a pillared porch. The escort rested like black statues in perfect formation, Grober leapt out to open Hambledon's door for him and a young officer appeared in the porch, took one look at the tableau before him, and came to an abrupt stop.

Hambledon got out, took off his driving gloves, extracted a shabby brief case from behind his seat, and stalked into the hall, taking no notice of the young officer.

"In this room," said Grober, revolving round him, "in here, if the Herr will be pleased to sit down for a moment, only a moment, while I inform the General, who will wish to gather his staff together to receive the Herr in proper form."

"Naturally," said Hambledon. He entered the room and the door closed behind him. It was a small room beside the front door, the window looked out upon the drive and was slightly open. He was thus enabled to enjoy the remarks being addressed by the officer to the sergeant in charge of the escort and what little they were allowed to say in reply, for discipline is extremely strict in the Russian Army. However, the sergeant was permitted to explain what he thought was wrong with the car and the officer said that it had better be taken to a garage at once. "Tell them that the job is of the highest priority and the work had better be good," added the officer. "You will take the car yourself, Sergeant, at once. Now."

"I thought I'd forgotten all my Russian," said Hambledon contentedly to himself, "but it comes back, it comes back. I wonder if dear Ludwig could speak Russian? Probably not. Nothing Russian among his papers."

The car moved away on five cylinders from before the windows and a blue haze followed it down the drive. The escort disappeared, the young officer turned on his heel and passed from sight into the porch, and peace settled upon the scene. When the door opened the Herr Ludwig Kirsch was sitting at the table so deeply absorbed in some mathematical formulae he was scribbling into a small pocketbook that he did not even look up.

"Mein Herr," said the young officer, smartly at attention, "General Ambromovitch has the honour to await the Herr Kirsch."

The Herr returned slowly from the depths of his absorption.

"What? Oh, the General. Yes, yes, of course." He put his notebook away and picked up the brief case. "What is the General's name again?"

"Ambromovitch, mein Herr."

"Lead me to him at once."

magdeburg

HAMBLEDON WAS SHOWN into a large room with windows looking out upon the garden. There were six or eight men standing about a long table and at their head a big bullet-headed man with the oddly hairless look which afflicts so many of the Russian leaders. It almost seems as though there must be something about Marxism which affects the eyebrows.

He came forward and said: "Herr Kirsch? General Ambromovitch," and held out his hand, which Hambledon shook enthusiastically.

"Ludwig Kirsch," he said. "Delighted, General."

The General introduced his officers one by one and there were stiff bows and the inescapable handshaking all round.

"Now," said the General, whose eyes had been set upon the scruffy brief case from the moment it came into the room, "let us sit down and see the beautiful present our clever friend has brought us." He spoke German rather badly, hesitating for words and plainly translating in his mind. Hambledon sat down with the others and slid the brief case along the table to the General, who seized it eagerly and struggled with a defective catch while the rest of the company watched in breathless silence. Eventually the flimsy catch gave way, the General opened the case and drew out its contents.

"What—what——"

He spoke in Russian and all the men at the table rose as though actuated by one lever and leaned across the table towards him; all, that is, except Ludwig Kirsch, who could not be expected to understand. He therefore kept his seat and gazed innocently out of the window.

He was roughly recalled by having his arm shaken by the man next to him, he looked up to find the General purple in the face and waving foolscap sheets of squared paper with neat calculations upon them. Kirsch sprang to his feet with a cry of horror, snatched the sheets from the General's hand, and clasped them to his chest.

"My notes—my manuscript examples—my life's work! I am engaged, gentlemen, in——"

The General interrupted with a Russian word which Hambledon could not remember ever having heard before, though there was no doubt as to its meaning, and added in German: "The Smirnov Plan. Where is it, where?"

"Ach! In the car. Concealed in the car, General. I go and get it." He turned towards the door and opened it. "In the car, well hidden, I go and—— Where—*zehn tausend Teufeln*—where is my car? It was outside the door I left it——"

The young officer, who seemed to be on butler fatigue that day, sprang forward to explain that as their distinguished guest had had trouble on the road he had at once sent the car to the garage beyond in order that the distinguished guest——

"Bring it back at once!" said the General. "At once."

Since all this was in Russian, Kirsch naturally could not be expected to understand a word of it. He therefore stood by, bleating: "My car, where is my car?" Then, remembering that he had a reputation for losing his temper, he picked up a china ash tray from the hall table, hurled it across the room, and thundered: "Produce my car at once! What den of thieves is this?"

By this time the young officer had run out of the house and Hambledon followed him to the front porch, still clasping his trigonometry samples and quivering with fury. The General took him by the arm, making soothing noises, and led him back to the long room; the other officers trooped after, avoiding each other's eyes and wiping a variety of expressions off their faces.

"It is a little mistake," said the General. "Your car was taken to the garage for a slight adjustment which your escort recommended for your convenience, Herr Kirsch. It is a very good garage. We ourselves use it in cases where a specially high standard of work is required. The Herr need have no fear."

Kirsch allowed himself to be soothed and offered vodka and a cigarette. He reclaimed his brief case and tucked his papers lovingly away.

"While we are waiting," said General Ambromovitch, "tell us, please, how you regained the papers?"

Kirsch put the brief case away and became in a moment the alert intelligent spy. His mouth hardened and his jaw came forward.

"I received the first message about the Smirnov Plan on the day before the Englishman passed through Goslar on his way back to England."

"He is gone, then. You are quite sure?"

"Certainly. I made quite sure that he had not got the plan before I allowed him to pass unhindered. I saw him being conducted to the train by some other Englishman who came out to meet him; I made enquiries and learned that he had flown back to England from Hanover."

"That is helpful, to know that he has gone home. We have been looking for him but now the search can be called off and the troops returned to barracks. Colonel Kaganov, you will give the order."

The officer on Hambledon's right assented and left the room. Hambledon drew a quiet breath. He had, of course, been angling for this.

"And Lentov," prompted the General.

"Lentov, I think, must have had difficulty in crossing the frontier; he arrived two days later. I did not ask him about his adventures," said Herr Kirsch drily. "He looked as though he had been sleeping in ditches—I do not know. Nor care. One of my people sheltered him and let me know, I went down to the house." Kirsch made a gesture of finality. "We buried him in the orchard. I took the plan and hid it on my way home. I will not, if you will excuse me, tell even you where it was. I will only say," he added, with a grim smile, "that churchyards are not normally the place for vulgar pranks or children's play, there are many hiding places in ancient tombs and the dead do not chatter. I am sorry if I deprived you of the pleasure of dealing with him yourself, but the——"

There came a knock at the door and the young officer entered. "The car is here."

"Good," said Kirsch, and left the room with long strides.

General Ambromovitch looked round the table.

"An odd man," he remarked, "the brilliant Ludwig Kirsch. One would say, two men. Did you notice how he altered when he turned his mind to our Intelligence work? I imagine that his devotion to his mathematical studies is equally wholehearted. He lives two lives, that man. Interesting."

Herr Kirsch came back a few minutes later carrying under his arm a thick and very grubby plank which he laid on the table, thus displaying what looked like a patch let in and held by two small screws. "This is the underneath of the plank, of course, it is part of the floor of the luggage compartment in the back of the car." He took a screw-driver from his pocket and drew out the two small screws, lifted the lid and took out the packet inside. "The Smirnov Plan, gentlemen, as I received it. I hope that egregious idiot Lentov has not lost any of it."

General Ambromovitch took it in both hands, laid it on the table, and tore open the covering paper. There, once more, was the large folded map upon stiff paper, the smaller sketch plans relating to marked areas upon the map, the pages of notes; everything, in fact, which the original package had contained except the note beginning: "This is the Smirnov Plan which was stolen." That note had gone back to London with the photographs.

Kirsch took a step back from the table. "I did but glance at the contents to see if they appeared to be the right thing," he said, with an unexpectedly deprecating smile. "I have never been a soldier; my eyes——" He touched his glasses. "General, you will wish to examine these in private. With your permission I will retire."

General Ambromovitch, who had been delightedly gloating, sprang to his feet and came round the table to take both of Hambledon's hands in his. They were indeed the right papers—they appeared to be complete—the gratitude of the Russian Command—their indebted-ness—the brilliance of the operation which rescued the papers—the intrepidity, the resource, the initiative——

Kirsch bowed, extricated his hands, and stepped back. He thanked the General politely, but entirely without enthusiasm, for what he had said. There was, however, no occasion for all this fuss. He, Kirsch, had been instructed to regain a stolen packet and he had accordingly re-gained it. Why not? An agent expected to be given that sort of order and was naturally expected to carry it out. A thousand thanks. "And now," he added, "I should like to return to Goslar. My other work awaits me and I am very busy."

They crowded round him, patting him on the back, those who could speak German saying that he must not go back yet, a few days' holiday among friends would be good for his health. "In any case," put in the General, "there is a dinner party tonight at which you, esteemed Herr Kirsch, will be the honoured guest."

Eventually Kirsch yielded; he would stay a day or two, not more. There was, of course, also the question of a new assistant in Goslar. "No doubt Grober reported that I have lost both my Goslar assistants? Yes, yes, one is dead and the other has run away. Let him go. He was becoming too well known in Goslar, people were beginning to notice him. Of course I have other men in my area but they are well posted where they are. If I were to move one of them he would have to be replaced and their local knowledge of their districts is their most valuable asset." Kirsch walked up and down across the end of the table and addressed the class. "It will be plain to you, gentl—I mean, comrades, that when a man has lived so long in one place he knows everyone in it and can spot a stranger on sight. When he is an integral part of the community and is known and told all the local news and can ask questions without arousing distrust, that man is a hundred times more valuable where he is than he would be anywhere else. That is clear, I hope? Good. In Goslar, where there are many visitors, this useful faculty would be wasted. I want a new man, a stranger. I want Gustav Ehrlich."

Kirsch sat down at the end of the table and absently nodded to the others to sit down also.

"Grober told us," said the General, "that you wished to have Ehrlich, but you ought to know that we cannot recommend him. He is not reliable. He is an agitator, useful in factories, no more than that. He is——"

"But do you not see that a man who can readily make acquaintances, who can talk to all comers and encourage them to talk to him, is precisely what I want? As for being an agitator, that may come in useful, but for the present he will say what I tell him to say and do what he is bid."

One of the officers said something to the General in Russian and Ambromovitch nodded.

"Walenski reminds me that Ehrlich fled the Western Zone because the police were after him for a civil offence, embezzling canteen funds or something equally stupid. He is not honest, he——"

"He will be honest with me," said Kirsch, and smiled unpleasantly.

"Very well," said the General. "Heaven forbid that I should attempt to teach a man like you his trade. We have put out an enquiry for Ehrlich through the usual channels; a further order of special urgency shall be issued at once. Walenski, you will see to it at once and report to Herr Kirsch tomorrow."

Walenski bowed and left the room.

"If he is above ground you shall have him," promised the General. "There is, of course, the point that if Ehrlich is wanted by the West German authorities for embezzlement or whatever it was, the Goslar police may have his particulars and be looking for him."

A slow smile grew across the enigmatical Herr Kirsch's face, he looked at the General and began to laugh quietly. He made no sound but his shoulders shook and Ambromovitch drew back.

"I have done it again," he said apologetically. "A life spent in the Army is my only excuse, I have always had to ask, 'What are you going to do and by what means?' I do apologise, Herr Kirsch."

"Not at all, not at all," said Kirsch amiably. "I myself am become tiresomely secretive over the most unimportant concerns of my private life. It is as well I have no wife, I should drive the poor woman demented."

On this pleasant note they parted. Hambledon's car having once more been removed—towed away this time—he and his luggage were driven to his hotel in a staff car with a soldier driving and another beside him. There was also a little pennon on the bonnet. It was a pity that the distinguished guest's arrival should have been marred by his suitcase foolishly casting open its lid and spreading upon the pavement his striped nightshirt, three odd socks, two clean collars, and a pair of bedroom slippers with holes in them. Hambledon picked up his dressing gown and stalked into the hotel with this garment trailing on the ground behind him, leaving the soldier escort to gather up the debris.

The dinner that night went on as Russian dinner parties usually do. It started with drinks at about half-past nine and finished with drinks towards three in the morning. Hambledon, who had endured Russian dinner parties before, swallowed a couple of olive-oil capsules before starting out and was thus enabled to be bright-eyed and still telling laboriously funny stories long after the General had fallen abruptly from his chair.

On the following morning he was at the garage, observing, with childlike wonder, the engine of his car dissected into its component parts. He explained that he was not a mechanic and illustrated this point by asking why there was a lump in the middle of the back axle and, following on from that, what was the principle of a differential? "So often," he said plaintively, "I have asked for this to be explained to me and even now I do not understand. . . . Yes, but if one back wheel goes round faster than the other, why does the tyre not wear out more quickly?"

Just before the chief mechanic faced the choice between insanity and suicide, two officers from the Headquarters Staff came along to the rescue. They were apparently delighted to find that Herr Kirsch was in full working order even if his car was not. One, who had been at the dinner the night before, introduced another who had not, saying that Lieutenant Lischtin, who could speak German and had taken an honours degree in mathematics, had been selected for the honour of taking the Herr Kirsch round Magdeburg and showing him whatever he wished to see. "There is a cathedral," said the older officer, who appeared to have a headache, "which I understand is interesting to those who like that sort of thing. There is also an exhibition of Soviet Art and Culture." He then sighed wearily and withdrew with lagging steps.

"This," said Hambledon to himself, "is it. They have turned a real mathematician on to me, how unspeakably painful. If he bowls me out it will be the end. Oh, hell's canaries, why did I come on this idiotic trip?"

Aloud he said, looking after the retreating Russian, that the poor man looked as though a Turkish bath would do him good. Lieutenant Lischtin laughed and said that poor Captain Petrov suffered with his liver, but he would be well again tomorrow. "I am entirely at the Herr's service this morning," he added. "If the Herr is really interested in the cathedral, shall we go there?"

"Are you?"

"Well, personally, I feel I've rather grown out of cathedrals," said Lischtin apologetically. "When I was about twelve I was frightfully keen on that sort of thing, but I seem to have worked it out of my system, as it were. But if the Herr would be interested to see it, I shall be delighted——"

"Not at all," said Hambledon briskly, and called himself a fool. Lischtin could hardly discuss cosines and cosecants in the precincts of a cathedral, or could he? If there happened to be a dome on the thing, he might——

"What I really had in mind," said Hambledon, "was, to be frank with you, beer. We made rather a night of it last night, as you may have heard, and I am left with a thirst. Have you learnt to drink beer?"

Lischtin said yes, indeed, since he had been stationed in Germany, and added that there was quite a decent café down by the river where one could sit on a terrace and watch the steamers. They set off at a good four miles an hour, since the banks of the Elbe were some distance away, and Lischtin babbled cheerfully on about the time when, as a schoolboy, he had wanted to be an architect and build cathedrals, but his father had sensibly pointed out that the demand for cathedrals in present-day Russia was likely to be limited and he would have his living to earn. "So I took up mathematics. Does not the Herr think that there is a good deal in common between mathematics and architecture? One starts with a foundation in the form of a problem and builds upon that, including the various factors involved as an architect would include arches soaring to clerestories and——"

At this point Hambledon became entangled with a woman pushing a perambulator and surrounded by five children, one of whom had a dog on a lead. By the time he had sorted himself out, Lischtin's flood of similes had at least been interrupted. "And if he talks about trigonometric functions of a constant variable, I can always be taken ill," he encouraged himself. "If only I had a small piece of soap I could have a fit." But fortunately for him there were, in the centre of the town, so many people upon the pavement as to make conversation impossible.

Lischtin's café overlooked the island upon which Magdeburg's Citadel stands; as they settled down at a table on the terrace, he pointed it out to Herr Kirsch.

"Excellent," said Hambledon. "Now, if the waiter will hurry up with the beer we can attend to our thirsts and look at the Citadel at the same time. What could be better?"

"Nothing," said Lischtin with conviction.

After a short but refreshing interval Hambledon ordered two more and asked Lischtin what he wanted to do with his life. "For mathematics," he said, boldly taking the initiative, "are not an end in themselves unless you propose to teach, and somehow I cannot picture you as a schoolmaster."

Lischtin said that possibly that had been in his parents' minds but, frankly, it was not in his. Captain Petrov had introduced him as a mathematician, "But I do hope, sir, that you don't suppose for a moment that I think I'm anywhere in your class. But I was particularly happy to be given the opportunity of talking to you this morning because there was something I wanted to ask you."

"Here it comes," thought Hambledon, and managed with an effort to look benign.

"The—the outside world," said Lischtin, blushing with earnestness. "Has the Herr travelled? In, perhaps, Switzerland, Holland, and even France? To Paris? Really, to Paris? Ah, tell me about Paris!"

A couple of hours later they had lunch together and then Lischtin reluctantly admitted he had to go on duty. "Such a privilege to meet you, I cannot thank you enough——"

"It has been a pleasure," said Hambledon warmly.

sausage factory

WALENSKI REPORTED that he had made enquiries at the various Record Offices and there was no trace of Ehrlich.

"He reported his return to the Eastern Zone," he said. "He was not received with any particular acclaim because he had behaved like an idiot." Walenski was a tall thin man with a hooked nose, black eyebrows over hooded eyes, and deep lines from his nose to the corners of his mouth. Bad-tempered, thought Hambledon, and obstinate.

"A man who has a job to do for Soviet Intelligence," went on Walenski, drawing his black brows together, "has no business to put himself in the power of the police by petty malefactions for personal gain. He is unworthy of the cause he serves. He is a scoundrel, and in my opinion should have been sent to the salt mines."

"Whereas he has now disappeared? To avoid being sent to the salt mines?"

Walenski frowned and said that trace of the man appeared temporarily to be lost. "It is reported that he said his nerves were affected by being hunted down by the police. He apparently gave a highly coloured account of his hairbreadth escapes. He said that he would find work somewhere for a time until his nerves were restored."

Hambledon remembered that it was Walenski who had volunteered information about Ehrlich's crimes to General Ambromovitch. Some personal animosity?

"Do you know this man yourself?" he asked.

Walenski said with emphasis that he neither knew Ehrlich nor wished to. "He is very small fry," he added contemptuously. "He would not appear at Headquarters. No, my interest in this unimportant matter is quite otherwise, and I shall now disclose it to you, Herr

Kirsch, because in my opinion it affects your security and effectiveness and that of all men in your position. Not nearly enough care is taken in the selection of men in your service and I contend—have frequently contended—that until we select candidates for Intelligence with much greater care than is used at present, we shall continue to be faced with the humiliating failures we too frequently endure at present. The selection is at fault."

Hambledon had recognised the type by this time, he had met it all his life in every country in which he had served. Walenski was the Bore with a Grievance and one finds his twin brother in every club in Europe. They complain to the secretary, poor man, whose emotions have been most movingly expressed in the Hundred and Ninth Psalm. With perfect respect, one sometimes wonders whether the psalmist was ever a club secretary.

"I see your point," said Herr Kirsch, "and I will bear it in mind. About Ehrlich——"

"He may have been taken on by some employer for a fortnight on trial," said Walenski. "It is not necessary to register at a Labour Registration Bureau until the employment becomes permanent."

"Thank you," said Kirsch acidly. "I am afraid I cannot wait for a fortnight. If your various Records cannot trace this man for me I suppose I must go and look for him myself."

"But——" began Walenski.

"In my vocabulary," said Herr Kirsch, glaring at the man over the top of his spectacles, "there is no such word as 'but.' "

He abandoned Walenski without ceremony and went to stroll in the painfully tidy garden, where he encountered General Ambromovitch.

"I have just heard that my car is now ready for the road, General."

This happened to be true, shorn of the garage's comments, which were to the effect that that car didn't want mechanics on it, it wanted a squad of fairy queens waving wands to turn it into a new one and that if they ever saw it again they would all run away and join the Army.

"I hope," said the General courteously, "that this does not mean that we are to lose the pleasure of your company so soon."

"Most kind," said Kirsch. "No, it seems that I have to drive to one or two places where I have introductions, to see if I can find Ehrlich. Captain Walenski's research into records has not been successful."

The General's eyebrows went up. "Walenski—well, Herr Kirsch, he is our liaison with Records so I felt obliged to ask him. He is," said Ambromovitch firmly, "a most conscientious officer."

"I am sure of it," said Hambledon politely.

"And, my dear Kirsch," said the General, throwing an enormous arm round Hambledon's neck and speaking in his ear, "I can't stand the sight of him."

"Transfer him, then!"

"He has been transferred so often," said the General sadly. "He has performed his duties with impeccable accuracy in practically every branch of the Army."

"You embolden me to ask whether he has ever served in Intelligence—I trust, General, that I do not offend?"

"Not a bit. You are no fool, are you? You don't mean to tell me that he has been trying to teach you your business?"

"He gave me a little advice," said Hambledon drily.

The General laughed loudly and smacked Hambledon between the shoulder blades.

"He advised our Inspector General of Military Intelligence in Berlin," he gurgled. "That was the point at which he was transferred to us. So you are going to drive off into the blue and interview masked men behind haystacks, are you? Heaven knows how you mystery men work but you certainly deliver the goods. Come back, my dear Kirsch, and we will have another party before you return to your dangerous work. It was a good party the other night, wasn't it? Come back and see me again. Good luck to you. I must go; there are six people waiting to see me." He shook Hambledon warmly by both hands and turned away.

"Jovial old boy," said Hambledon to himself. "Not a bad fellow at all, for a Russian."

But General Ambromovitch was coming back.

"About that man Ehrlich," he said abruptly, "you are quite wrong, you know. The brute is rotten to the core like so many of your stinking fellow countrymen. When he has betrayed you, remember that I warned you. You can either shoot him yourself or send him back to me. I will deal with him and what is left of the beast can go to the salt mines."

The fat hairless face looked grimly amused, but the pale eyes were merciless. He nodded and went away to join the group who were waiting for him; Hambledon, after a moment's dumbfounded silence, walked off to his hotel to pack Kirsch's clothes in Kirsch's suitcase, meditating on what had just passed.

"I shall never understand these people. What was that proverb father used to quote? 'Scratch a Russian and you'll find a Tartar'? How unpleasantly true."

He looked with distaste at Kirsch's scruffy dressing gown but threw it over his arm and picked up his hat and the suitcase.

"Of course, they are an oriental people, one must remember that."

He went out and collected his car from the garage, which seemed oddly glad to see it go, and drove out of Magdeburg, going south. It would, naturally, be quite idiotic to drive straight to Waldecke near Ilsenburg, the noticeable car would certainly be reported by dutiful police and his journey plotted from place to place. In a series of mystifying zigzags he traversed much of the province of Anhalt, stopping here and there for brief conversations with road menders and other readily available persons. He stayed one night in a village inn at a remote place called Wippra, which is miles from anywhere, and on the afternoon of the second day drove into Waldecke.

It was, indeed, a small unimportant place such as Britz had described, but it contained all the necessary ingredients. There were the great forests sweeping down close to the village with a few cottages tucked away in the very shadow of the trees. Was it in one of those that Micklejohn was first concealed? The village was unusually compact, probably because it had grown up in a clearing and had had no room to spread; one road ran through it and on to Ilsenburg. The houses stood upon the street for the most part; there were a few more beside a lane leading to the church. There was a farmhouse or two further back, and there was a sawmill beside a stream. It was all extremely peaceful.

Hambledon drove up the street at a footpace. One house at the end of a row was larger than its neighbours; the sausage factory perhaps? No, a faded board above the door announced the Volkspolizeiamt, the Vopo headquarters. It looked as though in happier days it might have been an inn. Tacked on to this were three small cottages forming a row of which the far end was a slightly larger double-fronted house with yet another board above the door. This one bore the name of Hans Muller and, below the name, the entrancing word *Wurstfabrik*; Sausage Factory.

Hambledon stopped the car and went in. Micklejohn and his friends would have received by this time the message telling him to trust Ludwig Kirsch, a friend. There would be no trouble, therefore, he had only to announce himself and a pathetically grateful undergraduate of BNC, smelling strongly of sausage, would leap out from some dark corner and greet him with decently controlled enthusiasm.

He walked in at the front door to encounter sausage-factory smells and a stout imperturbable man with gold-rimmed spectacles pushed up on a shining forehead. This man sat behind a desk in a small room used as an office; a door open behind him let pass the clank of primitive machinery and the smell.

"Good day," said Hambledon.

"Good day, mein Herr," said the man behind the desk. He went through the motions of rising from his chair without actually doing so and looked enquiringly at his visitor.

"Ludwig Kirsch," said Hambledon and waited for some reaction, but none came. "Ludwig Kirsch," he repeated. "Do I address the Herr Muller?"

"Hans Muller," said the fat man, with a bow. "Please sit down. In what way can I serve the Herr?"

Hambledon sat down, drew the chair closer to the desk and leaned across it to speak in a confidential tone.

"I believe that you have working for you a young man named Ehrlich, Gustav Ehrlich."

Muller's face became completely blank; not gradually in some process of thought but instantaneously, like a camera shutter.

"Excuse me a moment," he said, and half rose from his chair to shut the door behind him, that leading to the workshop. The lock did not catch at the first attempt. Muller rattled the handle to free it and slammed the door shut this time. "The noise," he explained and, indeed, it was immediately decreased. "I am, in any case, a little deaf. The Herr was asking for one Gustav——?"

"Ehrlich," said Hambledon, and spelt it.

Muller shook his head slowly from side to side and his glasses slid down on to his nose.

"I am sorry," he said. "I do not think I have ever employed a man of that name. Certainly I have no Ehrlich working for me now."

Hambledon hesitated. Perhaps a mistake had arisen somewhere along Britz's tortuous lines of communication, or perhaps this man was not in the secret. The name of Ludwig Kirsch had fallen quite flat. Yet that instantaneously blank look was certainly hiding something, though the something need not necessarily be an English undergraduate. It might equally well be black-market pork or illicit sausage skins.

"The name is not a local one," said Muller, "and I employ all local

159

labour. Is the Herr quite convinced that he has come to the right place?"

"I was told Waldecke, near Ilsenburg."

Muller heaved up his fat shoulders.

"In this wooded country there are so many places named Wald—something," said Muller reasonably, for *Wald* means a wood. "There is Wald Lobenklee, there is Oberwald, Unterwald, Waldboden, Waldklippe, Waldberg. I cannot but think that the Herr has been misdirected. Also, most places make their own sausages and my name is probably the commonest in Germany."

All quite true. Hambledon began to think that the locale of the story must have been shifted, perhaps quite inadvertently, from a place name strange to the speaker to one he had heard before—a very frequent mistake.

"Do you know if there is a man in this place called Otto Neumann?"

"Another common name, Neumann," smiled Muller, "nearly as common as mine. Not an Otto, no. There is a Widow Neumann, who is a little simple, poor thing. She has a small grandson called—what is it—Willi. Wilhelm, no doubt. His father was killed in an accident and his mother is also dead. He is I suppose about eight years of age. They are our only Neumanns, mein Herr."

There seemed no more that could usefully be said and Hambledon rose to his feet.

"Thank you very much for your courtesy, I must apologise for taking up so much of your time."

Muller stood up and came round the desk to shake hands, the eternal Teutonic handshaking. "Not at all, it has been a pleasure to meet the Herr, we see so few strangers in these lonely villages. I only wish I could have helped the Herr in his enquiries."

Hambledon knew what a wide network is comprised in undercover movements; the secret grapevine telegraph runs for miles in all directions. If this were not the right village it was probably somewhere in this area. Micklejohn would not have travelled far—if he left a word it might be passed on to him.

"If I may," he said, "I will leave my name and present address with you. If you should happen to hear of this young man, perhaps you would be so good as to let him know that I was asking for him."

He wrote "Ludwig Kirsch" on a piece of paper together with the name of his hotel in Magdeburg. "I shall be there for a few days longer."

Muller said that he was honoured with the Herr's confidence and would institute enquiries, for what that was worth, and they parted like old friends. Hambledon went out and sat in his car to think things over.

Curse Britz. This was obviously the wrong village since the name of Kirsch aroused no response at the sausage factory, and now he had no idea where to go. Thoroughly discouraging.

He looked at the Volks-polizeiamt and considered going there to ask for Gustav Ehrlich, since their records probably covered a larger area than this village. He hesitated for fear lest, if anything of this should ever leak out, reprisals might be taken against those who had sheltered Micklejohn. Besides, if he were seen going into Vopo head-quarters it would damn him finally in the eyes of the underground movement and neither of his messages would be believed. Confound Britz and Micklejohn, too, for a pair of infernal incompetent blasted nuisances. To think he had successfully pulled off the Kirsch imper-sonation only to go home empty-handed.

He lit a cigarette, started the car, and drove slowly out of the village, thinking deeply as he went. Five miles away he stopped the car and got out his map, for he had had an idea. Muller had mentioned several other villages with names which began with *Wald*; since Hambledon was in the district with a car, it would be worth while going to look at them. One only had to look for a *Wurstfabrik Muller*. Wald Lobenklee was easy to find, it was not far off, just north of the Brocken, but it seemed to be a stretch of country, not a village. Oberwald and his brother Unterwald, where were they? Waldboden, surely. No? How very odd. Waldklippe, Woodcliff, the sort of name one would expect to find in this country of woods and cliffs, but one would be disap-pointed. There were a dozen names ending in *klippe* but not one beginning with *Wald*. Waldberg struck a familiar note, but not here, it was far away in—in Württemberg, of course. Not far from the Swiss border. There might well be another Waldberg, since Germans are regrettably given to duplicating their place names, but it did not ap-pear on this map.

Hambledon drew a long breath and relaxed comfortably in his seat. Muller had invented all those delightful place names; Muller had lied. That instantaneous blank shutter across his face was no matter of il-licit pork, it was a reaction to the name of Ehrlich. Gustav Ehrlich, not Ludwig Kirsch. The name of Kirsch had apparently rung no bell, but that of Ehrlich had set off all the alarms at once.

The evening was closing in rapidly as it does in those narrow wooded valleys; the sun may still be shining on the Soviet-occupied hotel on the top of the Brocken, but under the trees by the streams in the glens there will be a dim green twilight. Work ceases in the woods and the workers go home to supper.

Hambledon turned the car and drove back until, a couple of miles from Waldecke, he found a cart track leading into the woods. The car bumped and rolled in the ruts as far as a clearing where it was possible to turn. It would be wise to leave it facing outwards, ready for a sudden departure. He was wearing his own crepe-soled shoes; he took a pocket torch and his Luger automatic and started to walk back to Waldecke.

micklejohn

HAMBLEDON DID NOT HURRY; he wanted to reach the village after dark. The sky clouded over and the night came on swiftly. He took what he thought would be a short cut and lost his way, in the event he did not arrive in Waldecke until it was so dark that one could scarcely see across the street, and in the small houses lights were going out one by one. The inn was still open and there were customers inside with steins in their hands. The Vopos in their headquarters were still astir, and at the corner by the turning to the church there was an oil lamp in an iron cage doing little but cast shadows. Hambledon retired into a deep doorway opposite to the Sausage Factory Muller, and waited.

There was no light in the house of Muller, though presumably he lived over the workshops; seen by daylight, there had been curtains at the upper windows and, in one, the back of a looking glass. Fancy living out one's days in a perpetual atmosphere of damp sausage. Now it would seem that either the Herr Muller had gone to bed or was out visiting his friends.

Down the street, by the way Hambledon had come, there were voices saying good night and a remark which was probably a jest, for laughter followed. The inn closing down for the night? Presumably, for a door closed audibly in the quiet night and there were footsteps, heavy footsteps of tired labourers, not the measured tread of trained men; not, for example, Vopos. Most of the steps went the other way but two men came up the road and past Hambledon's doorway. With eyes accustomed to darkness he could see them reasonably well, elderly men bent with labour; as they passed there drifted to his nose a mingled smell of beer, tobacco, and farmyard. Particularly farmyard. Their footsteps died away and complete silence settled upon the street, only broken by the church clock chiming half-past ten on a cracked bell. Early risers go early to bed.

Hambledon thought that he would give Muller until eleven to come back, if he were out; if he did not appear it would be time enough to rouse him up. The village would be in its first sleep and not easily disturbed. He looked up and down the street. Even the Vopos had gone to bed.

A quarter of an hour later there came to his ears the click of a key being turned in a lock, the rattle of a loose door handle. Across the street the door of the sausage-factory office opened cautiously and the light of an electric torch appeared.

Hambledon instantly bent his head down and put his hands behind him lest the light falling on them should betray his presence, but the man in the doorway merely looked up and down the road, listened for a moment, and said: "All clear. Come on," to someone behind him.

Two more men came out. One was of medium height or less, like the first, but the third was tall and slim and even in that dim light it could be seen that he moved and held himself differently from the others. He turned back to speak in a low tone to whoever was shutting the door after them and someone wrung him by the hand.

"Never," said the tall young man, "never, so long as I live," and only Hambledon's preternaturally sharp hearing enabled him to catch the words.

The tall man turned away just as one of his companions put out his hand to pull his arm and all three walked off up the street, with their heavy boots clumping on the dry road. The tall man was in the middle, the shorter ones upon either side and Hambledon, in his soft crepe-rubber soles, followed silently after.

"It is extremely good of you," said the tall young man, "to take all this trouble——"

"Shut your trap," said one of the men roughly. "Give us away at once if anyone hears. Nobody talks like that in these parts. And stroll, don't walk so fast. Nobody strides along this time of night."

The young man said no more and the three went on without speaking; Hambledon, following behind, had plenty to think about. No doubt the underground movement continually sheltered men on the run for one reason or another; hid them in attics and passed them from place to place by night. Where there is tyranny there will always be men evading it. It would be unwise to assume that this man was necessarily Micklejohn, though there was that about him which

164

strongly suggested it. He walked, even in those boots, with a lighter step than the others, he had the loose-limbed balanced swing of the natural athlete, not the heavy-footed tramp of the labourer, and he carried his head high like a free man. But it was his voice which had startled Hambledon. The young man's German was excellent; fluent, grammatical, and carefully pronounced. Too good, as the other man had said; extremely well taught, in fact, and almost certainly not his native tongue. It was not guttural enough; it was much too clear.

If the message about trusting Ludwig Kirsch had gone astray, this man could very well be Micklejohn.

At this moment some inner prompting urged Hambledon to drop back and let the three get further ahead: he slowed up and stopped by the entrance to a yard.

The three men ahead of him were much too far off for Hambledon to hear anything that was said in a low tone, or even, in that darkness, to observe small movements. One of the two shorter men had taken to glancing over his shoulder and the other noticed it.

"What's the matter, Franz?" he asked in a low tone, peering round the young man in the middle.

"I think we're being followed," answered the other, in an equally low voice.

"Why, did you hear anything?"

They all stopped together and listened intently; Hambledon, thirty yards behind them, slipped like a prowling cat into the yard and waited.

"Didn't hear nothing," said Franz. "I just felt there was someone."

"I hear absolutely nothing except the leaves rustling," said the tall young man.

"Wait here," said Franz. "I'll go back."

Hambledon heard him coming, one man alone, and went to ground behind the gatepost. The man passed the yard entrance, went a little further along the street, and paused for a moment before he turned and came past again to rejoin his companions.

"Find anyone?" said Franz's friend.

"No."

"Satisfied, then?" said the tall man.

"No."

Hambledon did not move from his place until he heard them all start walking again. When he put his head cautiously round the gatepost he saw them, against a lighted window, looking back over their shoulders.

Hambledon cursed under his breath, for now he would have to keep so far behind that it would be quite easy in the dark to lose them altogether. He went on with the most extreme caution, following only the sound of their footsteps until they passed out of the village and walked on along the road. He followed them for some distance, nearly half a mile, before the footsteps stopped and there came the clash of an iron gate being closed. After that, silence. Hambledon held his breath; a moment later he heard, very faintly, the sound of a closing door.

He moved more easily now that they were within some building which might, with luck, be identifiable by the iron gate. In any case, they would have to make some sort of light and no house is really lightproof.

The night was less dark by now; the sky had cleared and somewhere behind the hills the moon was rising. Hambledon came to a fence enclosing a big yard, weedy and overgrown with disuse and he remembered passing it earlier that day, when he first came. It had a faded and broken notice board still standing; since he had been looking for a sausage factory, he had read what was left of the inscription. *Möbelfabrik*. Not sausages. Furniture.

Hambledon climbed over the gate, there was a large shed across the yard, facing him. There were some balks of timber stacked up to his left, on his right a broken-down timber tug. He walked on to the big shed and circled round it. There was the door by which they had entered. The shed was built of wood and some of the planks were rotten and slipping. Further along, at the back, there was a faint light showing through a slit, a candle on a table, and three men round it.

Hambledon leaned his ear against the slit and listened.

"—have to stay here tonight," one of the German voices was saying. "Such short notice as that, no time to work out a plan, nothing arranged." The usual German discomfiture if every detail is not settled beforehand.

"I am very greatly obliged to you," began the educated voice, but Franz interrupted him.

"Not good of us at all," he said grumpily. "We only done it because you are a danger to all of us. If you'd been caught there, there'd have been shootings against a wall and we've had too many already."

"But I still find it hard to believe"—the young voice again—"that just because a man comes and asks for Ehrlich—he was told Ehrlich was not here and never had been——"

"Ach, but it was the man who came! It was that Ludwig Kirsch, as bold as brass, giving his name as though we had never heard of him! We know about him, the Russian spy in Goslar, he's here only to make trouble, he is. Hobnobbing with the Russian Army in Magdeburg. They gave him a banquet the other night, pity it didn't poison the lot of them. If you can't see nothing wrong you've got no sense."

"Well, you'll have to stay here tonight and we'll see about getting you away in the morning. You can sleep in the wood drier. Nobody will look for you there and you can have some sacks to sleep on."

"I hope there's a little more room than there was over the Vopo headquarters," said the young man cheerfully. "I couldn't move."

"Was that where old Neumann put you? Well, what a place! How did you get there?"

"Up into the roof and through an attic partition, you know; just planks between, but they'd got it all stacked up with boxes and I dared not move them."

"When was this, then?"

"When that man first came, Kirsch, you know. Muller rattled the handle of his door and shut it twice, that was the signal somebody was asking for me and I'd better clear out. If Kirsch had gone to the Vopos they might have searched the houses and that was one place we were sure they would not look into."

Hambledon abandoned his listening post, for he had heard enough. The tall young man was Micklejohn and the next thing to do was to go in and get him without being shot at sight. He made his way round to the door, slipping out his picklocks as he went, because if the door was not locked it ought to be. It was the only outer door in the place except for the great double doors in front, which had not been opened for four long years. He tried the handle of the small door and was rather indignant than otherwise when it opened at once.

"These amateur conspirators," he muttered, and closed the door carefully behind him—he could not lock it, there was no key.

The door had admitted him to a vast workshop; furniture making takes a lot of room. The three men were in a small room at the far end, probably once the manager's office, and the light from the candle showed through the broken glass panels of the office door. Hambledon, keeping close to the wall, thought it safe to switch on for a moment at a time the tiny pencil torch which kept him clear of disused machines and odd stacks of unidentifiable rubbish. He reached the door without attracting attention, turned the handle, and walked straight in.

"Good evening," he began.

The three men whirled round to face him, the two Germans with guns in their hands and their mouths open, but Hambledon went straight on.

"My name is Hambledon and I am an Englishman, come here to take out one George Micklejohn. You, I think, are George Micklejohn, are you not? We have never met but I have seen your photograph. I think——"

He was interrupted by a sort of muffled bellow from Franz.

"That is a damned lie! You are the Russian spy from the other side, Ludwig Kirsch. I saw you in the village this afternoon."

"Ludwig Kirsch is in gaol in Goslar. I came over here on his papers."

"Another lie. Kirsch was in Magdeburg the other day, sucking up to the Russians. They gave him a banquet——"

"They gave me a banquet," said Hambledon mildly, "but I am still not Ludwig Kirsch."

"Are you trying to tell us nobody noticed you'd changed your face?"

"They had never seen Kirsch," said Hambledon. "He has never been over this side."

Micklejohn intervened. "I will speak to him in English, I shall know at once if he is not an Englishman." He changed to English. "Mr. Hambledon, is this really true? I heard that there was someone of that name come to Goslar to look for me."

"Perfectly true. Your father asked for someone to be sent out and I got the job. You heard I was there, then, but you didn't get another message telling you to trust Ludwig Kirsch?"

"Oh, no, I didn't. But there was some trouble one day last week, somebody got shot. I expect——"

"That would be it," said Hambledon. "Damn those trigger-happy Vopos."

"Chattering away," said Franz angrily, "and we don't understand a word of it. How are we to know what you're saying?"

Micklejohn reverted to German.

"He's English all right—by the way, wait a minute. I've got a photograph in my wallet. Here it is. The Vopos took this when you went up to The Wire, Herr Hambledon, and a copy was passed to me asking if I knew you. I didn't, of course." He gave the print to the Germans, who peered at it under the candlelight. "You can see it's the same man."

"It's a Vopo photograph all right," said Franz's companion. "I've seen the like of that before."

"Yes, maybe, but that don't prove he isn't Kirsch," said Franz obstinately. "You're too simple, Ernst. Kirsch could have gone up to The Wire, like anybody else on the other side, couldn't he?"

Hambledon said: "Micklejohn, do you believe me?"

"I do, yes. I don't understand how you could have got away with impersonating Kirsch, but I'm perfectly certain you are English and not German."

"I don't like it," said Franz, but his friend Ernst, who never said much at any time, took the floor for once. He spoke a dialect so thick that Micklejohn had difficulty in following him.

"I don't see," said Ernst slowly, "as it matters to us, Franz. As I see it, we was asked to get him out of here because Kirsch was after him. Well, now, if he"—pointing a gnarled forefinger at Micklejohn—"is satisfied, if he wants to go with this man as says he isn't Kirsch, why should we stop him? We don't want him here, do we?"

"No," said Franz, "that's right. You're right, Ernst. You come over here," he went on, addressing Micklejohn, "wandering across, only *der lieber Gott* knows how, and you have to be fed and sheltered and hidden away and all of us in danger on your account as though we hadn't enough to worry about without you——"

"Believe me," said Micklejohn passionately, "I realise all that perfectly well, and when I think what some of you people have done for me, I—I can't——"

"All right, all right," said Franz, not unkindly. "So long as you do realise it. Well, if you want to go with this Herr Whatever-it-is, I say, go."

Ernst nodded agreement.

"Well, that's all right," said Hambledon. "I don't anticipate much trouble in getting you out, Micklejohn, you are my new assistant and I have permission to take you back into Western Germany with——"

The door at the far end of the shed opened without precaution against noise and a man came running, with an electric torch to guide his steps. He called out something as he came and Franz said: "All right. It's only Walter."

He came up to the door of the little office, looked round him at Hambledon and Micklejohn, and said: "Ach, good. I am in time, then." He leaned against the doorpost, panting. "I have run all the way."

CHAPTER XXI

137

HE WAS A WEASELLY LITTLE MAN, thin and in poor condition, but his eyes glittered in the candlelight. "There is news," he said, "from Magdeburg. Wilhelm Greiger's son August, you know? He works at the Russian Headquarters at Magdeburg, he is a waiter."

Franz was impatient. "That is no news, he has been there for weeks."

"Ach! As though I run to tell you that! This is something he heard while he was serving vodka to that Russian pig of a general and his guests. The news is that the Englander who came over here got back again the same day and went home to England at once, and the proof of that is that the Russians have called off the search for him and all their soldiers have gone back to their kennels. So, this man you all think an innocent Englander, what is he? A police spy. A police spy. Living here among us all——"

"Absolute nonsense," said Micklejohn sharply. "I am the Englander of whom you speak and I have never been a spy in my life."

"I myself," said Hambledon, "told the Russians that lie for the express purpose of having the search cancelled." But they were not listening to him, the damage was done. The three Germans were standing together by the door. Ernst's and Franz's guns were out again and all their faces were alive with fear and suspicion.

"Put your hands up!" bellowed Franz suddenly. "And get back the other side of the table! I never did trust either of you, and *Gottes Wort*, I was right!"

"Who is that?" asked Walter, the newcomer, pointing at Hambledon.

"Ludwig Kirsch."

"Ach! He who told the Russians the Englander had gone. Now he says he is not gone, eh? Very clever man, Ludwig Kirsch, it is said. He does not look so clever now, does he?"

"What do we do with them?" asked Ernst. "Take them outside and kill them? It will make a mess in here and leave marks on the floor."

"Quatsch!" said Walter. "There is plenty of sawdust and wood shavings on the floor. They will soak up the blood. Shoot them in here, I say; if we take them outside, they might escape."

Hambledon looked at Micklejohn, who had turned a little green, for it is one thing to face death with a decent degree of fortitude and quite another to hear oneself described as a mess on the floor. However, he managed a valiant if rather sickly grin.

Franz, whose weapon was a Russian-made automatic, told Ernst to keep the prisoners covered while he wrestled with his gun and something which he had taken from his pocket.

"What is that?" asked Walter.

"Silencer. Without it, these guns make so loud a noise, if there is anyone within half a mile—ach! These Russian weapons! If only I had one of our good German weapons, but this is——" The silencer jammed and refused to move on or off and Franz threw it down on the table. "I cannot see," he said angrily. "I get a light," and stumped out of the room.

"If I can make any sort of diversion," said Hambledon in English to Micklejohn, "go flat on the floor by the table. I shall do much better if I haven't got to worry about you."

"I've done some amateur boxing," said Micklejohn helpfully, "it seems a pity not to use it."

Hambledon grinned. "You can always bob up again, can't you?"

"Quiet there!" said Walter commandingly. "I do not like your jabbering together."

"And remember," added Hambledon, still in English, "no Queensberry Rules here. Kick first and apologise afterwards!"

There came from outside the room the sound of someone pumping vigorously; a moment later a bright light entered the room, carried by Franz, who set it down on the table.

"That petrol lamp," said Ernst uneasily, "it is not safe in here. Those things explode."

"Only when they become overheated," said Franz, picking up his gun again. "I can't see without it." He wrenched at the silencer and Walter came close to watch him. "Ach! The devil-damned thing——"

Even Ernst, who had kept his eyes and his gun steadily upon the

Englishman, could not any longer resist. He looked down at Franz's gun——

Instantly Hambledon moved forward and his knee came up under the table, tilting it away from him; the lamp fell over, rolled off the table between Walter and Ernst, and exploded. Burning petrol ran about the floor, the trampled shavings caught fire, and the flames began to spread. Hambledon threw the table over upon Walter, who failed to withstand it and cannoned into Franz just at the moment when Micklejohn dodged round the table and hit him violently on the ear and the nose and finally in the eye. He forgot Hambledon's warning about kicking, but Franz reminded him with a hack on the shin which brought him down.

Ernst fired off his gun several times in no particular direction till Hambledon, snatching out his own Luger, drilled him through the shoulder. He dropped his gun to clasp his arm and Hambledon hit him on the side of the head with all his strength.

Walter had disengaged himself from the mêlée and, having drawn a lungful of wood smoke, was clinging to the doorpost coughing his heart out. He was, in fact, a consumptive.

Micklejohn got up again, limping, and was about to resume operations when the flames reached a heap of shavings in a corner and blazed up in real earnest.

Franz uttered a shout of warning. "Get out, get out! The explosives!" He dodged into the doorway, taking Walter with him.

"Explosives?" said Ernst, shaking his head as though Hambledon's punch had rattled his brains. "What explosives?"

"Under the floor, you fool! Run!"

They ran, dragging the coughing Walter with them, down the long shed and out of the door at the far end into the night. The flames, encouraged by the draught from the door, ran up the partition.

"We'd better go too, hadn't we?" said Micklejohn, edging round the table.

"Not that way, I think," said Hambledon, tearing at an old tarpaulin which had been nailed to the wall like wartime blackout. "I think there's a window behind this—yes, there is. They might be waiting for us at the other end—you never know." The rotten tarpaulin gave way and the equally rotten window frame went out with a crash. "Can you get out or shall I—oh, good. I was afraid that fellow had really hurt you."

"Only hacked my shin and it serves me right. You did warn me," said Micklejohn as Hambledon scrambled out after him. "Now what?"

"Run," said Hambledon, "before the place blows up."

They ran off behind the shed and found a fence. They went over it like cats and dodged among tree trunks till Micklejohn came upon a path. They trotted along more easily, having their way illuminated by the leaping flames from the big shed, which, being made of old tarred timber, burned like a torch.

"They had better do something quickly about that fire," said Hambledon, "or they'll have the trees alight. Ever seen a forest fire, Micklejohn?"

Before Micklejohn had time to answer there was a sudden hollow boom; they took cover behind tree trunks and saw sparks and flame and burning timbers hurled high into the air to fall slowly over a wide area with pattering noises like the first heavy drops of a storm; something small and heavy crashed through the branches of Micklejohn's tree and thudded into the ground behind him.

"If that doesn't wake up the village," said Hambledon thoughtfully, "it's a poor lookout for the Last Trump."

Reaction seized upon Micklejohn, who leaned against his tree and laughed till the tears came.

"I was hoping to leave the district with my usual modest unostentation," added Hambledon, "but I don't think it's going to work this time. I've got a car, such as it is—here's the road."

They came out upon the road and began to walk along it, hearing excited shouting from the direction of the village and the sound of a car engine being started.

"Waldecke is awake," said Micklejohn.

The noise from the car increased suddenly and twin head lamps lit up the road as they came.

"The Vopos," said Micklejohn, "they've got the only car in the village," and he turned to dive into the bushes but Hambledon seized him by the arm and dragged him back.

"Stand fast," he said, "if you'll excuse my talking like a whisky advertisement, they've already seen you. Do the Vopos know you at all?"

"No. Never seen me, I took care of that."

Hambledon stepped into the road and held up his hand with a commanding gesture; the car slid to a halt with screeching brakes and a voice bellowed, "Volks-polizei!"

"I should hope so. Why the devil weren't you here before? Or don't you read orders on a Saturday night?"

"Mein Herr——"

"I come here on a special mission from Magdeburg," stormed Hambledon, "expecting to find you at your posts. I suppose you were tired. I suppose you were in bed. I suppose you think that orders from

General Ambromovitch can be left over till Monday. Why the hell weren't you surrounding the place as ordered?"

"What place—we had no orders——"

"What place! The underground subversives have a meeting place and a store of arms and explosives here, under your noses, and you don't even know it!" Hambledon shook his fists in the air. "When I report this——"

The car door opened and a fat agitated German hopped out. Over his shoulder it could be seen that the car was full of Vopos still hastily doing up buttons and buckling equipment. Hambledon flung open the other door.

"Get out and go and put the fire out! What do you mean, sitting in there doing nothing, do you think you're in a box at the theatre? *Aus! Aus!*"

The men tumbled out and ran towards the burning ruins of the *Möbelfabrik* shed and their unhappy commander turned to follow them. "Not you! I have cleared out this nest of vipers for you with one assistant and now I am going home. You can drive me to my car. Fritz"—to Micklejohn—"don't stand gaping there, get in the car." Micklejohn dived inside as the first of the running villagers drew near.

"But the men," bleated the commander, "the scoundrels who——"

"You can rake over the ashes in the morning," said Hambledon, entering the car and slamming the door. "You may find a few blackened bones—drive on till I tell you to stop—but I doubt it. There may be some pieces hanging in trees."

The Volks-polizei commander shuddered and drove on past the leaping flames, not very high now since the roof and most of the walls had been blown away. The commander had once been a major in an Army Commissariat branch; when his Army life came to an end with the war and there was, of course, no pension to be had, he had thought himself lucky to get a police post in a quiet country district. Waldecke was not within the frontier zone and the violent young men of the frontier guard were under a separate command, *Gott sei dank*. The commander had never been used to violence; all he wanted in life was a quiet office where he could sit filling up forms, for he loved filling up nice tidy forms and did it very well, not to be driving along dark roads in the small hours alone with this terrible man from Magdeburg and his downtrodden assistant. The commander discovered in himself an unexpected gush of sympathy for a young man appointed as assistant to a man like that. Dreadful.

"Stop here," said Hambledon.

The car stopped at the entrance to the cart track up which Hambledon had driven Kirsch's car earlier in the night. The Vopo commander leapt out.

"One word, I beg," he said. "I implore the Herr to believe that I received no orders for this evening from Magdeburg; indeed, indeed, I am most meticulous about opening orders at once. Mein Herr, the orders must have been misdirected—lost in transit—stolen——"

Hambledon, half out of the car, appeared to hesitate.

"I suppose that is possible," he said slowly. "I find it hard to believe that a man of your rank would deliberately ignore an order. Certainly, once the alarm was given, you brought your men upon the scene with commendable promptitude."

The commander practically wagged his tail.

"I was sure that the Herr's sense of justice would prevail. I will lodge a strongly worded complaint with Magdeburg about the non-arrival of these orders."

"Just a moment," said Hambledon, and drew his feet back into the car. "I don't think you had better do that. I don't think it would be wise. If, by any chance, the loss of the orders was not carelessness but deliberately arranged—you see what I mean?"

"You mean——" began the commander, and stopped.

"You have it. Your complaint would be looked for and abstracted like the orders, and endless confusion would result."

"Dreadful. Ach! Dreadful!"

"I am myself driving straight back to Magdeburg now and I will visit Command Headquarters first thing in the morning. If I myself give a full account of what has happened here—including the non-arrival of your orders—all will be made clear with no possibility of leakage. You agree?"

"But, of course——"

"And an enquiry can be set in train from the Headquarters end."

"Excellent. From every conceivable aspect preferable. In my report of tonight's doings, what should I say, then?"

"For your own records, a full account, naturally. As for a report to Headquarters it would be better to wait until you hear from them. I shall, after all, be making your report for you and will explain that you have qualms about entrusting it, in writing, to possibly unreliable communications. You will hear from them in due course by a reliable messenger."

"A thousand thanks. What a relief! I shall remember the Herr with gratitude to the end of my life. With apologies, I have a small flask of schnapps in the car, the Herr must be exhausted and thirsty, I should be so greatly honoured——"

"Thank you. I think a little something would go down very well."

The commander produced a flask which must have contained at least half a pint, pulled the cup off the bottom of it, unscrewed the cap, and handed both to Hambledon, who was, indeed, not sorry for a little restorative. It had been a crowded evening. He said: "*Prosit!*," drank, and asked if his young assistant might also——

"Oh, please——"

So Micklejohn had a small tot while Hambledon explained that though young and inexperienced he was really shaping quite well on the whole. "Now you, Commander. No, I insist."

"What name," said the commander, wiping his mouth on the back of his hand, "shall I be permitted to remember with honour?"

Hambledon got out of the car and shook hands. "In the branch in which I have the honour to serve," he said solemnly, "we do not use names. If you refer to X37, Headquarters will understand. *Auf Wiedersehen*, Herr Commander. Would you mind moving your car a few yards? Mine is parked away up this lane. Come, Fritz."

Hambledon led the way up the track with long strides, Micklejohn dutifully keeping half a pace behind. The old car started at the first attempt and they drove out into the road, past the saluting figure of the commander, and turned right for Ilsenburg.

"Congratulate me," said Hambledon, "for I have attained a lifetime's ambition."

"Certainly I do," said Micklejohn. "Congratulations, sir. What about?"

"For years I have had a secret longing for somebody to call me X37 and at last I've managed it."

"Sounds like a policeman to me."

"What? Oh. Oh, well, you may be right. I thought the name of Ludwig Kirsch had been bandied about quite enough for the moment. Policeman, eh? Never mind. I took some trouble to muzzle him for the moment, Micklejohn, because we've got to go back to Magdeburg to pick up our exit passes for Helmstedt. I didn't want him ringing up Headquarters early in the morning with a dramatic story about bangs in the dark and have old Ambromovitch demanding a full account of it tomorrow afternoon and probably well into the night. I want to get away as soon as possible."

CHAPTER XXII

dead or alive

THEY DROVE AWAY through the sleeping countryside; just before they reached Ilsenburg an odd light high in the air to the west caught Hambledon's eye. He slowed down, staring, and stopped the car for a moment.

"What in the name of Heaven is that?"

It was a great cross of glowing light and looked as though it were hanging in the sky.

"That," said Micklejohn, "is what they call the East German Cross. It's a huge wooden one about sixty feet high on a hilltop in the Western Zone near Bad Harzburg. It is covered all over with reflectors and on Saturday nights they floodlight it from the ground. You can see it for miles and miles into the Soviet Zone and people creep out after dark to look at it sometimes. You know. It rather awes me."

"I don't wonder," said Hambledon.

He drove on for some time and then stopped the car again off the road in a quiet spot.

"It is now a little after 3 A.M.," he said, "and only forty miles to Magdeburg. There is no sense in arriving there at 5 A.M., making people wonder what we've been doing all night. I simply loathe people wondering what I've been doing. Besides, the offices won't be open till eight. Let's have two or three hours' sleep. Can you sleep in this wagon-non-lit?"

"I think I should sleep if I were pegged up on a clothesline," said Micklejohn frankly.

"Sleep well," said Hambledon. He turned his shoulder to his companion, snuggled down into his corner, and closed his eyes, though how much he slept is another matter.

177

At six he woke Micklejohn by the simple method of starting the car and driving off. Micklejohn, whose young energies seemed completely restored by two and a half hours' sleep sitting up in a cramped space, woke up at once.

"Good morning," said Hambledon. "I hope you slept well."

"Yes, thank you. Good morning, Mr. Hambledon. I hope that you also had a good night."

"Passable," said Hambledon, slowing down for a herd of cows, "passable. Which is more than can be said for these beasts, isn't it? Let us talk German, shall we? They might overhear us and give us away. Take your fool's tail out of my radiator, Strawberry."

When they had passed the cows Micklejohn asked whether Hambledon knew anything about a thing called the Smirnov Plan. "I started it off to you as soon as I heard that you were in Goslar, but communications seemed a little——"

"I know," said Hambledon. "Difficult. But I got it all right. Want to hear the whole story? Listen."

Hambledon talked on to an enthralled audience and ended: "So after it had all been carefully photographed I brought it back as a nice present for the Russians. Not a very civilised people but they're great on presents."

"But why not simply remove it——"

"And have them thinking out a brand new plan we know nothing about? Not likely."

At Magdeburg there was no difficulty about the exit permits, as Hambledon had had the forethought to get a signed authorisation for them from General Ambromovitch's office beforehand.

"Breakfast?" asked Micklejohn.

"Certainly, breakfast. I know a pleasant café down by the river. Come on."

They sat on the terrace in the morning sunshine; since it was Sunday, a few church bells rang halfheartedly, but there were no little groups of people, prayer books in hand, making their way through the streets. The Communists do not encourage Sunday observance, as is well known, secularisation is the word of power, and traffic and people passed busily about as on a weekday.

"You wouldn't think it was Sunday," said Micklejohn. He emptied his second cup of coffee and attacked his third roll. He received no answer and looked round in surprise to see Hambledon sitting very still in his chair, with his hat tilted forward over his eyes. He was watching two men who were walking together past the café; one was a small neat man who looked across at Hambledon, raised his hat, and bowed. Hambledon made no response whatever. The other man was tall and lean, dark-skinned and saturnine, with a deeply lined face, he did not look in Hambledon's direction at all. The two men walked on quickly and could be seen to be deep in conversation.

The moment they were out of sight Hambledon sprang to his feet, threw a note upon the table, pointed it out to the attentive waiter, said: "Come on, Micklejohn," and walked rapidly away, leaving his coffee unfinished. Micklejohn abandoned his roll and hurried after Hambledon, who was already starting the car.

Micklejohn jumped in beside him, shut the door, and said: "Who were those two men?"

Hambledon swung the car off the car park and drove away without answering. When they were at last clear of the city and upon the road to Helmstedt he settled down to send the car along at the utmost speed of which she was capable.

"Those two men," he said, and laughed abruptly. "The small fair one is Lorenz Grober, a German in Russian Intelligence. He came to see Ludwig Kirsch at his house at Goslar. Kirsch being already in gaol, he saw me instead and as he'd never seen Kirsch I managed to persuade him that I was Kirsch. He then kindly arranged this little trip for me and even met me at Helmstedt, to ensure that I wasn't held up on the Russian frontier. The other man's name is Dittmar and he is probably the one man in the whole Soviet Zone of Germany who knows that my name is Hambledon and not Kirsch. Tiresome, isn't it?"

Micklejohn thought this over and considered that "tiresome" as a summary was a trifle inadequate.

"But he was the tall dark man—are you sure he saw you? And recognised you? I thought he did not look across at all."

"He saw me all right; that's why he didn't look again. As for recognising me, he was shadowing me round Goslar for a fortnight on Kirsch's orders, Kirsch was his boss. When things blew up and Kirsch and another man were arrested, Dittmar ran for it and got clear away."

"But what's he doing here with the other man, Grober?"

"All in the network of Russian Intelligence. I expect Dittmar knew him by name and where to find him. Dittmar had to get out of the Western Zone because the police were after him. No doubt he made his way here and went to see Grober to report and ask for another post. I ought to have thought of it. It's obvious, when you come to think of it. We ought to have had a pint of beer in a cellar for breakfast instead of coffee on a terrace, but I thought I was the illustrious Herr Kirsch still and it wouldn't matter if I was seen. They would know that I had picked up our exit permits, you see."

"Yes. For Helmstedt. And we're making for Helmstedt."

"That's right. It's only thirty miles from Magdeburg and we've covered more than half the distance already and the Russians simply hate getting up early and it's Sunday anyway. Grober is not a very important person, it may be some time before he can induce anybody to listen to him—I hope."

"And in the meantime we pass the frontier before they have time to stop us."

"That's the general idea," said Hambledon.

Micklejohn relapsed into silence to watch the kilometres coming up on the speedometer. The old car was going quite well.

"It was a bit of bad luck," he said suddenly, "those two men happening to come along together at that moment, wasn't it?"

"These things happen," said Hambledon calmly, "and one can't always expect them to be in one's favour. But it must have been quite a moment, mustn't it? There they were, strolling happily along in the morning sunshine and suddenly that harmless little twerp Grober says: 'Look. There is your employer, the never-sufficiently-to-be-esteemed Herr Kirsch.' And Dittmar says: 'The devil it is, it's that hellhound of a *verdammter Englander*, the Herr Hambledon.'"

"But if Dittmar knew that Kirsch had been arrested in Goslar, he'd report it, wouldn't he, as soon as he arrived?"

"I am not sure that he did know it," said Hambledon. "I think he was too busy running away. Anyway, we haven't been arrested yet, have we?" He patted the steering wheel encouragingly. "Come on, Boanerges. Another ten kilometres and then you can cool down."

Although the road was an important main road, it was neither wide nor particularly well kept. They were driving through a stretch of forest where the road was narrow but reasonably straight; some distance ahead there was someone at the roadside doing something with branches. One would say that he was piling smaller branches upon a larger one of beech which, being flat, would make a passable sled. When they drew nearer it became plain that this was, indeed, what the old man was doing. He glanced towards the oncoming car, the only one in sight, bowed his ancient back to take the strain, and dragged his timber out to block the road almost completely.

"Is he blind and deaf?" began Micklejohn——

180

"Just possibly neither," said Hambledon, and pulled up Boanerges within a yard of the obstruction.

The old man turned with a dramatic start of surprise, cupped one hand to his ear, and squeaked: "I didn't hear you. Just a minute and I'll clear—what say?"

He came doddering round to Hambledon's window, stuck his head in and said: "Name of Ludwig Kirsch? Thought so. Don't go on, they're waiting for you. Road block on the bridge two kilometres ahead and a Vopo post just round that bend. Orders to stop car and take you both, dead or alive."

Micklejohn gasped and Hambledon said: "Thank you very much indeed. How did you know?"

"Outside Vopo telephone box," said the old man, with a toothless grin. "They think I'm deaf, see? Can't hear nothing, I can't. So they repeat message, write it down and read it back. Car number GS 13579, name of Kirsch and friend. I know about you from Waldecke, see? The man with the message to say Kirsch is all right is in my attic with a bullet in his chest. Turn left here, keep going seven kilometres, and then lie up till dark." He backed away and dragged his wood round in the road to let Hambledon pass. "Go, quick, quick!"

Hambledon, who had not stopped the car engine, let in his clutch and swung left into a woodland track. In a matter of yards he was out of sight of the road. Micklejohn, looking back, said so.

"But not out of earshot," said Hambledon, thankfully changing into top on a downward slope.

"Tell me, if it's not a tactless question," said Micklejohn, "why do you handicap your mobility with this peculiar vehicle?"

"It's Kirsch's and he loved it, odd as that may seem. It's the only car he ever consented to drive and he lost his quite notoriously violent temper if anybody was tactless enough to cast nasturtiums upon it."

"Some obscure fixation," suggested Micklejohn helpfully.

"Obscure is right. Kirsch drove it, I am Kirsch, therefore I drive it. But I think we will find an early opportunity to dump it now that the name of Kirsch appears to be without honour in the land."

"Six kilometres coming up," said Micklejohn, with his eyes on the speedometer. "Seven, our old friend said. What do you suppose happens after seven kilometres?"

"Probably a road junction complete with police post." Hambledon slowed down, stopped the engine, and got out. "You stay with the car, will you? I'm going to walk on and see what there is to see. I shan't be long."

He came back twenty minutes later to say that there was indeed a police post on the road to which this track would lead them and that it was manned by alert Vopos. He climbed into the car, took out a map and brooded over it, merely making small grunting noises when Micklejohn asked questions until the young man gave up asking. Eventually Hambledon looked up with a grin, offered Micklejohn a cigarette, and pointed out a double dotted line on the map.

"Walker's track," he said. "I don't know whether we can get the car through but we can try. It turns off to the right about fifty yards ahead and meanders off. I think it by-passes this road ahead of us, which, if I am right, ends in a farmyard. We circumnavigate the farmyard"—he started the car—"and consequently do not have to cross the road."

"I see that," said Micklejohn, as the car moved on, "just like walking round the headwaters of a stream. But I thought we were going to leave this car."

"What, here and now? It isn't my idea of a car but it goes a lot faster than we can walk, you know." Hambledon changed down and put the car at a rise, which it charged gallantly. "It's in much better condition than most cars over this side. You must have noticed that. It's just a little too well known, that's all."

They rounded the head of a valley and turned south and east until Hambledon said: "I think this will do for the present. Can you keep awake for two hours? I want to sleep. Call me if anyone comes."

beanfields

As soon as darkness began to gather, Hambledon climbed into the car and said that it was time to start. "We ought to pick up some petrol somewhere. I didn't wait this morning. I thought that there was plenty of petrol in the Western Zone. Never mind. Some opportunity will doubtless present itself."

They drove on along one lonely country road after another, but always trending southwards, till the car hesitated, coughed, and hesitated again. Hambledon pulled into the side of the road and turned the petrol tap on to the reserve.

"Though even that would be more helpful if I had any idea whether the reserve tank held two gallons or one pint," he said. "You're very quiet, aren't you?"

"Nothing much to say," said Micklejohn. "I expect I'm hungry. Stultifying to the brain. I've noticed it before."

"We might pick up some sausage somewhere," said Hambledon soberly, "but don't count on it. The country people here are hungry too."

They came up to the top of a rise and looked down the further side to see, on the left, a house with lighted windows open to the warm night. Hambledon put the car out of gear and coasted silently down the hill. As they drew near the lighted house it could be seen that it was an inn; it could also be heard that there was a party in progress, for sounds of revelry floated out through the open windows.

The inn stood a little back from the road with a cobbled space before it. Hambledon drew the car off the road, ran it past the house to a patch of grass beyond, and stopped the engine.

"I'm going to have a scout round for some petrol."

"But this is an inn, not a garage——"

"I know. But they may have a pumping engine or something. It's worth looking."

"They are very drunk, aren't they?"

"All the better," said Hambledon, and slipped away.

There was a yard at the back of the inn. He turned into it and received the full blast of dissonance from two windows and an open door. Someone was playing an accordion not too badly, but he had chosen quite a different melody from someone else who was strumming loudly on a guitar. Some members of the party—it appeared to number about six—were singing whatever took their errant fancies from moment to moment. Hambledon was a man so nearly tone-deaf that he always said that the only way to recognise a song was by the words, but even he found this cacophony almost painful.

"But it's nice and loud," he said, and wandered round the yard looking for petrol cans. He did not find any, but he did find a car run into a shed with the doors closed but not locked upon it. It was a good car by Eastern Zone standards, which meant that it was an official car, and when he walked round it there was a little green pennon on the bonnet and several official stickers on the windscreen, which he identified as those of the Agricultural Produce Control Office, or words to that effect, for he had thought it wise to learn something about control offices.

He turned on the petrol, released the brake, and pushed the car backwards out of the shed without difficulty. Too easily, in fact, for the car dropped its back wheels into a surface drain just too deep for Hambledon to heave it out unaided.

"They wouldn't hear," he said, "if I started up a racing Maserati." He got in, confidently started the engine, and began to drive out of the yard without having disturbed the revellers in the least. But just as he was passing the open door a man came staggering out of it.

He stopped, stared, and let out a yell which quietened even the singers. The inn emptied itself into the yard with shouts and maledictions as Hambledon put the car into second gear and shot out, blowing the horn to attract Micklejohn's attention. He was already out on the road. Hambledon slowed down just enough to throw the door open and let Micklejohn scramble in, and then drove on down the hill.

"They're all blind drunk in there," said Hambledon.

"Not too drunk to run," said Micklejohn, crouching on his seat to peer out of the rear window. "Two of them have found Boanerges.

Here comes a third. No, he's fallen down. He's staying down. They've got Boanerges going and they're coming on. They're all over the road but they continue to come. They've switched the headlights on, dipped. That was a fine sweeping curve; d'you think the driver thinks he's skating?"

"This is where we leave them behind," said Hambledon, and put his foot down. "There'll be a road post soon and I want to get there comfortably first. Are those papers in that door pocket beside you?"

They were and Micklejohn dragged them out.

"Potatoes," he said, peering in the dim light from the instrument panel, "beets, cabbage, beets, potatoes, kale—what are we, green-grocers?"

"Far better than that. Greengrocers, indeed. We are the Ministry of Agricultural Produce Control——"

"We have them," said Micklejohn cheerfully, "only we call them the County Ag. Red lights ahead."

"Very good. Any sign of Boanerges?"

"No. Yes, I think—yes. Squinting slightly and far, far behind, but still pursuing."

"There must have been more in that reserve tank than one would expect. Never mind, so long as I can pass this barrier—stand by." Hambledon drew to a halt at the red and white pole, and a man in Volks-polizei uniform, who had been signalling to him with a red lantern, came up to the window.

"Good evening, mein Herr," he said, saluting the little pennon and the windscreen stickers rather than the individual driver. "Papers, please."

"What, again?" said Hambledon genially. "Franz, get those papers out again. Tell me, what is all the excitement tonight? This is the fourth time I've been stopped in the last hour."

"We look for a car," said the Vopo, "and though it is plain that the Herr's car is not the one, it is my duty to stop everyone."

"Naturally," said Hambledon. He took the papers from Micklejohn without looking at them and absent-mindedly laid them down. "I saw a car outside an inn three or four kilometres back—what make is it?"

"Composite, it says on the order. Two-seater body on long chas-sis——"

"But——" said Micklejohn.

"What number?" asked Hambledon excitedly.

"Western Zone number GS 13579——"

"That's the one! Was it not, Franz? Surely."

"That is right. All odd numbers and there was something funny about the car body," said Micklejohn eagerly.

"They were exceedingly drunk," said Hambledon. "They started the car as we came by and followed us. They were all over the road."

"They are coming this way?" asked the Vopo.

"Certainly. At least, they started this——"

"Look, look," babbled Micklejohn, pointing back up the hill. "All over the road——"

Dipped head lamps swooped and curved, appeared to hesitate and came on again.

"Look here," said Hambledon urgently to the Vopo, "I've got no fancy for being slammed in the rear by this drunken fellow. Let me through, quick, I'll stop the other side."

"Certainly," said the Vopo. He swung the bar to let Hambledon through and immediately closed it again, calling to his mate in a little telephone hut beside the road. "Hugo! Come out, this looks like our meat."

Hambledon drove on just far enough to be out of trouble, stopped the car and switched off the engine. In the sudden quiet Boanerges could plainly be heard approaching in a series of short bursts as the almost empty tank spared a few more drops to the starved carburettor.

Hugo walked forward to meet Boanerges while his fellow waved a red lantern. The car coasted down and ran over a bump which shook a last teacupful into the carburettor; the engine awoke with a sudden roar, the car swung across the road and butted the telephone box, which disintegrated. From white insulators above, on the telegraph pole, there came a sound as of harp strings breaking.

"Tara's halls," murmured Micklejohn. "I shall laugh in a minute."

"Be quiet. Look at that——"

The Vopos, one upon either side, opened Boanerges' doors and dragged out the occupants. These stood upon their dignity, such as was left to them, and addressed the Vopos by the German equivalent of "low fellow." The Vopos resented this and their captives kicked shrewdly. The butts of two Volks-polizei-issue revolvers rose up and fell sharply, with hollow-sounding thuds, upon the close-cropped heads of the captives. Their knees gave way. They were dexterously caught and laid out side by side in the cool grass of the road verges.

Hambledon's friend came, grinning, to put his head in at the car window.

"That's them all right," he said. "I thank the Herr for his warning. But our telephone, it is *kaputt*."

186

"Can I do anything? Take a message?"

"Ach, if you would! There is another post at a crossroads five kilometres on. I will write you a note. They can report this for us and then come up and help us."

Hambledon waited while the Vopo sprawled over his bonnet to write a note upon a small official pad with a printed heading: "The People's Police of the German Democratic Republic," which, as Micklejohn remarked when they drove on, is a fine example of words meaning what Big Brother says they mean and you can go and boil your head.

"Oh, quite," said Hambledon, placidly driving on through the night.

"But doesn't it make your blood boil——?"

"My dear boy, if I let things like that heat my blood I'd have died of spontaneous combustion long ago."

"But," began Micklejohn again. He then saw Hambledon's grim face in the shadow and abandoned, with a slight gasp, whatever he had been about to say.

The next road post duly materialised at a crossroads, a red light was waved, and Hambledon drew up.

"A note for you," he said, handing it out, "from Post 287 up the road. They have caught your fleas for you."

The patrol uttered a pleased exclamation and took the note to another man in yet another telephone box. He read it and came out, grinning, to ask for details of the affair at Post 287. Hambledon told him all about it.

"So all is well," he finished, "except that their telephone box is smashed to firewood and the wires down. They want you to go up and help them."

The man nodded. "They want to borrow our little radio transmitter-receiver," he said. "Hans, get your motorcycle going and you can take me along on the pillion. Oh, first let us dismantle this road post, it will not be wanted any more. You clear it away while I ring up posts ahead to pass the word 'Emergency Ended.' Then they can all go home to bed. The Herr may drive on now. He will not be stopped again. Good night."

"Thank you," said Hambledon meekly, and drove away.

They drove on and on, sometimes through deep and silent woods and sometimes through open farming country, until the stars faded and the sky grew light in the east. Here and there lights began to appear in cottage windows and the daylight broadened minute by minute.

"Where are we going?" asked Micklejohn, after a long silence. "Anywhere particular, or are you just looking for a likely spot, as it were?"

"We are making for a spot near a little place called Neuhof, where, for some reason which no one understands, there is a short length of frontier without a wire fence. There is the usual ploughed strip and a lot of Vopos, but no wire; on the further side of the ploughed strip there is a road which, believe it or not, is in the Western Zone. I wish it wasn't getting so damned light. I was hoping to cross in the pearly light of dawn, if that. It can't be far now." Hambledon put his hand in an inside pocket and pulled out a small folded map, which he passed to Micklejohn.

"Ah! The *Wanderkarte Camping!* When I first came to Goslar——"

"Look down in the left-hand bottom corner, outside the zonal boundary. Obersachswerfen, got it?"

"Obersachswerfen——"

"Oh, give it to me." Hambledon stopped the car and pointed with his finger. "There. Obersachswerfen we have just passed through, the next village is Branderode—about two kilometres—and we fork right just past the church. Then it's just over a kilometre to the frontier." He started the car again and drove on fast. "Please fold up the map again and put it in your pocket, I don't want it blowing about."

Micklejohn did what he was told and asked in a meek voice if there was anything else.

"If you know any nice strong prayers you might say them."

Branderode came into sight, a very small place with a few houses along either side of the road. There was, however, more than one lane turning off to the right and Hambledon slowed down.

"A right fork just past the church—not that. Nor that. Where's the church, for—there it is. Right fork. Good."

They turned off and left the place behind.

"Did you notice the Vopo office? No light on anywhere and no smoke coming out of the chimney."

"Nobody awake yet," ventured Micklejohn.

"No. And the Vopo patrols who've been on duty all night on the frontier will be tired and hungry and chilly and a bit dopey, I hope. There. Look ahead, across two fields, do you see a road? That's in the Western—dear me, how excessively fatiguing. Look to the left a little; two Vopos leaning on a gate. See them? The last time I was here

188

there were two Vopos leaning over that gate. Oh, so that's the roaring noise. I thought it was the blood rushing to my head. Now for a little innocent camouflage."

Hambledon leaned forward and pulled out the choke on the dashboard to its fullest extent.

The roaring noise to which he referred was being made by a farm tractor in some kind of trouble. It had just been started up in the road ahead of them, which had suddenly deteriorated to a mere cart track and came to an end in a field. The tractor was roaring on full throttle and the driver was clambering about on it with a spanner, no doubt trying to calm it but without much success.

Hambledon's car by this time was responding to the full choke by running unevenly and pouring from the exhaust a cloud of black smoke which drifted across the landscape and poisoned the pleasant morning air. He came up close behind the tractor, stopped, leaving the engine running, and got out.

The tractor driver could not have heard him but, in stepping down from his machine he bumped into Hambledon, who seized him by the arm and yelled in his ear.

"Do you know anything about cars?"

The man looked round and said he did, a bit, why?

"Mine's gone wrong. Come and do something!"

The man walked towards the car and then noticed the green pennon and the windscreen stickers.

"Agricultural Control," he said, and shied away. "I hates agricultural controls. We'd all get on a lot better if you was all stuck in ditches. I've got my own troubles. Governor's stuck and my tractor roaring her head off——"

"Come on," said Hambledon persuasively, and showed a roll of notes.

"Oh, well. Your mixture's too rich for one thing."

"The engine's missing," said Hambledon, and got the invariable reaction which always follows this remark. The man walked up to the car and cocked his head to listen.

Hambledon hit him hard under the jaw and caught him as he fell. Micklejohn jumped out of the car and Hambledon said: "Lay him down under the hedge there. Now hop on the tractor. On the side seat, there, I'm driving. I don't know much about tractors but they have gears like cars—hang on."

Hambledon swung the tractor round and out into the field ahead, there was a loud clatter behind, and Micklejohn reported in a horrified voice that they were trailing a cultivator but it was in the up position.

"I am more interested in the Vopos; are they in the up position too? Across this field and the next and we're free. They don't seem particularly interested at the moment, do they? They probably think we're in training for tractor races or merely—what the hell have you done?"

Micklejohn, scarlet with effort and embarrassment, was heaving with all his strength against a long lever. The tractor had slowed abruptly to about half speed because the cultivator had been dropped into service and the six long curved tines were tearing up the ground.

" 'Cast four anchors out of the stern'?" asked Hambledon lightly. "We are now entering upon a field of beans, the farmer will be pleased, won't he?"

"I thought this lever would let the trailer drop off," wailed Micklejohn, "and now it won't even come up again——"

"There's probably a catch on it somewhere," shouted Hambledon above the uproar. "Like what you have on a hand brake."

They were cutting a beautiful swathe through the beans and the accumulated harvest was packing more and more tightly under the hooked tines. Micklejohn found a small lever and pressed it, the big lever came back suddenly, the tractor leapt forward, and Micklejohn fell off. Hambledon, who was not normally given to swearing, produced an expression which startled himself, the tines fell down again, and Micklejohn ran alongside and jumped on once more. The two Vopos, now only some fifty yards away, doubled up with laughter and clung to each other, pointing.

At this point the farmer who owned the beanfield came running to cut them off from the gap for which they were making. He yelled, waving his arms and gesticulating, and signalled to the Vopos, who left off laughing and unslung their rifles. Another thirty yards to the road.

"Could you repeat that trick?" shouted Hambledon. "You can leave out the comic turn at the end."

Micklejohn hauled the long lever forward again and held it this time. Another fifteen yards—ten——

Something smacked into the tractor framing just in front of Hambledon and sang off, leaving a bright streak on the metal. He glanced over his shoulder. The Vopos were both firing though they did not look particularly steady. One of them threw himself down to take aim.

Hambledon drove across the ploughed strip, across the road beyond, through a hedge and straight into another field of beans on the further side.

"We're safe," shouted Micklejohn, releasing the lever in his excitement, "you can stop now, we're safe."

A bullet passed through the sleeve of his coat and smashed the oil-pressure-gauge glass just in front of him.

"Are we?" said Hambledon grimly. "Lever again, please," and he drove on.

Some men working in the field came running, white in the face and very angry.

"Who are you—this is not allowed—who will pay for the damage—look at my beans—at my hedge——"

Hambledon looked back at the road. Two motorcycles roared up to the corner, each with two men on it in the smart black uniforms of the Mobile Police. They pulled up, Hambledon sighed with relief, stopped the tractor, and cut the engine. The sudden silence was like a blessing.

"The police shall arrest you and shall throw you back," raved the Western Zone farmer. "Who shall pay me for all this damage?"

Hambledon got down from the machine, staggered momentarily, and leaned against it.

"Here is one perfectly good Russian-made tractor," he said, patting it affectionately. "It is yours, it will more than pay for the damage."

"No. We shall have to give that back. We cannot keep it."

By this time there were a score or so of people round Hambledon and Micklejohn; men who had been working in the fields, women from a little cluster of cottages near by, round-eyed scared-looking children. They all stared at him and their eyes were not friendly.

Three out of the four Mobile Police came through the gap in the hedge which had been made by the tractor and walked towards them; instantly the people milled round them instead, all talking at once. This trouble was not their fault, it was these two who had come across from the other side, they should be thrown back at once——

The police put them aside and the sergeant in charge came up to Hambledon and asked him who he was.

"You have heard of the young Englishman who went missing? That is he; his name is George Micklejohn. I am Thomas Elphinstone Hambledon, also an Englishman. The Chief of Police in Goslar knows me."

The sergeant made notes and spoke in a slightly more friendly voice.

"I have had instructions about gentlemen bearing those names but, the Herren will understand, their identities must be proved. It is my duty to conduct the Herren to Goslar."

Hambledon looked round at the ring of frightened hostile faces and beyond them to the ploughed strip, the *Zonengrenze*. Beyond this again there were the bent, sullen figures of the fieldworkers in the Soviet Zone all looking the other way; the square brown figure of the farmer shaking his fists over the long swathe cut in his beanfield; the Vopos—six of them now—standing about with their guns ready in their hands.

"To Goslar," repeated the sergeant.

"Certainly, Sergeant. I cannot think of anything which would delight me more and the sooner the better."

"In Walkenried," said the sergeant, "I will call up a police car. This way; it is not far."

They turned and walked away together.